W9-AQL-116

Hermes and the Golden Thinking Machine

Hermes and the Golden Thinking Machine

Alexander Tzonis

A Bradford Book
The MIT Press
Cambridge, Massachusetts
London, England

This book was set in Palatino by Compset, Inc. and printed and bound in the United States of America.

Library of Congress Cataloging-in-Publication Data

Tzonis, Alexander.
Hermes and the golden thinking machine / Alexander Tzonis.
p. cm.
"A Bradford book."
ISBN 0-262-20076-7
I. Title.
PS3570.Z66H46 1990
813'.54—dc20 90-5711
CIP

to L.L.

He reversed the traces . . . turning the front behind and the behind in front . . . and hurried through the shadowy mountains and . . . his dark alley. Then he destroyed the evidence with fire and . . . covering the black ashes with sand . . . he sneaked through the keyhole like the autumn breeze and like the mist.

—*Hymn to Hermes* (c. sixth century B.C.)

Contents

Acknowledgments

This book differs in at least two respects from other fiction. It has a bibliographical postscript at the end and acknowledgments at the beginning.

I would like to thank colleagues and friends for their contributions: First of all Bob Berwick, to whom this book owes its existence, for his unique cognitive subvention, encouragement, and inspiration; Marilyn Matz, for sharing her insights and always so generously; and the members of the Improving Design Methods research group, Joop Doorman, Marc Cohen, Leo Oorschot, and Robert Seidl, for the stimulating environment they provided. Alexander Koutamanis contributed at every stage of the work, naming heroes, drawing up bibliographies, and drawing diagrams. Toos Schoenmakers assisted in the preparation of the manuscript.

Most helpful were the comments of Douglas Hofstader, Richard Ingersoll, Janet Murray, and Nancy Stieber. The book benefited from the V. F. Program of the Dutch Ministry of Science and Education. I would also like to thank Rena and Takis Adamidis, Lazaros Kotanoff, and Stathis Eustathiadis. Of great importance for the work has been what is surely the most beautiful courtyard of the Mediterranean, at the Hotel Miranda of Hydra.

I was very fortunate to have the invaluable aid of everyone at MIT Press, in particular of Helen Osborne and Cornelia Wright. I would like to express a special gratitude to my editor Betty Stanton of Bradford Books, who proposed the book in the first place and then provided the supportive framework needed for its completion.

With this project my co-author Liane Lefaivre and I agreed to specialize. I would carry out the writing of this book, on crime, while she would be occupied in finishing her own, on eros. In reality things worked out differently, and now I wonder why she is not the co-author and we had to stick to our agreement.

A.T.
Delft

The Cast

Hermes Steganos, archaeologist

Robert, Hermes' ex-roommate

Philippos Agraphiotis, professor, archaeologist, Hermes' uncle

Eleni, Hermes' distant cousin

Haralambos Karras, the examining magistrate

Nina, a first-year student in electrical engineering, Eleni's daughter

Esther, Hermes' editor

Paul, her husband

Professor Votris, an old family friend and a genius

Sophia, his housekeeper

Brigadier General Krypsiadis, also studied electrical engineering

Kiki Nikolaki, telex room operator

Gerald, the "cinnamon man"

Donald, a philosopher of photography

Melania, a medium

Elpis, her sister

Pat Sloan, a business man

Kate, his wife

Aby Wind, millionaire and patron of archaeology, collector

Dorothy Evans, chairman of the department of archaeology

Agnes/Circe/Tina/Doxa, a waitress

Mrs. Mitchell, a guest of the Sloans

Manolo, the cook

Daphne, the stewardess

The captain of Sloan's yacht, a Maltese

An AI singer

Baron and Baroness de Vouët-Vuillard, guests of the Sloans

Lekkerkerkerkerker, a welfare bum

A conscientious driver

Various policemen in short sleeves and/or dark suits and glasses

Various taxi drivers

Two security guards

A Customs official and three assistants

Hermes and the Golden Thinking Machine

Chapter Zero

It started to snow in the late morning. Thick flakes came down fast, covering the road, the sidewalk, the front yard. Hermes watched as the snow erased the paths, wrapped the bushes, extended over the stairs leading to the house.

He was tall, with a long oblong head—dolichocephalic, as his colleagues in the archaeology department referred to it. His face was striking yet hard to read, a face that wore a pleasant, almost archaic, smile but gave away nothing else.

He touched the keyboard. The screen came to life:

> For some time now I have been working on a study of human artifacts, trying to encompass all the possible kinds of man-made objects that an archaeologist would encounter on a site. I have been reconstructing the thoughts of those who made the objects, whether they were stories, solutions to problems, or just acts. I have been looking at each of them—stories, solutions, and acts—to see what it is in the mind that makes them different and what is common to all.
>
> Let us look inside each. A story, for example, could go something like this:

A Memorial Day in Cambridge

"A thinking machine?" Hermes asked.

"A *golden* thinking machine," the voice shouted back. "Behind the Shrine of the Lilies." The last words were warped. "I finally tracked it down . . . Took six months to excavate. Extraordinary . . ." There was a long whistling tone. "A thinking machine. Pure gold . . ."

"But you never mentioned this before," said Hermes, pressing the receiver to his ear.

A pause. "I meant to keep it as a surprise." The voice at the other end was muffled, barely surfacing above a low buzz. ". . . of the greatest significance for archaeology . . . It crowns my career . . ." Suddenly the voice was forceful again. "This find strengthens your theories . . . And, my dear nephew, the inscriptions on it are very similar to the ones you deciphered in your dissertation."

Before Hermes could respond, the voice snapped back, "See you tomorrow then. I'll be expecting you here. Come straight over from the airport. I'll be flying in from Santorini tonight. That will give me time to prepare lunch and to polish my little thinking machine . . . a centerpiece for the table."

"Yes. I suppose. Thank you. All right. I'll be there," said Hermes and hung up.

It was quiet again in the room. The whole house was still. Outside the wide-open window nothing moved but branches that rustled faintly in the air. No cars. Not even people. It appeared that the apartment, the building, the whole city of Cambridge had been deserted, peopled only by the breeze and the trees that late Memorial Day afternoon.

His watch showed he had two more hours to get to the airport. He got up, looked around. On the floor near him, clothes, food, utensils, papers and books, some with their spines slashed and their leaves loosened. Farther away, envelopes, boxes, drawers, their contents emptied. All lay scattered, in shambles, where they had been flung.

Hermes set to work. He moved among the heaps swiftly, splitting them and joining them. He carried with his right hand, picked up and placed with his left. He did not interrupt except to check the time and, once, to answer the telephone. There was no one on the line. He stood for some time holding a mute receiver as the silent, empty end of the day closed in.

Slowly, small neat heaps emerged. The floor appeared to be divided into a strange matrix. To a mathematician it might have looked like a physical model using discrete objects to accompany the demonstration of a problem. To an archaeologist, on the other hand, it might have seemed like a table in a laboratory covered with sherds, sorted in piles according to some typological system, or like a table for ordering hieroglyphs drawn on paper, set up to interpret an arcane ancient inscription.

Since his childhood in Greece, Hermes had been intrigued by numbers, structures, arrangements. But he had been equally absorbed by distant alphabets and archaic graffiti. Perhaps this dichotomy had stemmed from his parents' background; his mother was a Polish-born mathematician who had never practiced her profession, while his father was a very prominent Greek archaeologist.

The split persisted after Hermes had entered Harvard. Initially he had entertained the idea of studying architecture "to reconcile my two hemispheres," as he had said at the time, but then, while reading *The Decipherment of Linear B,* he discovered a different solution: archaeology, although of an unconventional kind.

He specialized in the decipherment of proto-Hellenic texts using modern cryptanalytic methods. Nine years later he received a doctorate from Harvard in archaeology for his work deciphering archaic texts; he had developed a reputation for his brilliance in mathematics and his erudition in the classics.

Copies of his dissertation were read with equal attention by archaeologists, philologists, cognitive scientists, and AI researchers. One reader commented that "the work contributes to making precise and explicit what we have referred to, rather vaguely, as 'archaic' or prerational mentalities in the development of human consciousness." Another wrote that "the research takes a computational approach. The results, far from being reductive, offer a fascinating insight into human intelligence as a super deciphering machine." A third noted, "I never realized until now that a rigorous study of problems that one would think amount to nothing more than cryptanalysis could yield so much knowledge about the workings of the human mind."

There were negative remarks as well, of course: archaeology should concentrate on its traditional objects rather than on such alien techniques, there was too much speculation about the human mind unsupported by hard physiological evidence. Hermes' responses to these objections were considered prototypes of exactness, thoroughness, and succinctness, which only strengthened his academic reputation.

But Hermes had also attracted the attention of nonacademic groups, including members of the business and intelligence communities, especially since the popular press discovered his work: for example, *Time* magazine published a short but laudatory paragraph under the title, "The Code to End All Decoding?" and printed his photograph. The face that gave away a pleasant, almost archaic, smile and nothing else. Hermes gave his photograph but refused to be interviewed or to comment on the text.

To understand just how Hermes' writings appealed to such diverse circles, how this somber work, loaded with jargon and hieroglyphs, excited so many, and to comprehend the strange events that followed, one must take into account the context within which all this occurred.

Ours is called the epoch of information—more people are occupied every day in the handling of messages than in any other work; more information is processed than at any previous time by humans and machines of varying degrees of intelligence. Hence the interest in everything that helps the processing of information, such as cognitive studies, the design of brainlike machines, and artificial intelligence.

Hence the belief also that the control of information is more important than ownership of resources or means of production. The investment in the accumulation of information is matched by the fabrication of misinformation, by censorship, interception, eavesdropping, tapping. Global spying has brought with it the omnipresence of secrecy. Millions of dollars are being invested in supercomputers for enciphering. Thousands of researchers are trying to invent the impenetrable code or the universal decipher key and are monitoring who's-who in the world of code making and code breaking, who develops what, for whom, and where the upcoming talent can be found.

Thus it happened that Hermes, close to finishing his undergraduate honors thesis in which he interpreted half-a-dozen proto-Hellenic inscriptions and presented an appendix containing a technique for solving a cumbersome combinatorial decoding problem, came to be invited to lunch by an enthusiastic middle-aged Harvard alumnus.

Soon after the clam chowder it became evident that the alumnus was an expert in international financing who had no understanding of archaeology and no interest in acquiring any. Over pralines and cream ice cream, Hermes was offered the job of assistant "crypto-designer" in the data security section of a major stock brokerage business in San Francisco.

There Hermes lasted for eleven months exactly. Much to the regret of his employers, on a Monday morning, following a Saturday visit to a Berkeley bookshop where the sight of a book with the title *Greek Myths, Machines for Thinking?* caused him a brief blackout and cold sweats, he resigned.

Four years later Hermes finished his doctoral dissertation, deciphering more inscriptions using artificial-intelligence-related theories of language understanding. At that point more invitations for eating out arrived: three times for nouvelle cuisine, twice for Japanese gastronomy, once for a North African feast in New York. And each time he passed up an attractive employment opportunity.

But success in research also brought Hermes more bizarre experiences. He realized he was often followed; his office was searched, his mail intercepted, and his telephone tapped, generally not very discreetly. One night he arrived home to find his apartment broken into, the purpose transparently frisking rather than theft.

All this might explain why, after his very first year of teaching, Hermes unexpectedly applied for a grant that would permit him to get away "for a year to work under the freest possible conditions." The grant had been awarded to him. But how the wishes of men diverge from the commands of the gods. Little did Hermes know that he was already heading toward a rendezvous with greater trouble.

An hour had passed since he had begun arranging his intricate matrix landscape on the floor. In a way Hermes was going over a routine for which he had once written a computer program (a modification of BAGGER, an existing, simple expert system for bagging groceries), which contained his best backpacking techniques. Hermes' experience was vast because as an undergraduate he had made many amateur photographic excursions to national parks with his backpack as his only companion, and he had written a computer program to advise his archaeology colleagues on how to pack for a dig. A few years earlier Hermes had written a similar program for his college roommates and had called it KNAPSACK. He was alluding, of course, to the famous cryptanalytic problem and to the mathematical problem of the same name—with a knapsack of fixed size to fill up, selecting from a number of fixed-size objects in such a way that there would be as little unutilized space left as possible. Hermes' problem had to do with how to put his belongings in boxes before leaving for vacation.

All the bits and pieces had found their place, some in extra-large orange plastic garbage bags that he carried to the backyard, some in cartons pushed against the wall with notes on them: "Please give to . . ." or "This is to be kept in the basement" or "This is for you." Hermes' dark hair and smooth olive skin were covered with dust.

The large room was bare. At its center stood a full knapsack and a strange contraption of minimal size and elegant proportions, in a soft black leather case. Its unrevealing black boxiness made the object appear to explode with power. And for 1983, the year Hermes is taking off on this trip, this year of the spies and the Mafia, this disturbing year when the unthinkable was being thought of in at least two places in the world, this "laptop" machine was at the cutting edge of technological achievement and at the high end of the centuries-long art of the artificial.

The machine had been given to Hermes by a student named Black, a *bricoleur,* an amateur musician, and a person of great powers of persuasion, who arrived one day in Cambridge to do graduate work in electrical engineering. To Black, space and time occupancy had a theological identity as evil powers to be purged through shrinking; his only dream was to make the smallest and most powerful thinking machine on earth.

Days and nights passed. Black calculated, struggled, constructed, and one day appeared at Hermes' doorstep with the prototype finished.

Hermes was stunned. "It feels like a musical instrument."

"It's like watching the movies," Black added timidly.

Most of the machine's hardware parts existed already; Black had put them together differently or in a different context. The same with the software modules of its demonstration program. Black, with the help of Hermes, created a condensed supermenu of different styles of machine thinking, a compact programming environment. It was "a tool kit" that, as Hermes said, could easily be telescoped into a mind factory or, in the words of Black himself, could be "walked around as a garden of endless wanderings," and in the words of the chairperson of the archaeology department, was simply "a conceptual thesaurus."

Black wasn't completely content with his product when he delivered it to Hermes. He had whispered, "One day I hope we'll make a machine for alternative types of logic, a machine that will make it easy for us to think in ways we can't yet think. We'll write stories in archaic cognition style and essays in the ultimate cryptogram code."

Hermes never saw Black and his twin computer again. Nor did any one else in Cambridge. Black never got his degree. Instead he officially entered the list of the Missing Persons Bureau. Hermes inherited the computer Black had left with him, and the copy Black was known to have kept vanished, probably to be devoured as an industrial prototype.

There was nothing left to do in the room. He showered. From the refrigerator he took his last bottle of Perrier. He leaned back his long head, dolichocephalic, as it was referred to in the archaeology department, and drank slowly.

A breeze was coming in from the sea through the open window. The magnolia trees rustled, as if the backyard was filled with invisible things moving smoothly, nearing the house, and then retreating toward the shadowed fence. He shut the window.

He called for a cab. The room was getting darker. The cab was late. Maybe somebody was trying to stop him. The telephone rang again. He picked it up. He waited. Once more, nobody on the line.

Suddenly the clean room, the vacant house, the serenity of that Memorial Day, gave off an exhilarating aura of freedom. Greece was so remote from worries, constraints. Just a place with an apartment waiting, a couple of distant relatives, a few crumbs of memories, the Archaeological Institute, ruins, coffeeshops, and perhaps a "golden thinking machine."

He put the knapsack on his back and hung his laptop computer on his left shoulder. He opened the door. The corridor was dead still. He closed the door and locked it. He put the key in a small manilla envelope and slipped it under the door. He went down the corridor and came out onto the front porch.

The street was empty as far as he could see; only a small brown van dozing on the right. The sun was setting ahead of him. He closed his eyes, sensed the air, and heard the taxi honk.

Over the Atlantic: Robert

When Hermes reached his seat on the plane, the place next to his was occupied by a person holding a newspaper very close to his nose and upside down.

"Robert!" exclaimed Hermes.

"How did you guess?" The person emerged sideways from behind his newspaper. He wore sunglasses with leopard-skin frames.

"What are you doing here?"

"Trying to be incognito."

"By being conspicuous?"

"It's my cover," said Robert gravely.

"A little transparent."

Robert feigned surprise. "You never approve of my tactics. You think you know everything about concealment. Just because they've made you professor of decipherment doesn't mean you're omniscient," he said, folding his newspaper.

"That's for sure. For instance I can't figure out what you're doing here." Hermes placed his knapsack and his laptop in the overhead compartment and sat down. He turned to Robert and smiled. Robert took off his glasses.

Robert looked like something between an angel and a mouse. He had the blue eyes, curly golden hair, and dimpled smile of a cherub together with the prominent nose and subdued chin of a rodent. A notorious nonstop talker to an almost fatiguing degree, loquacious but never informative, he had been one of Hermes' roommates in college.

Hermes had first taken notice of him when Robert had told a friend to lock the door from the inside on his way out of the room. Robert's conversation had been riddled with paradoxes—people who claimed things like "all Cretans are liars" and that they themselves were Cretans. Hermes had never tired of Robert. To the contrary. Robert became Hermes' indispensable companion, and people said that this was living proof of the old saying that opposites attract each other.

After majoring in English, Robert, like Hermes, had stayed on in Cambridge. But Robert did not go to graduate school. He kept himself busy getting a string of part-time writing jobs through a seemingly endless supply of contacts. His irregular enterprises would take him away from Cambridge for a few days, and then he would be back again at his old seat at the Club Casablanca. It was from there that he continued to propagate his unreliable, aporetic tales. But since Hermes almost never had time for the Casablanca, they had met only by chance in the last five years.

"I'm on a journalistic assignment," Robert said, and laughed. He always laughed at the end of a phrase, as if to cast doubt on what he had accidentally revealed. Then he would add, "Of course, I'm joking," and laugh at that too.

Hermes looked sideways at Robert and stretched his long legs. "Sorry if I doze off, Robert," he said, "I haven't slept for two days. I'm going to close my eyes now."

"I've been commissioned to write 'A Guide to Greece for Those Who Know It Extremely Well,'" Robert continued, unperturbed by Hermes' attempt to get some rest. "What about you?"

"On a Guggenheim," Hermes yawned.

Robert jumped up in his seat. "You didn't tell me that last time I saw you in the Square."

"Didn't know about it myself," said Hermes, his eyes still shut.

"You're getting to be like me," said Robert, "an unpredictable freelancer," and laughed again. "And what about your new job at Harvard? So young and already retired?"

"On leave of absence for a year," said Hermes, raising his eyebrows without opening his eyes.

"Is everything going well?" Robert asked.

"Just great." Hermes opened his eyes and looked at Robert. "How are things with you?"

"I'm doing all right, I guess."

"Still working on that novel?"

"I'm giving it a little rest," said Robert, removing his sunglasses and contemplating their pattern.

"I hope we'll have the chance to see more of each other in Athens," said Hermes.

"Give me your address."

Hermes took a deep breath. Alert now, he dived into his pocket, took his address stamp from it and stamped the border of Robert's newspaper. "The apartment my father used to live in."

"You still keep it?" said Robert, eyeing the address. "I didn't think you ever intended to go back to Greece."

"A distant cousin of my father's takes care of it," said Hermes, putting the stamp back into his pocket and stretching out again.

"I won't be staying very far from you, in between my assignments."

"Oh, I didn't know you knew Athens," said Hermes.

"It's my home away from home," Robert said, joking now.

"That's news to me."

"I never fail to keep my best friends in the dark," said Robert. "And you? Don't tell me you're finally going on an excavation."

"No. It's only to write a book," said Hermes.

"What about?"

"Proto-Hellenic intelligence."

Robert's face took on a pained expression. "Is it archaeology or artificial intelligence this time?"

"As always, both."

"I can still see you reading Turing with your morning coffee and Herodotus in bed. And what about that poster of the Rosetta stone? Do you still have it on your wall over your computer?"

"What a memory."

"I'm just as impressed as ever with how you can keep working at something that has no definition. For the last ten years you haven't succeeded in giving me a clear idea of what intelligence, let alone artificial intelligence, is. Any progress yet?"

"You're misquoting me, Robert. I said artificial intelligence is hard to define because intelligence itself is hard to define. But when it's used in phrases like 'every day we understand human intelligence better' and 'every day more intelligent thinking machines are being produced,' we know very well what it means."

"I must congratulate you. I find that answer sublimely vague. I'd stick to archaeology if I were you."

Hermes protested. "It's vague, Robert, because to describe intelligence you have to describe all the things that people think the mind does—solve hard problems, know the world, use knowledge in remaking it, produce true statements, and prove their truth by creating and applying rules."

"Preachy as ever, I see. That's good for your undergraduates. But you and I know that the most exciting things the mind does are lie, laugh, and create chaos."

"Is this the prelude to your standard defense of poetry?"

"Can't I have standards too?" Robert threw back his head and let out a laugh. Then in a confidential tone he added, "Do you know what Sir Henry Wotton, the Elizabethan ambassador to Venice, advised a diplomat one day? Always to tell the truth. This was to keep the enemy, by nature predisposed to disbelieve him, permanently misinformed."

"I'll take note of that," said Hermes, pretending to be searching for something to write with. "I'll try to include it in my work on intelligence."

"You should take two notes of it," rejoined Robert, "because Wotton was also a great philosopher of gardens. Read his book. He wrote that gardens should be made of the opposite of truth and rules. He called it 'agreeable disorder.'"

"I didn't realize you were into gardening."

"I'm trying to be multidisciplinary like you. As far as gardening is concerned, wasn't it you who tried to initiate me into 'garden path structures,' 'search trees,' and 'pruning'? Anyway, Wotton was just a spy specializing in misinformation."

"Now, back to the subject of intelligence. I believe you are misrepresenting my views," said Hermes lightly.

"Impossible. You know that since I don't believe in the possibility of representing anything, I don't believe in the possibility of misrepresenting anything."

"You know I believe intelligence is all the things you mentioned. Why are you misrepresenting me?" insisted Hermes.

"Simply to make you more expressive, Hermes. You're not only pedantic. You're hermetic. You'd be an incredibly dull hero in a detective story."

"I don't intend to get into one, thanks," answered Hermes, covering his head with his hands, as if to protect himself. "All I want to do is finish my book in peace."

"How can we still be on speaking terms after all this?" Robert responded with a tragic air, mirroring Hermes' gesture.

They both laughed.

Discussions of this type between Hermes and Robert had always been a game and a ritual. And as happens in games and rituals, neither Hermes nor Robert tried to find out why they kept recurring periodically. They went on.

The lights dimmed and the vessel continued voyaging over the vespertine ocean.

The flight lasted ten hours. Robert had talked incessantly and Hermes had not succeeded in getting any sleep.

"I have people to meet immediately, and the flight has made me over an hour late," Robert said while they were waiting in the passport control line. "I'll call you later."

"I may be out," Hermes said. "I've got an appointment with this uncle of mine, Agraphiotis."

"Agraphiotis? Does he have something to do with graphics?"

"He's an archaeologist. An academician."

"But I thought . . ."

The family in front of them had just finished with inspection. It was Robert's turn. They clasped hands in haste.

"I'll give you a ring tomorrow morning," Robert yelled as he rushed away.

Minutes later, at this crowded crossroad of east and west, Hermes walked toward the queue of taxis in front of the terminal.

The House with Green Shutters

The taxi left Hermes in front of a narrow gap separating two massive luxurious apartment houses close to the old Royal Gardens. The blazing street was deserted. He loaded his bag wearily onto his back and went through the gap down a long passageway. A shaded space the size of a small square, formed by the backs of buildings, appeared at the end. Accident, human greed, and the building code had come together in the design of this oddly idyllic clearing. In the middle stood a one-story villa, a doll's house, with light pink walls, a colonnaded portico, a tiled roof, and green shutters. It looked about a century old. Huge Roman pines surrounded it. A breeze tiptoed softly through their needles.

Hermes almost stumbled as he climbed the steps of the portico. He raised his head. There was a nameplate on the door: *Professor Dr. Dr. P. AGRAPHIOTIS, Academician.* He lifted the polished brass ring that hung from the ears of a helmeted, Athenalike figure and rapped it against the tips of her armored breasts. The door opened and Hermes was received by a grinning, excited man.

The man was tall and bald, with a white bushy mustache. His skin, including the bald part of his head, was uniformly tanned. It looked like expensive, red-brown leather. His eyes were sea-sky blue. He was dressed lightly in a short-sleeved ultramarine shirt, ultramarine slacks, and ultramarine cotton beach shoes. Hanging from his neck was a tiny platinum anchor.

"It's been so many years," exclaimed the man, Professor Dr. Dr. P. Agraphiotis, stretching out perfectly manicured and scented hands.

Hermes had not seen his uncle for almost twenty years, and then only once. His parents were still living. Of that very distant encounter he recollected that his mother had laughed at all of his uncle's jokes. But Hermes also remembered that his father, a researcher of international reputation, had said that Professor Agraphiotis had written only one book and in it had plagiarized the unpublished research of a friend who had died accidentally.

"I assume you had a good flight," said his uncle cordially. "You certainly travel light. Leave your luggage here," he added, looking askance at the knapsack and the computer.

"It was exhausting, actually. I didn't get much of a chance to rest," said Hermes, leaving his Spartan belongings by the entrance next to an amphora filled with umbrellas.

The academician objected, "Skipping a night's sleep at your age doesn't matter. Come on. I'll show you around the place."

Hermes ran inquiring eyes over Professor Agraphiotis who had now turned his back to him, his index finger directed to the wooden beams above them.

"The building was designed by a retired Bavarian army veterinarian for himself a hundred and thirty years ago. I was lucky to find such a charming place, a well-protected 'chalet' to rent in the middle of this asphalt jungle. Smoke?" he asked abruptly. Hermes was offered a rare Swiss cigarette.

"Never smoke."

Professor Agraphiotis lit a cigarette for himself, inhaled deeply, blew smoke toward the beams, and pushed Hermes into the room on the left of the entrance hall.

The plan of the house was immediately apparent. A series of large rooms placed one after the other, lined up *enfilade,* with all the doors ajar, revealing a view of the building from one end to the other. The room they entered, twice as long as it was wide, was filled with Biedermeier furniture. His uncle referred to it surprisingly as "my rare Louis XVth collection," and Hermes cast a tired look at the objects from behind half-shut eyes, a mild smile still hanging on his face.

As they passed a small crystal mirror inclined on a high rosewood pedestal, Professor Agraphiotis stole a glimpse of himself and straightened his shoulders.

All around them the fresh gleam contrasted with the blue walls.

on the mud. It is the same with me. I can reconstruct a whole temple from the fragment of an echinus. But don't ask me how. It just happens. I can't explain it. I can't tell you how I find what I search for. Like a hunter, I have hunches. I sense signs and I act. I'm not a scientist. I don't prove."

The mustache of Professor Agraphiotis bristled confidently.

Hermes was not impressed. "But scientists do more than just prove," he said.

Professor Agraphiotis grinned happily. "Yes, yes."

Hermes went on, in a didactic tone: "A basic part of scientific thinking is inventing problems, asking questions, making hypotheses, starting with some minimal information and ending with a whole theory. All this has its own rules."

"You're talking about professors who try to justify their theories with rules. I'm talking about intuition." Professor Agraphiotis looked satisfied with what he had said.

"Making a hypothesis doesn't preclude making a rule," Hermes countered. "Construing the state of the world from a fragment has rules of its own. Special rules. Very different from those used in justification."

"Hermes, Hermes! You look for rules everywhere," his uncle said in a jocular tone. "Come now. Intuition comes in a flash, you can't capture it. It's mysterious."

Hermes turned a thin smile to his uncle. "Intuition only appears mysterious because we have no means of representing it yet. We can represent justification though, thanks to Aristotle's groundwork. But in the time of Homer, when these rules had not yet been invented, justification was thought of as the speech of gods to mortals. It was as mysterious as intuition is today."

Professor Agraphiotis continued to grin.

"Following leads is a property of human intelligence," Hermes' gaze moved slowly over the map contours, "common to hunters and scientists alike, a method built into the mind by evolution. History redefines it at each period, now for hunting, now for science."

Agraphiotis quickly glanced at Hermes. When Hermes was finished, he started to talk, as if from a prepared text, ignoring what

Hermes had just said. "Oh, but hunters are altogether different from archaeological methodologists." He looked at the photographs of the bare, still unexcavated hills of Santorini. "Hunters and *field* archaeologists, on the other hand, are very much alike. They sniff here and there, read traces, follow leads. You need lots of talent, patience, a fancy for outdoor life, and to be ready to return with an empty satchel. Lonely work, too. That's why the hunter and the archaeologist are both dreamers. It's the long solitary hours groping for clues. Then the threat of failure. Ah! Small wonder the greatest stories come from hunting societies. About pheasants as big as cows with iridescent feathers." He unfolded his long arms like wings. "About foxes, with fur this long." He stretched his arms measuring the imaginary fur. "About deer with golden horns." He propped his tanned hands up on his head like antlers. "Of course in these stories the spoils would never make it back home. The hunter would say that they had been stolen by a huge winged panther, transformed into a ridiculously small mouse that had run away, or they had inexplicably melted into a polychromatic smoke."

Hermes' eyes shifted impatiently around the room. Professor Agraphiotis elaborated, his face turned up toward the heights of Thera on the map. "Some archaeologists still make up stories." He put his tongue in his cheek. "But you're not a field worker. You're a great theoretician. You write articles. Archaeology needs both." He winked once more. "I'm a field archaeologist. Pragmatic *and* lucky. I bring back my spoils."

Hermes seemed confused.

Professor Agraphiotis looked at him, pleased. "Together we can work miracles. Let's go back to the dining room and drink to it," he said. They returned to the dining room and moved to a round table close to one of the half-shut windows.

Hermes said, "I don't think it would be very wise of me to have a drink just now."

"Come now, Hermes. Let us celebrate. This is my housekeeper's afternoon off, you see. But we'll survive. We've got some delicious cold dishes for lunch," announced Professor Agraphiotis.

The table was crowded with covered platters, bottles, crystal, and silver structured in seemingly perfect shape correspondences. He spotted an imprecision in the alignment of the napkins and rushed to correct it.

"I'm not terribly hungry," Hermes said. He tightened his lips, closed his eyes, brought his hand to his forehead and rubbed it hard with his fist. More words poured out of the mouth of Professor Agraphiotis.

"*Voilà,* my dear nephew. What's your heart's desire? There's tarama, and some marinated mackerel, trout with mayonnaise, fava cooked Santorini style with onions and tomatoes and imam baildy. Do you remember imam baildy? You know, it means 'the priest fainted.' Then there are dolmadakia and spanakotyropita." As Professor Agraphiotis announced the content of each dish almost ceremoniously, he uncovered the platters one after the other.

Hermes looked down at the crystal glasses half filled with ouzo and took a deep breath. Aromas wafted up from the dishes. He swallowed and shook his head while the academician added ice and water to the glasses. The transparent drink turned milky. Then, with one hand raised for a toast, Professor Agraphiotis triumphantly lifted the cover of the centerpiece.

There, on the platter in the middle of the table, instead of a roast, lay a complicated system of superimposed and interlocked disks, pinions, wheels, worm wheels, cogs, and rotors of some kind. The object was slightly larger than a pocket calculator and the parts, more than a dozen, were roughly cut and almost completely covered with inscriptions, notches, incisions, punctuations. Dark spots stained the mechanism, but it looked as if it might have been made of gold.

Hermes blinked and drew his eyebrows together. "Unbelievable," he said. His lips moved to speak again, in a lower tone: "But I can't . . ."

Professor Agraphiotis interrupted, "*Et voilà.* The Golden Thinking Machine. It's all ours. Go ahead—pick up my little toy if you like. Examine it." He took a sip from his ouzo and glared at Hermes, his nostrils flaring and contracting.

Hermes had turned very pale and had his eyes half shut.

"Aren't you feeling well?" the uncle finally asked, surprised, noticing Hermes' moist forehead. "You're sweating."

"I'm afraid not," said Hermes, "I had a dizzy spell. I'm sorry. It happens to me occasionally. I guess I haven't slept for almost three days."

"But I thought your flight had been enjoyable." Professor Agraphiotis appeared not to be giving up easily.

"I'm afraid I'm going to have to go straight home."

". . . your room is ready for you here."

"I think I'd better go straight to my apartment." Hermes' voice was low, plain, and definitive. "Eleni's waiting for me at my father's apartment."

"Is that so." Agraphiotis mumbled an objection as his expression clouded over. "I had called her explicitly to . . ."

"I called her to ask her to prepare it for me," Hermes added with some effort. "Besides, don't you have to work on your find this afternoon?"

The professor's own forehead glistened now. "Of course, of course. We can compare notes tomorrow morning. You'll grab the theory side very easily, I'm certain."

Relief was already apparent on Hermes' face.

"You'll have to get a cab. There's no other way to get around the city. Except by car, and I'm not foolhardy enough to drive one. It's the law of the jungle out there."

The farewells were brief.

As he stood waving good-bye in the doorway, Professor Agraphiotis had the face of a confident man, a man who had encountered many happy days in his past and who was sure he would encounter many more.

Hermes hastened down the narrow passage between apartments, carrying knapsack and laptop. A taxi cruised toward him as he reached the street. He entered it and gave the address of his apartment in a tired voice.

The Apartment

"Let me show you around the flat," said Eleni to Hermes. "I hope you like the way we've arranged things." She went ahead of him and guided him. Eleni was tall and bony, her movements resolute and graceless. A thin mustache grew over her upper lip.

Eleni's husband had died when Nina, her only daughter, had been a few months old. She had worked as a teacher to support Nina and herself.

From the small entrance hall they walked into the living room. The long room led to the kitchen at one end and opened onto a small study at the other. Behind the study there was a door to a bedroom. All rooms had access to a narrow balcony that ran the length of the L-shaped flat. The facades of the apartments across the street stood only a handshake away.

All the furniture was covered with white dust sheets, an old Mediterranean summertime tradition. Eleni had carried it out thoroughly from one end of the house to the other. The flat looked like a landscape model of an arid mountainous region somewhere in the Caucasus.

"It's all so well ordered," remarked Hermes, looking around. "All so meticulous."

"For a while I thought you might stay with Philippos," she said. "That's what he told me this morning over the phone. He was very excited that you were coming. He said you had to work on something right away."

Hermes shook his head, annoyed. "I told him that I could only stay for lunch. Actually, I felt exhausted and I left without even eating."

"I'm sorry. I can't invite you for supper tonight," Eleni interjected nervously. "Nina takes her last exam in two days. She's finished her first year in electrical engineering. I promised her I'd be back soon. She concentrates better when I'm around." Then, observing Hermes more carefully, she added in an authoritative tone, "You do look very tired. You look like you have a headache."

"I do," said Hermes, "I haven't slept for three days. I actually feel like I'm coming down with something."

"You'd better go straight to bed then. But before you do, you should know where everything is. It won't take long. Tomorrow I'll help you set up your study. Now that I think of it, where are all your books? You always used to go around carrying piles of books with you. Have you had them sent by mail?"

"Oh, I've changed my habits. I guess I don't have such great demands anymore," Hermes said self-deprecatingly.

As she was demonstrating the contents of the refrigerator she started. "Oh. I almost forgot," she said, "somebody called you."

"When?"

A car braked outside in the street. There was a sound of shattering glass following the squeal. It made Hermes start but for Eleni it did not seem out of the ordinary.

She said: "An hour ago. He didn't leave any message."

As soon as Eleni left, Hermes went to the well-stuffed refrigerator and got himself some fruit. He studied the map of Athens for a few minutes. He uncovered part of the large dining table, placed his laptop on it, took a chair, sat down, and turned the machine on. Symbols raced across the screen, filling it as he typed.

A few minutes later half of the screen had been erased and in the clearing an image started emerging. A circle in the beginning. Then more circles of different sizes. Some concentric with the first circle. Some overlapping with it like epicycles. The whole gradually resembled the geometry of the centerpiece on Professor Agraphiotis' round mahogany lunch table.

Hermes stared carefully at the figures. His fingers moved fast over the keyboard. Other shapes appeared, free, threadlike, knotlike, choking the regular figures of the background, cluttering the whole screen like wild weeds over an unkept field. Hermes' eyelids hung heavily, and his glassy eyes peered through thin slits.

An hour later he shut the computer and stood up. He went over to one of the bookcases, lifted the dust sheet hanging there, and got behind it. He re-emerged with a volume of Thucydides in hand and went to the couch. Ten minutes went by. The book was lying on the floor. Hermes, his body stretched across the couch with his hand still touching the book, was sound asleep.

The setting sun sent its last rays deep into the flat, turning the peaks of the white-sheet landscape orange and gold and filling the valleys with purple shadows. Commotion and noise were just resuming in the streets of the city. The telephone did not ring again.

The Telephone Call

A glowing light, noise, and frenzy. They came from the wide-open windows of the apartment. From somewhere else in the clatter he heard the restless twitter of a telephone. Hermes opened his eyes, raised his head, and leaped up. The telephone was ringing next to the entrance. He rushed to it in his bare feet.

"It's me."

"Robert!" Hermes answered.

"Did I wake you up?"

The facades of the buildings across the street cast deep vertical shadows. Hermes mumbled, "I just woke up and my head is aching. Must be noon by now."

"It is. I couldn't call you earlier," Robert apologized.

"I guess I'm still jet-lagged. How do you feel?"

"Listen. There's news." Robert stopped. "Are you listening?"

"Yes."

"It's about your uncle. Agraphiotis."

"What about him? Is he after me? I had to run away from him to get some sleep yesterday."

"I'm sorry. Listen. He's been shot."

"Is this a joke?" Hermes said. The sound of a drill down the street was deafening. There was an ear-splitting noise from where Robert was calling, too. "What did you say?"

"I'm calling you from the street," Robert was saying. "It's all over the afternoon newspapers. Just out. Your uncle was murdered in his house. Yesterday. Early afternoon."

"But I was there. I saw him."

"I know. You told me you were meeting him."

"I don't know what to say."

"I have to leave Athens. My plane leaves in less than an hour. I'm on an assignment—I can't postpone it. Are you there?"

"Yes," Hermes said.

"What'll you do?"

"I have to think."

"What a mess."

"Yeah."

"Listen. I'll be back in a week. Maybe less."

"You better catch your flight. I'll manage."

Hermes hung up but stayed next to the telephone with his head bent. His eyes darted from one side of the floor to the other. Slowly he rubbed his thumb over his chin and felt his unshaved face. He started toward the couch where he had slept. His clothes lay neatly on its arms.

Ten minutes later he stepped into the elevator. It took him straight to the basement of the building. Then he deciphered what the letters and numbers meant on the control board, pushed the right button, and came out at ground level.

He was surprised at being addressed by his last name, firmly and politely, as he stepped out of the apartment hall onto the sidewalk. A young man presented him with a photograph sealed in a plastic identity card. A security policeman. He wore civilian clothes and looked like a Mediterranean football champion. The drill down the street was still blasting.

The First Interview

Hermes was asked to get into the front seat of a very small blue car waiting in front of the apartment. The young man got behind the wheel and started the engine. The car jerked before joining the rest of the frenetic traffic. It was then that Hermes realized that there was a third person inside the vehicle, in the back seat. It was an uncomfortable feeling.

They rushed through the busy streets for about half an hour to what was obviously a kind of police headquarters. Without uttering a word, the third man slipped out of the car as soon as they stopped and disappeared before Hermes could get a good look at him. Hermes was ushered by the driver through a number of complicated corridors to a small windowless hall surrounded by doors. All the doors were shut. The driver retreated, leaving Hermes in the company of a lazily revolving ventilator.

A few minutes later someone opened the door on his right and invited him in. Hermes faced the silent backseat fellow passenger in a bare room, sitting behind a bare gray metal desk.

The man's face was long and thin. Its paleness contrasted with the charcoal-black hair that was freshly cut with extreme precision. The suit he wore was also tailored with precision and, like the haircut, strikingly out of fashion. Hermes was asked to take a seat on a heavy gray metal chair.

The door opened. A head emerged. The man behind the desk waved it away. The head obeyed. The door was shut. They were alone in the room again.

"Do you prefer to speak English?" the man asked him in English.

"No. It's the same to me," Hermes answered in Greek.

"I am the examining magistrate," the man said, switching to Greek, "in charge of the murder case that concerns you."

"You mean of Philippos Agraphiotis, my uncle," Hermes answered.

The examining magistrate looked intensely displeased. He went on, "Professor Agraphiotis was found shot dead yesterday night. You are the last person we know to have seen him alive." He left his statement suspended.

"I see," Hermes said.

The examining magistrate continued in the same disagreeable tone. "You landed in Athens yesterday." Once more he left the phrase suspended, not indicating what the other person was supposed to make of it.

"Yes, about eleven o'clock," Hermes volunteered.

"A delayed flight," the magistrate commented, bending his head but keeping his eyes on Hermes.

"Indeed, the flight was late," confirmed Hermes.

The magistrate seemed to be listening to something outside the room and continued to appear dissatisfied. He said in the same manner, halfway between a statement and a question: "You decided not to stay with your uncle."

"No. I'm afraid I knew my uncle very little," Hermes said.

"He'd invited you to stay with him, though," remarked the magistrate, adding, "his housekeeper told us."

"I have exchanged many telephone calls with him in the past year," Hermes clarified, "but he invited me to stay in his house only after I arrived here."

"So, after years of silence you started calling him on a regular basis," the magistrate said.

"He sent me a letter congratulating me on my dissertation," corrected Hermes.

"You sent him your dissertation."

"No, I didn't," Hermes corrected again. "He found out about it in a review."

"And you received other congratulations from Greece," the magistrate said.

"No. I didn't," Hermes asserted.

"Your parents . . ." started the magistrate.

"By the time I got my diploma my parents were both dead," Hermes interrupted. "My mother died while I was still in college, my father a year before I finished my dissertation."

"You came back when your mother died," continued the magistrate.

"No."

"When your father died."

"Not then, either."

The magistrate turned curious eyes to Hermes and repeated, "Not then, either."

"I was out of reach both times."

"Out of reach," the magistrate echoed.

"It was summer, I was away from the university, and I hadn't left a forwarding address."

"No address," the magistrate echoed again.

"I was in a national park. I had a summer job."

"On an archaeological site. No address."

"I was working as a photographer. It was a biology expedition."

The examining magistrate remained silent, looking at Hermes with disaffection. Then he said, "You didn't correspond with your parents much, then."

"Rarely."

"I see," said the magistrate, "but you responded to your uncle's one letter by telephoning him."

"No. I wrote him a short note."

"And he wrote back."

"No. He called me. Many calls followed."

"He invited you to do excavations here."

"He did invite me to come work here, but not on excavations. My work doesn't involve excavations."

"No excavations. But you worked on other sites outside Greece."

"I've *never* worked on a site."

The magistrate seemed surprised but still unhappy. "You graduated in archaeology and you never worked on an archaeological site," he recapitulated finally.

"My studies took another path," Hermes explained. "I combined classics with mathematics."

The examining magistrate's eyes flickered. "Only theory. You never worked outside the university."

"I did. After college graduation. My academic experience in deciphering archaic texts was useful for doing some commercial work."

"Like antique dealing," said the magistrate, as if to himself.

"No. I did cryptographic work to protect the records of the company," specified Hermes.

". . . company."

"Finance company."

"You worked there for several years," the magistrate said monotonously.

"A year. Later I went to graduate school, in archaeology," stated Hermes.

"No more mathematics."

"Well, not really. My research still followed a computational approach."

The magistrate blinked.

Hermes continued. "I used artificial intelligence tools."

"Intelligence . . ." echoed the magistrate.

"Artificial intelligence," insisted Hermes.

"Intelligence," repeated the magistrate in a dull manner.

"Artificial intelligence. It has to do with computers," Hermes explained.

"Computers," the magistrate said again, and focused his eyes on the far left corner of his desk with intense fascination. "Now, after your uncle's commitment to support you, you found it convenient, given his position and affluence, to come to Greece."

"I'm here on a grant."

"Nevertheless, at the very last minute you decided not to stay in his house," the magistrate went on.

Hermes hesitated for a moment.

The magistrate added insistently, "Your uncle's maid said that you'd been expected to stay with him."

"I already told you he asked me to stay at his house only at the very last minute. As for my decision to come here, it has nothing to do with any invitation. I received a grant that covers my expenses. I don't need any other supporters."

"And what about your mother's relatives?"

"My mother had no relatives, here or anywhere else that I know of. She was Polish. No one on that side of my family survived the war."

"Do you know who inherits your uncle's estate?" asked the magistrate, slowly beginning to scratch the back of his neck.

"No."

The magistrate focused on Hermes' eyes. "Your uncle has chosen the Academy of Greece as his sole inheritor."

"In that case I hope the robbers left enough behind in the house for the academy to inherit."

"The robbers? How do you know there were any robbers?" The magistrate seemed animated for the first time.

"Who else would have killed him?" Hermes asked.

The magistrate scanned Hermes' face carefully. "Nothing seems to have been taken from Professor Agraphiotis' house." Then with an unexpected change of approach, he asked, "Can you please tell me everything. Where were you and what were you doing from the moment you set foot in Greece through to this morning?"

Hermes related his story in great detail.

"Now, can you give me a better description of this archaeological object?" The magistrate visibly suppressed a yawn, bringing his hand over his mouth.

Hermes described the Golden Thinking Machine as best he could.

"Those specifics are vague for an archaeologist," the magistrate reflected aloud in a bored tone.

Hermes tried to meet his gaze, but the magistrate was now paying intense attention to the near left corner of his desk.

"I didn't have time to memorize the thing," Hermes said between his teeth.

"Are there any other similar objects?" the magistrate tossed out. "I mean in museums."

"It's difficult to say because I'm not certain what the artifact was about. What I remember is something like a miniature hodometer, a device used in chariots to calculate the length of a journey. There are a few of those around. It also seemed to me like a mechanism that probably permits homocentric, eccentric, and epicentric motions through its cogs, something like a horologium, an anaphoric clock, that calculates the movements of the sun through the zodiac and the position of the moon and the constellations. In fact, if I recollect correctly, a similar object was recovered from the sea near Antikythera at the beginning of this century."

The magistrate turned his head slightly and looked at Hermes out of the corners of his eyes.

"What is peculiar," added Hermes, "and what makes this object stand apart from the others it resembles is that although I guess it is a Hellenistic artifact, it was found on an archaic site, and that it bore seemingly proto-Hellenic inscriptions. The site was abandoned during the Hellenistic period. What's strange too is that it was made of gold. Neither hodometers nor astral clocks are made out of such material."

"Could it have been used for anything else?"

"The way the symbols seemed arranged around the disks, it also could have been an encryption machine, a very early one, working on the principle of transposing ciphers and jumbling letters. Something like the one developed by Alberti, the Renaissance architect, but considerably more sophisticated."

"Why's that?" the magistrate asked, adjusting his tie.

Hermes shrugged. "Because the origins of Alberti's idea, using rotating disks for jumbling and transposing, doesn't seem to go back much earlier than the medieval theological, divinatory instrument, the *Ars Magna* of Raymond Lull. In addition, the Santorini object appears to be much more complicated than Alberti's device."

"Many people must have known the treasure had arrived in Athens," the magistrate remarked, averting his face from Hermes while his eyes remained fixed on him.

"No, I don't think so. I have the impression I was the only one," said Hermes.

The magistrate let his eyes rest on Hermes' face without speaking.

Hermes went on, "What Professor Agraphiotis did was very irregular. You can't take artifacts from their site, their context, just like that, and go around with them. I don't understand how he could have brought it to his house and shown it to me."

"It seems he trusted you." A joyless smile looked like it was about to surface on the magistrate's face but did not.

"Still, it's very irregular," said Hermes.

The magistrate took a breath and asked, "Did you notice anyone outside your uncle's house when you left?"

"No one," answered Hermes.

The magistrate insisted. "Nobody in a car for example, or doing some kind of a job in the court?"

"No one," Hermes repeated.

"And you had no difficulty getting a taxi at that time."

"None."

"And you went straight to your apartment, where your relative was expecting you."

"I called her from Cambridge a day before I left," explained Hermes.

"You corresponded with her."

"Occasionally. She took care of the apartment."

"She knew you were going to visit your uncle first."

"She did."

"And you told her that you were going to see a new find there."

"No, I didn't."

"You hid it from her."

"No, I didn't. I only talked about business with her, things like bills for the services of the apartment."

"Do you have a lawyer here?"

"Yes. But I never met him. My cousin deals with him, too."

"I see." Then, shifting his tone once more, the magistrate asked, "What do you think your uncle did after you left?"

"He mentioned that he was planning to work."

"He was disappointed you left so quickly."

"I think he was."

"But you left anyhow."

"I was very tired. I had a headache. I still do."

"And you left," repeated the magistrate.

"I felt uncomfortable imposing, even if he was a relative." After a short pause Hermes added, "and I found it embarrassing to see this archaeological treasure just sitting there."

"There is no longer any trace of this treasure." The magistrate was looking at Hermes straight in the eyes now.

Hermes flinched. "I thought you said nothing was missing."

The magistrate seemed not to have heard Hermes. He said, "Well, that's all for the moment. Except for one more thing I wanted you to know." The magistrate paused. "A neighbor heard your uncle calling out a name about the time we suspect he was murdered. Twice. That name was yours."

"What?" said Hermes and ran the fingertips of his left hand through his hair. The magistrate's eyes chased the fingertips.

Then the magistrate tapped the top of his desk softly. "I would like you to inform my office if you plan to take a trip outside Athens. I might need to . . . interview you again. And if you have any additional thoughts, please call me. Here is my telephone number. My name is Haralambos Karras, and . . . my condolences."

He handed him a piece of paper and looked even more dissatisfied.

Hermes moved to the door. The examining magistrate dismissed him with displeasure without rising. His hands remained behind the desk as if pressing a switch.

It took Hermes several minutes to find his way to the street after wandering through many heavily fumigated corridors painted in different tones of blue-gray, returning to Karras' door many times. In the end, he reached the exit.

The glare was painful. He stepped down the white marble stairway with his eyes almost shut. At the bottom of the steps he found a taxi. The driver asked, "Should I take you to a hospital?"

Summer Flu

When Hermes arrived at the apartment Eleni was already there. They had agreed she would keep a key to the place.

"Hermes," she said, "you don't look well. Didn't you have a good sleep last night?" There was noise in the kitchen. "That's Nina." She shouted toward the kitchen. "Nina, come and meet Hermes."

A young woman walked in from the kitchen. She was lean and tall, taller than Eleni, about the same height as Hermes. Her black hair was like his, only shorter and spiky. She greeted Hermes, scrutinizing every detail of his face.

"How alike you two look!" said Eleni. "It's astonishing." Before Hermes had time to say anything she added, "Nina, you leave now. Hermes needs to rest." Then, seeing the girl's disappointed eyes, she added, "She'll call back after her examination tomorrow."

Nina murmured some words about returning after the exam and left the room. The door of the apartment banged shut.

Eleni turned to Hermes. She hesitated, then said, "A detective came this morning. He was inquiring about you. It was in connection with Philippos. I guess you heard the news."

He nodded.

"The funeral's tomorrow. Tomorrow at eleven."

Eleni left the room. Hermes went straight to bed. The telephone rang right away and rang again. By then Hermes was fast asleep.

Hermes opened his eyes. He was lying on his back in bed. The afternoon sun entered the room. He looked at his watch; he had slept for over twenty-four hours.

There was a strong smell of gas coming from the street. He shut the shutters and windows. He went to the kitchen, found some fruit, and brought it back to the living room. He washed and dressed.

He took a low stool, sat in front of the small computer, turned it on, and traced the same superimposed circles, the same twisted loops.

Gradually radiant formulas began to parade upon the screen, replacing the drawing.

Then the telephone rang.

"Dr. Steganos?" a slow, deliberate voice asked.

"Yes."

"Dr. Steganos, Votris here. Votris." The man cleared his throat. "Please accept my condolences."

By the time he hung up the phone, Hermes had an appointment for the next day at noon.

He went back to his computer.

The Cousin's Deal

It was nearly evening. Hermes was still sitting on the low stool, working. All the shutters were closed.

There was a soft tapping at the door. Hermes stepped out quietly into the entrance hall. The tapping started again. Hermes listened.

"It's me. It's me."

He turned on the light and opened the door. "Why don't you ring the bell?" he asked.

"I didn't want to disturb you." Nina strode in past him. She saw the computer turned on. "Oh I'm sorry. I thought you were sick."

"I'm not sick any more."

"Is this a computer?"

"Yes. A laptop."

"Laptop. I've never seen anything like it before."

"Of course you haven't. It's a prototype. One of a pair."

She looked at the machine in amazement and walked over to Hermes' other side without letting her eyes leave the computer. "Wow. What happened to the other one?"

"As far as I know a company is trying to mass produce it." Then he asked, "How did your exam go?"

She answered with contempt, "Very well." She shrugged her shoulders. "Boring."

He pulled together his eyebrows. "Why?"

"Just some trivial calculus problems. Took less than an hour to finish. I have one more in September."

"What's it in?"

"Organic chemistry, a required course for all first-year students. God knows why. What are you working on, anyway?" she asked, going up to the screen. Narrowing her eyes she said, surprised, "I don't understand a thing!"

"There's nothing much to understand. Just notes."

"What language are you using?"

"LISP."

"What's that?"

"A computer language for manipulating symbols in a humanlike manner. Have you done any programming yet?"

"Some FORTRAN and some PASCAL. Taught myself." Turning away from the screen she said, "You must be a pretty unusual archaeologist."

He smiled. "Why?"

"What do you use your computer for?"

"For reasoning."

"Reasoning? I thought computers were for calculating."

"Sure. Initially they were used as numerical machines. But as early as the 1940s people realized that these machines could do more if they used symbols and human-like thinking instead of just ciphers."

"Cybernetic robots in action. Science-fiction stuff. I know."

"Cybernetics are very applied. They're not fiction."

"I know. Control mechanisms and communication systems. But not reasoning. That's only in cybernetic SF."

"Sure. But at the time cybernetics was invented it was thought of as a global scientific program that investigated information processing broadly, the same way artificial intelligence is today—AI, as it's called."

"Artificial intelligence! More science fiction!"

"Not true, AI is . . ."

"What makes it different from cybernetics?" she interrupted.

"In cybernetics, information was expressed through numbers and statistics, and it was employed mostly for guiding machine operations through numerical computations. It wasn't used to control symbolic knowledge and it wasn't applied in inference machines for qualitative reasoning."

"And what's LIST?"

"LISP, you mean. It's just a computer language. It came in with AI and was developed very much in response to AI's needs for symbol systems. Cybernetics didn't need sophisticated programming languages like LISP. Artificial intelligence depends heavily on them."

"You speak as though you are lecturing, and it's gloomy here. Can we have some light, please? Can I open the shutters?" She moved toward the balcony.

Hermes drew open the shutters. They walked out to the balcony. Nina sat on the railing. Hermes brought his laptop and placed it on a little card table that was already out.

"And how long does it take to learn LISP?" asked Nina.

She leaned backward on the railing. One foot lifted off the ground.

"Don't!" Hermes burst out suddenly, almost upsetting the little card table as he got up. "Watch out!"

Nina rolled her eyes. "I'm used to it," she said. But she stepped down anyway. "Well, how long?" she insisted.

"Depends on what you want to do with it. LISP isn't like other languages." He added a few more details about the language. "It's a flexible, open-ended system you can adapt in a number of ways."

"And to get a general idea?"

"I'll tell you after I've seen you working on it for a week."

"You mean I can use your computer?"

Hermes thought for a minute. "You can when I'm not using it. But you must take very good care of it. It's an irreplaceable machine."

"What program do you use?" She touched the keyboard without pressing the keys.

"Like the machine, the program is a prototype also, a special program designed by the same person who made the machine." Hermes touched a key and the symbols disappeared from the screen.

Nina whistled. "That's fast. What's special about this program?"

"It's like an encyclopedia of methods, a development environment to make your own programs in."

She made a face. "Will you help me learn it?"

"You can also use a tutorial by yourself. It's part of the overall system."

Nina looked disappointed.

Hermes added, "It depends on my research."

"I know. You have so many things to do. Your book. To solve the crime."

Hermes jumped in his seat. "What crime?"

"What crime? Philippos' murder, of course. I think it's fascinating," said Nina. "I can help you solve the murder. Especially if you help me with LISP. We could combine forces in detection."

"What? This mess has nothing to do with you or me."

"Come on, what kind of idiot do you think I am? You're in trouble. You're the prime suspect."

Hermes stared at Nina, confused.

"I spied on you. When Eleni kicked me out of the room and I was supposed to go back home. I hid in the kitchen. I listened to everything you discussed with her."

"What?" whispered Hermes.

Nina continued excited. "I know. It's unforgivable. But you think you could work out a super-program to solve his murder? You've solved much harder mysteries before. You must have. I could assist you. I could be your Watson. We could use the crime as a case study for my education. You said yourself artificial intelligence is mostly about problem solving. Detection is a kind of problem solving. We could call the program 'Sherlock 2000.'"

"2000?" asked Hermes.

"Why not? The century is coming to an end soon," she announced solemnly. "Just a few more years to go. We have to prepare for it. In my department they're still in the Stone Age. The only thing professors ever talk about are projectiles. Catapults at the beginning of the year to analyze motion. Six months later stones thrown from moving chariots to introduce frames of reference in relativity. Finally, before exams, bombs and targets to explain goal-directed systems. It's so boring."

"You have a point," Hermes sympathized. "It must have been different when Galileo lectured about ballistics for the first time."

"But this is now. Today war is carried out through intelligence services. Why not teach through spy stories?" Her eyes danced.

"Well, spies aren't substitutes for missiles, either in warfare or in the classroom. But spy stories could be useful to talk about information-processing systems, I suppose."

"Do you think we could work out some demonstrations?" Nina jumped to her feet.

"I'm only an archaeologist," said Hermes, raising his hand noncommitally.

She shook her head. "With all the computers and artificial intelligence?"

"Every educated person should be familiar with computers and AI."

She pointed to him. "I have a theory. You're here to work for the CIA. Philippos, the royalist, was KGB. That's why you murdered him."

"Listen," Hermes said, suddenly impatient. "That's enough. This kind of talk can be dangerous."

"I'm sorry." She blushed at his abrupt explosion. She stirred uneasily as if tired of standing. "I didn't realize . . ."

"Why don't you take a seat," said Hermes, calm now.

"I'll tell you the truth," she began. "I'm fed up with studies here. I want to go to the States and study artificial intelligence. I know more about it than I pretended. I mean I know enough to be seriously interested. I know also that you're not just an archaeologist. Please don't get angry." She hesitated. "I went through some of your computer files—those I could get into that is, most of them were inaccessible—while you were sick. You were asleep for so long! I thought you'd never get up."

"What?"

"I read your notes about solving problems."

Hermes looked at her, astonished.

"Yes. Artificial intelligence. That's what I want to go into," Nina concluded, taking a deep breath.

"You'd better prepare for years of study," said Hermes trying to get up.

"I have all the time in the world," she said. She pushed him back into his chair lightly. "Each day we'll discuss just a small part of the theory. Then I'll study it by myself and put it in the computer. Each day, as you'll be gathering more facts about the crime, I'll be feeding them into the machine. And soon Sherlock 2000 will solve the crime."

"I wish you would stop referring to the 'crime.' Murder's a serious matter. I wish also that commonsense problem solving were as simple as you think."

Nina ignored the remark. "Is it a deal?"

Hermes hesitated, then said, "It's a deal."

"When do we start?"

He looked at her, amazed.

"Where do we start?"

He said, resigned, "With representation."

"Representation?" She looked disappointed.

He started solemnly, "Representation is a set of conventions to make descriptions with."

She appeared puzzled.

He continued, "To solve any problem, whether with our mind or with a machine, you need descriptions. They capture information on the basis of which you can act appropriately. To provide an answer to a question, to reason how to carry out a task, you need to have a good description of where you are, where you aim, what lies between the two, how many ways you have to go over the gap. Good descriptions make better solutions."

"What's a better solution? You either solve something or not."

"You can come closer, and faster, to a target if you have the right representation."

"If you're talking about photographs and maps, pictures, I see what you mean. I see they could have been of great use for Holmes and Watson in *Appledore Towers,* and for us if we had to enter a 'silent and gloomy house to search it without turning on the lights,'" she quoted.

Hermes laughed, "I didn't know you knew Conan Doyle's *Charles Augustus Milverton* by heart."

"Read it six times." She started to recite. "'With our black silk face coverings which turned us into two of the most truculent figures of London . . .'"

Hermes cut her short, "There are many other ways of representing besides pictures. Pictures are good to describe objects in space, form, position, texture, color. Pictures are also easy for humans to remember and consult. But they're not as good in helping us answer questions about complex time or cause relations. Pictures also can give computers a tough time. Alternative representations that use words, numbers, or some symbols of logic might be preferable in this case."

"More objective."

"I didn't mention objectivity. It's more a question of interest and fit."

"I don't get it."

"A representation is good with respect to what you want to do with it. Replacing Roman numerals with Arabic ones made arithmetic easier, not more factual."

"Objectivity doesn't count?"

"I didn't say that either. I meant there are many other things that count. Descriptions of problems represent what we have in our mind to solve problems with, which might relate not only to objects that exist now but also to objects that existed in the past, and to some other objects that can or could have existed under certain conditions, or even some that could never have existed."

"Why bother?"

"Because out of such objects we can make hypotheses, predictions, plans."

"Sounds good. I'll keep it in mind. Now give me an example of a representation of a problem. That's what I need."

"I'll give you a very simple one. It deals with dangerous crossings. You know the story of the farmer who wanted to find a way to cross the river with his possessions, a fox, a goose, and some grain, by boat? The boat could only hold the farmer and one of his possessions, and the farmer could not leave the fox alone with the goose or the goose with the grain without fatal consequences."

"Of course I do. It took me five minutes to solve it more than ten years ago."

"Not bad. How did you do it?"

"I found a carton, an apple, an onion, a tomato, and a pepper, and I pretended they were the boat and the three heroes of the story. A long rug on the floor became the river."

"Not bad again. Your representation through objects permitted you to concentrate on the essentials: the passengers, their arrangements on either side of the river, the crossings. But it didn't offer you an overview of the problem. Now we'll try another representation for the same problem. We'll use links and nodes. It works like this. Each node stands for an acceptable allocation of the farmer and his three possessions on either side of the river. The links for the crossings. Let's see if this representation can help us."

"Let me try." Nina grabbed paper and pencil from the table and walked out on the balcony.

She was back soon. She shouted, "Definitely less time than my previous record. Here is the solution, ten permissible allocations linked by possible crossings."

"That was quick. How did you do it?"

He took the paper from her hands and looked at the scribbles:

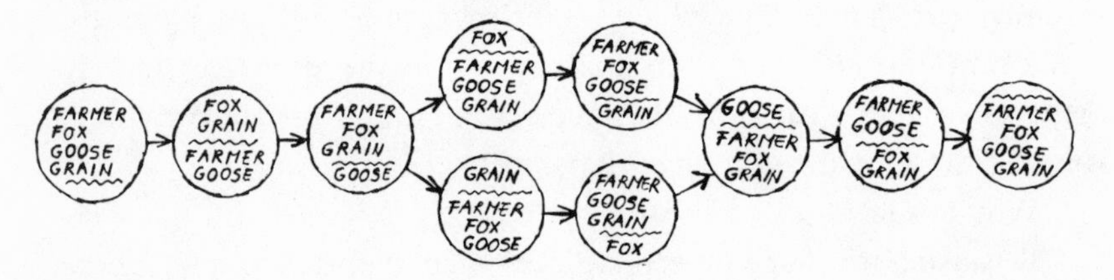

She spoke fast. "Well. There are the two sides of the river, and during each stage of the crossing we can find the farmer, goose, fox, and grain, in different arrangements. In fact sixteen possible ones . . ."

"You have a talent for combinatorics."

". . . out of which only ten are safe." She halted. "The rest involve murder!"

Hermes turned his eyes away from the paper and looked at her.

"Next," she continued, "I simply had to link these nodes, to describe the possible crossings. I calculated how many links are between all nodes. Forty-five. But accepting only those that are permitted in the story, I cut them down to ten."

"Very well done."

She was beaming. "Correct. This *is* a good representation. Somehow it directs your mind. It gives you an overview of the problem. A change in the representation can make you see regularities and symmetries inside your solution that can simplify the solution radically.

You realize, for example, that you don't have to solve the parts of your problem that are like the ones you're already solved."

"Sounds good for transportation problems. Now, what about Sherlock?"

"It's good for Sherlock as well. It's good for any problem that involves states, transformations of one state into another as a result of an action."

She got a glimpse out of the window: "Difficult crossing problems. Hmm. Your problem has made me think of another thing."

"What thing."

"Philippos."

"Philippos?"

"Think of it. His assistant, the maid, the treasure."

"Yes."

"They're a threesome. They commuted between Athens and Santorini. They had to cross the Aegean many times," she said quickly.

"So?"

"The maid, if left alone with the treasure, would steal it. And the assistant, if left alone with the maid, would make advances to her."

"I see some similarities. But . . ."

"In the later version the peasant is eaten."

"What are you driving at?" Hermes looked at her suspiciously.

"Obviously something went wrong. The rules weren't respected. I tell you what. Philippos fooled around with the maid and was killed by the lovesick assistant. *Crime de passion.* Then the maid ran away with the treasure."

"Nina! Where did you get all that? Philippos . . ."

". . . made advances even to me. He was a Don Juan."

"To you?"

She watched Hermes without answering.

"But the maid is over sixty," he ventured.

"And Philippos was over seventy," she asserted.

"And the assistant? Who's he?"

"He committed suicide the same day Philippos was killed." She added quickly, "Didn't you hear about it?"

Hermes studied Nina, puzzled. "What? That's interesting. How did you know?"

"It was in the newspapers. Nobody paid attention, though."

"That brings in a new factor. I wonder," he said gloomily.

"You shouldn't."

"Why?"

"Because I invented him."

Hermes gawked. "You invented him?"

Nina nodded.

"Why did you do that?"

"Because there has to be an assistant."

Hermes was silent.

She smiled. "Don't you see? There were three objects in the representation."

"I see. Nodes and links, by replacing words, gave you the competence to grasp the problem. At the same time, they invited you to fly away from it. Are you seriously interested in scientific methods or in wild fiction?"

Her eyes pleaded. "Give me a point to start with, a hypothesis, and I'll stop being wild. Don't you see that we should have had a hypothesis by now? Isn't that the first thing to do in a scientific investigation?"

"Choosing the proper representation is the first step toward a hypothesis, the beginning of solving a problem. Anyhow what I don't understand is why you have to be so far-out in going about it."

"Frustration."

"At not having a hypothesis yet?"

"This, and at your face."

"My face? What is wrong with it?'

"You're withholding things."

"I'm not. Why are you so suspicious all the time?"

"Because I can't read you. Have you told me everything about Philippos? All the hunches?"

"Of course I have."

"And the facts?"

"And the facts."

"You have to tell me everything you have done and everything you have encountered from the moment you landed, and maybe before that. I have to see."

He sighed.

Nina smirked. "And then will it be possible to save all the hunches and facts in the memory of Sherlock 2000 so I can be consulting him without taking more of your time?"

"We can, but we have to make him remember first, build a data base where all these hunches and facts can be stored."

"Let's."

"But I warn you. It'll be a provisional structure, just a shelf, where we can leave our notes in labeled files. Later, little by little, we'll transform it into a more intelligent, mindlike memory organization."

She lowered her eyebrows, ready to speak.

He didn't wait. "I think you've worked enough for today. We both need some sleep now."

She stood up but did not go away. "Will Sherlock 2000 solve problems during sleep?"

"While we sleep, yes."

"And while Sherlock sleeps?"

"That's much more difficult. To make machines emulate the way people solve problems while they are asleep, we'll have to endow them with a subconscious."

"We'll have to work on that."

But Hermes had gone back to the keyboard. She went to the door, then hesitated and swung around. "If you're not a spy, why did you have to work behind closed shutters"?

"You're incorrigible . . ." said Hermes, without taking his eyes from the screen.

The door shut. She was gone. He said to himself as he worked on the keyboard, ". . . or very bored."

Two hours later Hermes was still on the balcony. It was cool and quiet. It was past midnight. The laptop was still on the card table. The screen shone under the clear starry night. A moth that had been flying in circles for the last hour rested on the computer screen. It started climbing up its surface, wandering through the glowing symbols and in and out of a window on the top right side of the screen filled with figures of superimposed and interlocked disks and rotors.

The Professor Problem-Solver

The address Votris had given for the appointment belonged to a big purple Modernist building in the heart of the noisiest part of the city. In the early 1930s it had been a luxury apartment house for successful professionals. The building was smeared all over with signs of different sizes, shapes, colors, and lettering. Smaller signs surrounded the entrance, advertising foreign language lessons, Japanese stenography, obscure political parties, and minor agencies. There was a sign for a bus company that traveled to any part of the world, another for "natural" counterpoisons, and a third for the protection of widowed mothers. Next to it was the faded color photograph of a large, long-bearded priest in dark glasses surrounded by a woman and seven children. The most prominent place over the door was taken by the aluminum plaque of a company that imported Czech crystal and miniature retractable scissors.

Inside, propaganda and commercial brochures covered the walls of the marble entrance hall, which still impressed by its generous size. Publicity and announcements littered the way to the elevator.

The elevator, an old metal cage, was obscured by similar commercial epigraphs and some handwritten messages. One read "Entrance to the Many Entrances: tel. 777–7777." Next to it was "Man is a Name."

Once out of the elevator on the top floor, the scene was very different. Bare polished walls, an intense smell of turpentine, wax, and varnish, and one door with no name plate on it and no bell to ring. Hermes knocked.

The man who opened the door was old, short, and thin. On his frail body was an aged head with thick, disheveled long hair, a leonine head. Behind him stood a woman of the same height, but very

round. The impression of roundness was accentuated by her almost perfectly circular face with the hair tied behind, forming a tight sphere.

"Votris," said the man and shook Hermes' hand vigorously. The woman waited on the side. Hermes entered a small hall covered with green patent leather. The woman shut the door, its back also covered with green patent leather. Suddenly it was oppressively quiet. Hermes was guided to a second hall and then to an enormous room, divided into two parts. At one end were a long dining table and chairs, at the other a group of huge overgrown sofas. A double row of glass sliding doors covered by a layer of complicated shiny aluminum shutters opened onto a wide balcony. The shutters were drawn, pleasantly filtering the midday sun. The walls were covered with photographs in uniform black frames of individuals or groups, of laboratory equipment or machine installations or instruments set up on plains, valleys, mountaintops. No city noise reached inside the room.

The old man turned ceremoniously to Hermes and finally spoke.

"It has been a very, very long time." Votris had a surprisingly youthful voice and spoke in strong but mellifluous tones. "You remember Sophia," he said introducing the woman. "Yes. A very long time indeed. It is 1983. The last time you were here was the 25th of March, 1960, to be precise. I remember it because it was the day I received the announcement of an honorary degree in medicine from the University of Lisbon for my papers on astroepidemiology. I, of course, proposed your father for the same honorary degree. He had written a monumental paper on lead poisoning in Ancient Greece. The rector of the university, a medical doctor himself—a very good friend of ours from the time of our studies—wanted very much to honor your father. But your father wouldn't hear of it. He insisted that the investigation had nothing to do with medicine. Your father was a most humble and demanding man. Most demanding. Our greatest archaeologist," Votris said somewhat awkwardly.

Hermes coughed.

Votris continued. "Your father and I shared a room for three years during our studies. Later on, we never let a month go by without dining together." He paused momentarily. "Your mother could have had a great career as a mathematician. She did some first-class research in Poland just before the war, improving the capabilities of the Enigma decoding machine. With the collapse of Poland she escaped with the rest of the team, as you know, to Rumania. From there she could have gone to France with the others. She had her own contacts. She kept up a correspondence with André Weil. But in the confusion she lost touch with the rest of the group. She was chased by the Iron Guard and moved south. Her final stop was Athens. She spent the war years in hiding. Your father saved her life. I helped too. I think I can say this to you in all earnestness—I don't think she ever quite recovered from those ordeals. There seems to have been no place for mathematics in her life after the war."

Votris cleared his throat uneasily. Hermes coughed again. Votris turned to Sophia. "I think Dr. Steganos would like some sherry," he said. Then he led Hermes toward the center of the room.

"Take a seat, Dr. Steganos. I want to hear everything about your work. I understand it has to do with deciphering ancient inscriptions and it has some general implications for information processing. Most interesting. You see, I'm an information theory specialist and a bit of an expert on cryptanalysis myself. It's only natural, of course, given my background. I helped establish the communications security system of this country some decades ago and I had some pet projects. I equipped our clandestine commando forces with enciphering machines similar to the Enigma, disguised in portable scales, using weights as coding devices. Decades later a similar device was applied in another part of the world. I also created a scandal when I almost succeeded in deciphering extraterrestrial messages. It sounds like a strange thing to do. But it is a curious story, still unresolved. They used the duration of silence intervals in their system. But the transmissions just disappeared suddenly one day. That was also the early nineteen-fifties."

Then, lowering the register of his voice about half an octave, Votris muttered, "I'm sorry about your uncle. The Academy is very grateful for his gift. But he didn't lead a very prudent life and he wasted too much time outside science. Science demands sacrifice and discipline. Well, well. Your mother found him amusing." Votris gazed into the void.

"She never spoke to me about her life," Hermes said simply. "She tutored me for school and the only thing she insisted on was that I leave to study in the States."

"Yes," said Votris, clearing his throat once more. "Tell me about your stay here so far."

Hermes recounted all the events since his arrival at the airport. Votris made no comment. Instead he said, "Now, tell me about your work."

Hermes reported the results of his research along very general lines.

Sophia moved quietly on the other side of the room, preparing for lunch. As Hermes' presentation approached its end, she invited them to take their seats at the table.

"I believe your work is most interesting," said Votris. "But I'm afraid you are choosing the easy path."

"Why shouldn't someone choose a simple method instead of a complicated one?" Hermes asked.

Votris answered: "Why are words, everyday vocabulary, simpler than numbers, I would say. You're scared of formalizing your ideas. You're scared of general mathematical methods, you say, because they're too general and of numbers because they're too precise. But hasn't all scientific progress been accomplished through generalization and precision? I don't want to say that what you tried to do is not scientific. But I do have the impression that you, like the rest of your generation, shy away from the hard problems and seek out easy, soft answers in the name of pragmatism. I find that disappointing."

Sophia brought in a dish of stuffed peppers and left. "I know," Votris continued, "that there have always been opposing points of view in science. They come in waves and shake up people at regular intervals. Each generation expands what the other has just touched on. Your generation is breaking this continuity."

"I don't believe the situation's any different from what it was before. Your generation initiated so many revolutions."

"That's what they were called, although we never claimed our theories were incommensurable with the old, and we never made conceptual catastrophism our credo."

"You might not have used these words, but you advanced through shifts and leaps, not through marginal improvement."

"I don't agree. Do you know how I started my career?"

"You were a mathematician first," remarked Hermes.

"Correct. I got my degree and the first prize in the university when I was twenty-one. Numbers fascinated me, but only as long as they had to do with the real world. My first job was in the Bavarian Railway's scheduling bureau and I did an excellent job. Soon there was a competition to design a new route passing over the mountains. Each alternative route involved a combination of connected points, and each had different costs—excavation, construction, sheeting, bedding, expropriating land—and different benefits. I tried to enumerate all possible combinations. I considered the parts of each route as points of a network with a negative or positive value, the costs or benefits of a particular route. I realized that I had spent too much time trying to identify all these alternative passages and that very little time was left to submit a solution.

"I remember it was the last weekend of the carnival, very early that year. I decided to go away for three days to a mountain inn to concentrate. I was very anxious, so anxious I couldn't work on my calculations that first night. Instead I gazed out of the window at the blizzard, the chaotic multitude of the snowflakes coming down, forming patterns in front of my eyes. I didn't see flakes, I saw clusters."

Votris went on, intoning melodiously. "This image made a great impression on me, and it has followed me for years. It had a great influence when I was dealing with information processing and recognition, but that night it gave me the idea of looking at my alternatives and my calculations more as patterns than as isolated objects. It occurred to me that I could reduce the number of my calculations if I examined the various branches of the network selectively and eliminated the need to calculate paths that I could prove in advance could not offer me a better outcome. I was groping with what came to be known as an optimization algorithm.

"Well, I finished my calculations a day ahead of the deadline and was awarded the first prize. They were impressed intuitively with the results without paying much attention to the method I had followed.

But I looked at things differently and decided to go back to school. First I studied civil engineering, then mechanical engineering. It took me three years to get both diplomas. My thesis for each study was a version of the same problem. In fact I kept on explaining the approach I had accidentally hit on that night in the mountains. But instead of dealing with the rational organization of paths in space, I turned to scheduling in order to rationally schedule operations in time. In civil engineering I studied the order of succession of production functions to construct a railway bridge, and in mechanical engineering the order of succession of production functions to manufacture a new type of diesel train engine. At that time I was fascinated more by railways than methods.

"Only after the war," Votris went on excitedly, "did I realize that I had actually discovered what came to be known as 'critical path method.' I didn't care, because by then I was in information theory and even deeper into combinatorial optimization."

Votris paused. He took a breath. "I'm going through these old stories to show you how science progresses incrementally by facing new questions and expanding the old solution to new problems, replacing one physical model of the world—*ein physikalisches Weltbild,* as Max Planck would have said—by another that contains a larger amount of correct information. This broadens the area of application of the theory, while it limits the possibility of errors excluding quantities that cannot be measured. Science does not improve by claiming to be soft and lenient while it *is* in fact getting soft and lenient."

Hermes protested at this point. "But introducing qualitative reasoning doesn't mean getting softer. Experts use 'rules of thumb,' qualitative reasoning, all the time."

"Oh, yes! You mean expert systems," Votris said in an animated voice. "I know. They're taking over. They're even replacing critical path method. I wonder who can trust such an eclectic stimulus-response bunch of associations. How can they predict anything without a theory? And have you heard how they treat probability formulas? An insult to human intelligence."

Hermes protested again. "You're talking about a very limited application of qualitative machine reasoning," he said.

Votris paid no attention. "And just when computers were getting bigger and faster, 'inexact' reasoning was brought back to science, not reasoning 'under uncertainty' mind you, but reasoning 'inexactly.' How do they think we will be able to optimize?"

"Einstein," Hermes suggested, "didn't like it when your generation abandoned continuity and causality in favor of indeterminacy in physics. Maybe engineers are no longer interested in optimization today."

"Not interested in optimization? After centuries of struggle to develop optimization methods?" Votris' look was angry now. "Optimization isn't a fashion. It's nature's principle. It's everywhere, from the compact hexagonal shape of the honeycombs to the icosahedral symmetry of spherical viruses, in each organ, in each form of growth. Optimality is present in nearly every domain of physics and biology. Engineers just follow nature's example. But in order to exercise this selection you need to be able to enumerate alternative solutions, measure and compare their structure, their operation, their performance. And to do that, you need numbers, not qualities."

Votris' whole body was quaking. But Hermes caught the cold calculating eye of the professor trying to weigh his audience's reactions.

Hermes remarked, "What do you do if you can't collect all the data you need for your calculations, or if your data are purely qualitative, or if you simply have not enough time for your calculation? You're too much of an engineer, Professor Votris. You can't tolerate anything that is not precise. Anything outside the diet of numbers makes you allergic."

Votris jumped up excitedly. "Doctor Steganos! Hermes, if you will permit me! *You* are an engineer. *You* are the one who's thirsty for results. I don't measure proofs by the yard, as Frege said. I don't want to emulate the way people chit-chat. I'm interested in valid thinking. I want the closest possible relation between signs and things. I'm rather curious as to how you developed such a pragmatic taste, you an archaeologist," said Votris with some sarcasm.

"It is not pragmatic taste," said Hermes smiling. "I look at rules of thumb, symbolic computations, and numerical calculations as different kinds of tools invented in the course of history to match specific problem contexts. I don't value them abstractly."

"But you just said the opposite," protested Votris.

"I said some tools are preferable to others with respect to a given context. As an archaeologist I am interested in such tools in a dual capacity. On the one hand as means of studying certain phenomena that concern me. For example, deciphering a number of inscriptions—and AI methods have proved successful where purely numerical calculations have not. And, on the other, as phenomena in themselves. I'm interested in studying the world from within the human mind, I'm interested in thinking. I'm interested in how the human mind represents the world and what the primitives it uses are and how they are structured. You look at the world from the outside, you try to make models, to describe and explain the insides of stars, the shapes of their swarm behavior, fractal Medusas. I see the photograph on your wall." Hermes pointed to a photograph of a volatile liquid substance on the wall.

"But if you are interested in the insides of the human mind, my dear boy," Votris snapped back, "you may be searching at the wrong level. The heights of physical symbol systems won't give you the answers or universal concepts or representation primitives. You should be looking down at the level of molecular transformations that take place at neuronal sites. But I'll wait until the next time we meet to challenge you on this point. Maybe you would like to rest now. Or maybe . . ."

Although only half closing his eyes, Votris was unable to hide their sparkling. "You have some questions to ask me about the climate—I mean the situation at large here—as you've been away so long."

"I do want to come back to this discussion because we left it open at a most crucial point," Hermes said. "But, before I leave, I did want to ask you . . . How serious do you think the Agraphiotis case is? Could it create any problems for me? As you know, I was the last person to see him alive."

"Yes. Now I remember somebody mentioning that to me yesterday after the funeral, at the Academy. The Academy is one big gossip center . . . Not all my colleagues are as busy with their subjects as I am. Well, let's go over to the sofas. It's more comfortable."

They moved to the other side of the room. "Take this seat." Votris pointed to the sofa across from the window. "I can see your face clearer there." Votris took his place, his eyes riveted on Hermes. "So you've been wondering. It's a good coincidence that I called you then."

"I believe it is, Professor Votris," Hermes said. "I have been interviewed by the examining magistrate."

Votris nodded. "I heard something about that too." He cleared his throat. "My dear Hermes. There is a dilemma that I hope the police will not face: either to indict a young brilliant professor, or leave the murder of an old, grandiloquent academician unsolved."

Hermes was listening attentively.

Votris went on. "I sat next to Agraphiotis at the meeting of the Academy a week before you arrived. We chatted for a few minutes. Then he started asking about you. I didn't like his questions. That is all I can tell you for the moment."

"And what do you advise me to do?" asked Hermes worriedly.

"You have already taken the first correct step." Votris nodded his head approvingly. "You have come to see me. Many of my old students are close to the national security department now." His face turned to Sophia, who had just brought the coffee. She nodded to Votris positively. "I will introduce you to a person who can be a good consultant, let us say. A man of method *and* experience. He is an advisor on investments in communication, you might say. Of course, getting back this golden machine will be essential." His eyes shone as he added, "Describe the machine once more, please."

Hermes described the object one more time.

Votris listened as one listens to an encore, anticipating the familiar delicious moments to arrive, losing himself a couple of times in perplexity, then rising toward a state of ecstasy at the end. "For certain it is an analytical machine. I can't say anything about its archaeological value or dating, or about the symbols you mentioned in the readings, but the function is computation. Hermes, we must get it back. We must," he pleaded.

After that he closed his eyes, rested his head on the back of his sofa, and went to sleep. Or so it seemed.

Sophia took Hermes to the door, and he was once more out in the cluttered street under a scorching sun in search of a taxi.

Registering at the Institute

Hermes awoke at sunrise. A pink reflection caressed the wall opposite his window. Metallic shopfront shutters were being rolled up with a great clatter down the street.

He ate a peach, some white cheese, and some bread, and worked for an hour at his laptop. At half past seven he left home. He went to the Institute on foot, passed it, then entered the park that climbed the hill behind it. He wandered among the pine trees for a while. The temperature was rising.

When he went back to the Institute, at half past eight, a young woman asked him if she could be of assistance. He introduced himself.

"Hermes!" she said, focusing on him eyes in which particles of gold and gray spun amid a surrounding tumult of green. "What a name! Oh. There's some mail for you, and the director asked if you'd arrived. He wants to meet you. The librarian too. She has your mail."

The librarian stood on the third step of a wooden ladder.

"We were expecting you the day before yesterday," she said, without getting down.

"My airplane was delayed," said Hermes.

"We checked. You disembarked as scheduled," was her reply.

"Could I have my mail?" Hermes asked, impatient.

"I like to distribute mail at the end of the day," she answered.

"But perhaps I'll be busy in another library by the end of the day."

"Our residents receive their mail at the reception. When they're out of town for longer periods, I keep the mail."

"Well, I'm not out of town," Hermes said. "Can I pick it up? Please don't bother stepping down."

"I certainly will," she said, with greater annoyance. "I'll give you the mail myself."

She climbed down and went to the other end of the room.

"We had a meeting yesterday about reassigning places for reading. We're short of space."

"Whatever you decide."

"Don't you think you should have informed us you'd come late? There's so much happening in airports these days."

"If anything had happened to my plane, you would have learned about it from the newspapers."

"Here it is," she growled, and handed him three envelopes.

He moved to the exit of the building. The young woman stopped him again.

"One more letter. It just arrived. She wants to check all the letters you receive," she whispered, pointing toward the library room. "She's a snoop. But take it anyway."

Hermes gave her a smile and went out in the garden of the Institute. Sitting on a marble bench in the shadow of a citrus tree, he opened the first envelope. It contained a welcome note, a schedule of events, some background on the Institute's history, and a few pages describing scholarly facilities in Athens. The second was from Cambridge, a bank statement. In the third envelope he found a card from Robert. It had been mailed from the airport and said that he would make every effort to come back as early as possible. In the envelope that had just arrived, there was an invitation to an evening party at some "Villa Emma" in Psychiko.

The librarian stood behind one of the tall windows of the building surveying him. He pretended not to see her, folded everything into a packet, put it in his back pocket, and got up. Not much time left before his appointment.

Lobby to the Telexroom

The instructions, delivered by Eleni on behalf of Sophia who was, in turn, under Votris' orders, resembled spy-thriller routines. Hermes followed them precisely.

He entered the hotel from the side street. He did not cross the crowded marble lobby. Instead he turned right and climbed up the ornate blue-carpeted stairs. Churchill, they said, had dropped some ashes of his cigar on that carpet. Hermes reached the mezzanine, turned to the left, and continued to the end of the platform to a small elevator door. He entered the tiny cabin. The directory read *Bar, Mezzanine, Telexroom.* He pressed the button for the telex room.

He stepped out of the elevator and faced a hand-written sign, *Telexroom,* and an arrow under it pointing to the right. He followed the arrow and found himself at the entrance of a cool, long, wide, lemon-colored penthouse bar. No one was there. He proceeded to the end of the bar where a small oasis of potted palm trees stood serenely, camouflaging a small alcove behind it.

In the alcove were two doors. The oval brass plaque of one was engraved with large italic letters, *Private.* The other, in small Roman print, read *Telexroom.* A female voice behind the telexroom door delivered endless figures of agricultural product prices in a half-incantatory, half-reportorial tone, a soft, monotonous monologue. Rings, clicks, and mechanical tapping accompanied the recitation.

A table with four armchairs surrounding it occupied the center of the alcove. Hermes chose one and sat down. The *Private* door opened and a short, stocky man walked out briskly.

"Brigadier General Krypsiadis," he introduced himself, and shook Hermes' hand. "Very hot summer," he said.

"You have a very nice place up here, General. They told me this is your office."

"No, no," said the brigadier, "I only hang around here." He jutted out his chin, extended his arm and slowly traced the outline of the room with his index finger, as if surveying a field. The finger seemed to hover in the direction of the telexroom.

"I'm retired. I just do a little business here and there. You know, small investments, placing my own savings. Some advice for friends, too. That's why I have to be close to the telex, to receive the news as soon as it comes in. The usual thing. Keep an eye on the floating notes, the Euromarkets, U.S. futures, company retails. Information is the alpha and the omega of good business, you know."

The brigadier looked at Hermes with the overbearing amiability of a Middle Eastern carpet dealer through small but bulging eyes. The tip of his tongue pointed hesitantly beyond his slightly open lips toward his pug nose and touched his short black toothbrush mustache. It flicked back into his mouth at great speed. He said, "I met your father twice at Professor Votris' home."

"Professor Votris told me you were a consultant on communications investments."

"A retired man's excuse to keep active," said the brigadier with modesty. "Up until two years ago," he continued, "I was in charge of the communications hardware of National Security. I owe this honor to Professor Votris, whom I met when I was still a student at the police academy. During the war we belonged to the same organization, the Grapevine, in contact with the British Near East Command. He's the one who suggested I study electrical engineering, and after the war I followed his advice. I'm still grateful to him. Later I returned to the Ministry of Security in their technical staff; Professor Votris advised us on how to set up the whole communications apparatus."

Then the small door of the telexroom opened. Out of it emerged a woman in her mid-forties. She wore very high heels on which she seemed balanced almost by an intrinsic stability system, a miracle of equilibrium among coordinated moving masses. Every part of her body, including the rich hair, oscillated, waved, and attracted every other part in a seemingly random manner. A closer observation revealed the periodic impulses, the natural interaction, the accuracy with which the fluctuations alternated or ran parallel, the perfection with which the homeostasis was achieved.

Krypsiadis smiled at her with awe. The woman smiled back but without awe. She handed him a yellow slip. Her fingers were yellower than the slip. She smiled at Hermes, too.

Krypsiadis was absorbed in studying the message. The woman said, "Should I call them to bring up some coffee?" Her voice was tough, tired, tender. Her aroma was exactly the opposite.

"Of course, of course." Krypsiadis half jumped and turned to Hermes. "Sorry I forgot to ask you." Then he said, "Kiki, do me this favor, will you? Two coffees? Thank you for the note too." He gave back the piece of paper to the woman. "This," the brigadier said, almost unable to contain his pride, "is Miss Kiki Nikolaki."

The woman smiled again. The brigadier introduced Hermes as a "telecommunications specialist from abroad." The woman said very politely, "Very nice to meet you, sir. I hope you have a good and productive time in Greece. If you need any of my services I am here every day from eight in the morning till six in the evening." She left the room.

The brigadier focused his small eyes on Hermes once more. He said, "The telex girls are very friendly and *very* trustworthy." Then in a different tone, "How is your research coming along? Have you gotten into it yet?"

"Not really."

"You need to settle in first."

"Yes, I guess that's it," said Hermes vaguely.

"You also need to solve this, this . . . other problem," the brigadier added in a reassuring tone. "I'll help you. But you have to tell me about it first. As much as possible."

Hermes explained his situation. The brigadier listened, his tongue flicking occasionally from his half-closed mouth to his mustache and back. When Hermes had finished, Krypsiadis said, "The case requires professional care. Method."

At this moment the waiter brought in the coffee and disappeared without a word.

"What is the value of the missing artifact?" asked the brigadier.

"Difficult to say what museums are willing to pay for such objects."

"What's valuable about it?"

"Its antiquity. Its uniqueness. If it's an early computer, its significance is, of course, enormous."

"Describe it for me once more. And slowly please."

Hermes complied, speaking slowly and clearly.

Krypsiadis narrowed his eyes and glanced in the direction of the potted palms. Hermes looked in the same direction. A Venetian mirror hung at the end of the corridor; anyone entering the long hall would be reflected in it. No one had.

"It seems the magistrate, Karras, who is no stranger to me, is cultivating some theories about this object and about you," the brigadier said.

"He wants me to supply information," Hermes volunteered.

"Perhaps, perhaps. Now," the brigadier began, as if delivering a lecture, "let us examine the essence of this problem. As Professor Votris has said many times, detection is the most difficult form of problem solving. We should first look at the solution space and identify alternatives in a consistent, unarbitrary manner. We *must* be systematic. I'm a professional. Karras is a professional, too. This might be a more professional case than it seems."

"Meaning what?" asked Hermes, vexed by the brigadier's increasingly didactic manner.

"To be a professional," the brigadier continued obliviously, as if lecturing Hermes, "means to develop a search method appropriate to the nature of the search space at hand."

Krypsiadis dived his right hand into his trouser pocket and fished out a little pad, the kind children play with, with a gray plastic surface on top. He rested it on his knee. Then he produced a fat black and gold Mont Blanc fountain pen from his breast pocket, looked at it with admiration, and returned it to the pocket. Now his left hand emerged with a ballpoint-like pen. He applied the pen to the surface of the pad, and the pen left a black line. He wrote "Golden Thinking Machine" on it. Then, with a smug smile, he lifted the plastic sheet. Everything had been erased.

"Not truly safe," the brigadier said. "It leaves traces on the layer below. But good for everyday use, to note stock prices on." He smiled again. "I hear it's used even in the U.S. Embassy in Moscow." He put back the sheet and started drawing points and lines that he then connected. The tip of his tongue pointed in the air until he had finished.

"This is an illustration of your situation. You are involved in a search problem. You want to find the solution, the Golden Thinking Machine. Let's call it the G.T.M. for short." He wrote the initials G.T.M. on the sheet. "Now I will teach you about the methodology of search and search trees. Imagine you are a hunter," he said.

"A hunter!" said Hermes.

"Yes. A hunter. And, at the end of one of the branches," the brigadier pointed to the G.T.M. sign on the paper, "your prey is hiding. Now, how do you go about capturing it?"

Hermes raised his eyebrows, suggesting ignorance.

Krypsiadis smiled generously at his new pupil. "It goes like this. As you see, I have sketched a diagram made out of nodes and links. It looks like a tree. We can also say it looks like a maze. It doesn't make much difference. It is the abstract properties we are interested in here. It starts from a node—like a root—and keeps forking into spokes. It expands like the branches of a tree do—like a family tree. You can see several levels of generations of branches, children springing out of parents. Indeed, each node can have ancestors, chains of them, with the exception of the root node, which is, let us say, like Adam. Each node can also have descendants, again chains of them, with the exception the terminal nodes. We assume this tree represents your problem. You now stand here in the root node. It is your starting point. Your goal is to find your G.T.M. It must be in one of the terminal nodes of the tree. We call this the goal node. Between root node and goal node are intermediary nodes. These represent the states you go through searching as you come closer to your search goal, the solution to your mystery."

Is he going to describe all possible problem-solving procedures now? Hermes wondered.

Krypsiadis continued, "How do you know one node brings you closer to the G.T.M. than another one? How can you evaluate each alternate state?" For a moment Hermes believed Krypsiadis was asking a real question. But it proved merely rhetorical. "How can you select the path that will lead you from the root node to the goal node? Which search procedure should you follow?" The brigadier beamed happily.

What a windbag, Hermes thought. Now he's probably going to speak about systematic search procedures.

And indeed Krypsiadis, with half-closed eyes as if visualizing the search tree in front of him, began. "We call the precise description of a method for solving a particular problem, and in our case the orderly exploration of a search tree, an algorithm. The word *algorithm,* of course, is a corruption of the name of the Arab mathematician Mohammed ibn Musa al-Khwarizmi."

The historical reference triggered in Hermes' mind a train of thought about al-Khwarizmi, or Algorithmus, as his name was latinized. His *Science of Reduction and Confrontation* was the first book on algebra translated into Latin and introduced Arabic numerals to Western Europe. The Algorists, the followers of Algorithmus, were forbidden to use the system officially and employed it as a secret code in commercial transactions. Hermes wondered why the ancient Greeks, who had first employed algorithms, well-controlled step-by-step procedures of computation where each step applied the results of the preceding one, had not invented "the craft of using figures," as the *Carmen de Algorismo* of Alexandre de Villedieu, written around 1225, had called the decimal system.

At this moment Krypsiadis returned to the tree drawn on his pad. "One idea, in trying to find a path from the root node to the goal node, is to adopt what is called a depth-first search. Now, in the depth-first search, you start from the root node and proceed with the node ahead 'in depth,' all the way to the end of the branch. If the Golden Thinking Machine is there, then the search is over. If not, you *backtrack* directly to the first node from which another alternative branch starts and you start again. You proceed 'in depth' once more, but downward on a single path to the end of the branch. You follow the procedure until you reach your goal."

Krypsiadis traced the line on his pad from top to bottom until he rested his finger once again on the G.T.M. node.

"And what do you think of that?" Krypsiadis was especially pleased with himself.

"Makes sense," said Hermes. But he'll soon say I'm wrong, he thought to himself.

"Aha! I've got you there," the brigadier indeed said, with a great show of self-satisfaction, happily shaking his finger at Hermes. "You're wrong. It does *not* make sense. Not always, that is! That's because it's just an effective search procedure. It establishes an orderly exploration of all branches and guarantees success. It would make old Algorithmus happy. It is not an efficient way of proceeding, however. It might make you waste too much time if you start with a branch that leads to many long, deep, fruitless branches while the Golden Thinking Machine waits at the next short branch, just next to the root node."

Krypsiadis looked up at the ceiling sadly, as if the branch with the unpicked fruit were right there. "For such kinds of trees a different search procedure might be equally effective and more efficient for tracking down your goal. Let's try one that instead of advancing in depth, moves in breadth," he continued.

"Yes. Let's," said Hermes. He was approaching the brink of exasperation.

"Here you explore nodes in order of their proximity to the root node. First all the first-generation nodes. If the goal is not discovered, you continue with the next node generation, to the lower level, till you find the optimal transmitter to purchase." Krypsiadis interrupted himself. "Oh, sorry. I made a mistake. I got carried away. We've been applying these methods to purchase equipment. They are general-purpose scientific methods. I meant to say until you find the G.T.M."

"Provided you have the time," added Hermes hastily.

"Correct, correct," said the brigadier, picking up where he had left off. "The search is not efficient for trees that branch out excessively."

Hermes had to struggle to keep from walking out. Now he'll start apologizing about the fact that such systematic explorations are uneconomical and that they lead to computational difficulties and that they are no good for problems of certain size and beyond, he said to himself.

And indeed, "Breadth-first and depth-first are the most basic search approaches," Krypsiadis said. "You can improve them if you know how far each node is from your goal and you make good use of this information."

Krypsiadis quickly wrote numbers next to each node. "These numbers here indicate the distance from the stolen treasure," he said proudly. "Given this information you can develop what is called a heuristic. You remember Archimedes, of course?"

"Yes! He shouted 'Eureka!'"

"Precisely! Leaping out of his bathtub," countered Krypsiadis. "Today, 'heuristic' means a method that improves efficiency of a search, in other words an effort-saving device."

Hermes visualized Krypsiadis running nude and dripping water all over a marble floor.

"Extremely important. Because an orderly exploration, counting all nodes in a systemic, exhaustive search, can be very long."

Krypsiadis opened his arms wide, then his fingers, then his eyes, simulating with his body the way a tree grows from trunk to branch, from branch to shoot, from shoot to web and leaves. "Heuristics 'prune' the search tree."

Krypsiadis started to snip away at imaginary branches up in the air, using his index and middle finger as blades. "A simple, general-purpose heuristic is the 'nearest-neighbor algorithm,' which suggests at each step of a search the locally superior alternative. I'll give you an example."

Hermes wondered if he was going to hear again, as he had countless times in college, about the troubles of the traveling salesman who had to visit, once only, a number of cities connected with each other by road and who needed to figure out the shortest route. It might appear logical to those who do not have a good sense of the uncontrollable inflation of time to try all possible combinations. This would have caused certain bankruptcy to the naive salesman as the number of cities rose, modestly, to more than a dozen. The experienced salesman, on the other hand, settled for a *satisfactory* rather than the *best* route. He started with one city at random and kept on visiting the one that was closest to where he found himself at each stage of the tour.

Krypsiadis narrated the story with a modification. Instead of a traveling salesman there was an inquiring countersurveillance officer.

"Good method," said Hermes. We may be getting to the point at last, he hoped.

Krypsiadis breathed deeply. He touched Hermes' hand to make sure he was following him. "There is a danger, on the other hand, with heuristics. They might reduce the search but they don't guarantee an optimal, satisfactory, or even *any* solution. Beware of methods that yield attractive intermediate results and deliver nothing in the end."

"This is indeed very rational, General," Hermes said.

A generous grin appeared on Krypsiadis' face.

"Now can you suggest . . ."

". . . something more practical?" Krypsiadis completed Hermes' phrase. "I will. The success of search algorithms and their heuristics depends on their match with the form specifics of the search tree. The more you know about the nature of the search tree, the better the chances to choose the right heuristic."

Hermes said, "And what kind of tree is my problem?"

"Too soon, too soon to ask that," said Krypsiadis. "By the way," he added, narrowing his eyes, "are you sure you didn't get out of your apartment, after you were taken there by taxi from your uncle's, until the next morning?"

"Which part of your tree does this question correspond to?" Hermes asked. And in his mind he said, Is he trying to hypnotize me with his search procedures to catch me off guard for a crime he thinks I have committed?

Krypsiadis smiled innocently. "I just wanted to make something clear." Then he added dreamily, "There was a witness, I overheard someone say." He put his palm behind his ear. "A witness who was passing by Dr. Agraphiotis' house around the time he was shot. He didn't hear shots. A silencer obviously must have been used. But he did hear Dr. Agraphiotis shout a name. Twice." Krypsiadis stopped. "It was your name." He stopped again. "Now. Back to our tree."

Hermes examined Krypsiadis' happily blinking small eyes. "I already heard about this shouting. The magistrate told me."

"You didn't mention that he told you." Numerous wrinkles branched across the forehead of the brigadier.

Hermes ignored his complaint. He said, "It was a mistake."

"Of course. It can also be a remarkable resemblance that fooled your uncle," added Krypsiadis.

"What I want to know is, can I be considered as a suspect?" asked Hermes impatiently.

"Certainly," announced the brigadier plainly, adding proudly, "Professor Votris wouldn't have sent you to me if that was not the case. And that is the second thing you must keep in mind."

"What's the first?" Hermes asked.

"Methodology."

"Ah!" exclaimed Hermes.

"Oh!" exclaimed the brigadier. "I know, I know. You don't believe in methodology. But, I assure you, serious cases require methodological assistance. And discipline, of course. This is the last point I want to make today. I am sure you are a chess champion."

"No," said Hermes rather emphatically. "I never had the time."

"I don't mean playing," corrected the brigadier, "methodology. I am not a player either but I am an expert of strategy. The 'forking move,' for example. Always try to apply it. You know . . ."

"I know. Attack two pieces at the same time . . ."

Krypsiadis rubbed his hands together rapidly. "You see. Take the 'horizon effect.' I'm not a great friend of it, delaying a major blow by giving away a minor pawn. Now tactics. We must follow strict professional rules. You should never try to communicate with us directly, only through the 'grapevine.'"

"What?"

"Our information network, as I mentioned. Your contact will be Melania. Melania is a medium. As soon as something interesting occurs pass on the news to her immediately," ordered the brigadier, adding instructions about how to contact her and following with a crash course in countersurveillance straight out of a thriller. "In general you should behave as if all telephones are tapped and all rooms bugged, as if you are being tailed all the time." And the brigadier concluded, "You should never volunteer any information to anyone, and you should maintain an otherwise normal and transparent life."

Hermes raised his eyebrows.

"It's not difficult. It's a good habit to have, anyway." Krypsiadis advised like a doctor now. "About your visits to the medium—in a moment of crisis you turn to mysticism—you might imply that you visit a clairvoyant to communicate with your parents, for example."

Hermes listened.

"Good," said Krypsiadis and went over his mustache once more with his thumbnail.

"What will this cost me?" asked Hermes.

Krypsiadis laughed. "I'm not running a detective agency. I have a genuine scientific curiosity in the case." He stood up. "Like Karras." He finished abruptly, "I don't like him."

"I thought you were friends with the magistrate."

"The magistrate?" Krypsiadis repeated. "Some magistrate. Karras is a superinvestigator of a very special kind. And it is not a good sign for any case when he gets in, apart from the methodological angle that makes the case challenging."

Hermes began to ask, "Is it a case . . ."

"Speaking about method, you should have some practice now. I'll show you how you can leave this hotel without being noticed by anyone." He rubbed his hands together enthusiastically. Hermes caught sight of the brigadier's left hand. The scar of a old wound marked the back of his hand.

He emerged from the narrow rear service alley. A flock of dusty doves flew up, scared by his passage. He turned his head up to where the birds were moving, to the crumbling cornice of the building, mottled by what could have been bullet marks.

Hill Climbing on Flat Ground, with a Lesson in Pruning

"It's as if World War II never ended here. What does all this have to do with me?" said Hermes, walking toward Nina.

She was slumped in an armchair facing the laptop, with a plate of grapes beside her. The computer screen was off. The machine was on. Hermes pushed up the top. The screen came to life.

```
(SETF (GET 'S 'CHILDREN) '(L O))
(SETF (GET 'L 'CHILDREN) '(M G))
(SETF (GET 'M 'CHILDREN) '(N))
(SETF (GET 'N 'CHILDREN) '(F))
(SETF (GET 'O 'CHILDREN) '(P Q))
(SETF (GET 'P 'CHILDREN) '(H))
(SETF (GET 'Q 'CHILDREN) '(I))
```

A diagram stood next to it.

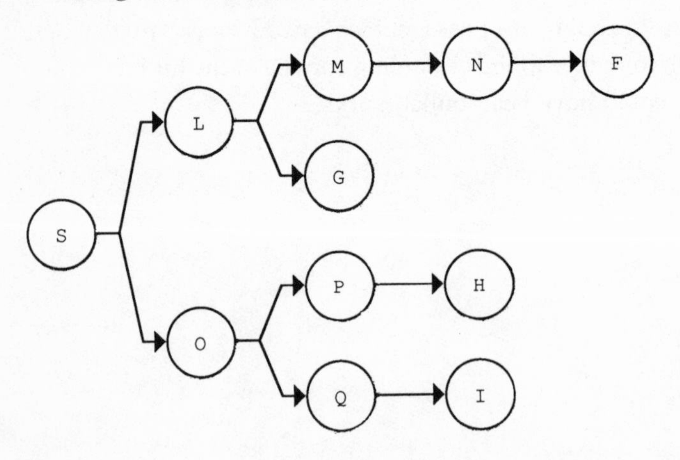

"Not bad," he said loudly, "especially as telepathy."

"Oh!" she jumped up. "This is an invasion of privacy." She shut the cover.

"Not bad," he repeated. "It captures the structure of a search by means of a tree."

"Just a tryout. And I wish you wouldn't snoop around in my notes."

"Sorry. I didn't realize you objected to snooping."

"What's this about telepathy?"

"Trees."

"What trees?"

"Search trees like yours. You were thinking about them the same time we did."

"What did Krypsiadis say? I thought he was going to help about Agraphiotis."

"So did I. But it seems he only likes to pontificate about general methods. He looks down on applications."

"Are you sure Krypsiadis wasn't trying some trick on you? They say he's a fox."

"Who do you mean by 'they'?"

"My mother. Did he really talk about search trees?"

"Uh-huh."

"And you?"

"I just listened."

"I bet."

Hermes continued with half-closed eyes as if reminiscing. "I was searching in a dark forest and not along the branches of a tree in the open as Krypsiadis did."

He raised the bunch of grapes from the plate up in the air and looked through it as if trying to identify a path from stem to stem.

"What kind of search?" Nina picked a few grapes from the upheld bunch.

"Hill climbing."

"Trying to find the Golden Thinking Machine hidden at the top of the hill?" Nina asked.

"Precisely. You *are* telepathic."

"And what happened during your hill climbing?"

Hermes went back to his reminiscing tone: "I was in a thick forest and the fog came down and closed in. I was looking for the top of the mountain but all I could see was the area around me. I could only check if the immediate ground was going up or down. It was getting very late. I couldn't waste much time. I chose the most promising direction, I kept going up, following only the paths that ascended. Eventually . . ."

"You arrived."

"Possibly . . ."

"Unless you had only climbed another shorter hill by mistake that appeared to be a hilltop while it was only a local peak. In that case you would have been stuck."

"Correct."

"As you would have been stuck if, in this dark forest on a vast flat area, giant granite buttes had soared up abruptly, unexpectedly, impossible to view from a distance because of the fog and the trees, where any rational attempt to improve your position locally would have been unworkable, or in a region of endless ridges you could not perceive a way to ascend."

"I see. You've gone through to the end of the chapter on search methods, and you reached the land of wicked landscapes where hill climbing, like parameter optimization, is hopeless."

"That's right," Nina said, "and I know what a bad kind of blind search your hill climbing can be if you use it across these ill-omened moors: long hours of lonely walks and no Golden Thinking Machine at the end."

"You should say the canyons of Athens."

"Do you think Krypsiadis might have been so vague on purpose?"

"I don't think so. He's simply one of those people who got fixated on certain events and ideas once in their life and keeps repeating the same routines."

"And what's his fixation?"

"World War II operations research. He sees spies and optimization everywhere."

"What's your conclusion?"

"I have no conclusions. In the beginning he made me mad. I was frustrated because he had wasted so much of my time. But as I was coming back, the absurdity of his paranoia made me see that we have overreacted, that we have been paranoic as well."

"No need for Sherlock 2000?"

"Not for any practical purposes. Finding the murderer isn't my job or yours."

"Maybe, but I still want to go on with Sherlock, just in case." Her eyes flashed. "For my education."

"No objections to that."

"When are we going to grow our own murder mystery search tree? First you have to give me more information. Your description of the Golden Thinking Machine is incomplete and fragmentary. Second . . ."

In vain Hermes tried to interrupt.

". . . second, your data base, where I keep on opening files recording what you tell me about the case, is no good for real investigation work. It just keeps on accumulating facts next to facts."

"I told you. It's only a logbook."

"You don't take me seriously. I'm struggling to put down all the facts you told me about Agraphiotis and link them in some way to build a search tree. For that I need a genuine search system. Not a theory."

"I do take you seriously. But it's too early. You have to look at the problem in terms of constraints first, before you turn to search trees."

"Do trees scare you that much? Why constrain them before giving them a chance to grow?"

"I'm not afraid of trees. Although they do have the natural tendency to grow, branch out, and then burst into vast combinatorial explorations. But if you start by identifying constraints, then you might avoid thickets."

"That's too theoretical. Can you give me an example?"

"I'll give you an example from cryptarithmetic."

"Aha. Your secret profession."

He jumped, "Who said that?"

"What are you getting upset about? Just Philippos, to Eleni, over the phone, when they were arranging about your arrival."

"Philippos talked too much."

"What do you mean? Did he have anything to hide? Anything about you?"

"Of course not. I just don't believe in unnecessary chatter."

"Neither do I. Let's come back to our discussion about constraints."

A smile ran across Hermes' lips. His fingers touched the keyboard and a new set of characters appeared:

Problem no. 1:

```
      C R O S S
+     R O A D S
_______________
    D A N G E R
```

Nina made a face. "What is it? A code message?"

"Just a simple puzzle. But you can see clearly how constraints posed by the nature of the problem domain, properly identified, can cut down useless search."

He typed again and more characters rushed onto the screen:

Problem no. 2:

```
      D O N A L D
+     G E R A L D
_________________
      R O B E R T
```

He continued, "Both problems call for replacing each letter with a distinct digit such that when each letter is substituted, the assignments provide a correct addition."

Nina asked, "Is this how cryptograms work? And do your problem heroes always come in threesomes, like the fox, the goose, and the grain?"

"That's a coincidence. You're always looking for hidden associations."

"I thought this was how detectives worked. And what's the code here?"

"These are only puzzles. They involve transposition of symbols, which of course is a general principle cyptography applies in many complicated ways. Puzzles of this kind have attracted cognitive scientists and computer engineers because their solution suggests interesting aspects of the human mind."

Nina protested, "Aren't you going to teach me how to solve cryptography problems?"

Hermes went on calmly. "Back in the nineteen-sixties Newell and Simon, two pioneers in artificial intelligence, tried to document how people dealt with puzzles like the ones on the screen and to identify how the mind solves problems so they could then program the computer to solve them."

"Why not go straight to the computer?" said Nina.

"Some did. But Newell and Simon believed that psychology had priority. They thought that by finding out how people worked their way through complex situations like cryptograms, they could see how the mind worked in terms of limits of memory and strategies of search, and not as a neurobiological organization."

"Why didn't they look straight into the neurobiological structure? Isn't that where thinking comes from? Function is the result of structure. Even at the Polytechnic they told us that."

"Correct principle. But not much was understood about the neurological structure of thinking at that time, and it's still too early to derive any conclusions."

"And the study of puzzles?"

"It did yield very useful results about how the vast search space that problems like cryptanalysis require can be cut down by identifying restrictions that are built into the domain the problems belong to. It's shown how to exploit constraints, thus reducing the number of possible alternative solutions to be tested. That's what good heuristic pruning, based on constraint exploitation, is all about."

"I thought heuristics were what Krypsiadis talked about and almost bored you to death with!"

"But he talked about them as general tricks, abstractly. Here is how the intrinsic structure of a problem leads to specific ways of simplifying its solution. For example, in our last puzzle, we have to assign ten numerals to the ten letters. If no intelligent pruning is applied, there are about three and a half million potential trials to carry out. Think of that. Let's see, on the other hand, what happens to the size of the search if we consider as constraints the rules of arithmetic, or the admission of only positive numbers, or the very specifics of the puzzle."

Hermes stopped and typed:

```
D = 5
```

He said, "Assume you start with this tip. You have then to substitute only . . ."

```
T, L, R, A, E, N, B, O, G
```

appeared on the screen.

". . . with the numerals . . ."

```
1, 2, 3, 4, 5, 6, 7, 8, 9, 0
```

"We start with the first alternative assignment for . . ." and he typed:

```
T = ?
```

"We try to see now if we can infer it directly from the constraints of the cryptogram, and if the possible alternatives we generate when testing these against the constraints of the puzzle lead to a contradiction. With this strategy, instead of complete enumeration of every branch of the search tree, we arrive soon at a fruitful end, and in our case to the conclusion . . ."

```
T = 0
```

"Take the next assignment now . . ."

```
L = ?
```

"Since no inference can be made directly from the constraints of the problem, as before, we have to try our luck with the first alternative in order that is . . ."

```
L=1
```

"Given the initial problem constraints, together with the new one accumulated from our recent discovery, that the numeral zero is assigned to T, we can easily find that our hypothesis leads to a contradiction because it implies, out of the third column constraint, that . . ."

```
R = 3
```

"which leads to the inference from the sixth column of the cryptogram, as you can see, that G is a negative number. But this contradicts the initial constraint of the problem that the numbers must be positive. As a consequence we have to drop the hypothesis . . ."

```
L = 1
```

". . . immediately." He continued. "This hypothesis failed to comply with the assumed constraints of the problem. Although this is a failure, it's good news in the long run. Because we see immediately that dropping it has a good effect on our search: we don't have to try any more the numerous assignments of the rest of the search branch that follow from the hypothesis. Instead we backtrack to *L* to generate a new hypothesis, and we try the next alternative on the list . . ."

```
L = 2
```

Hermes pointed at the screen again. He said, "Once more, exploiting the specific constraints of the domain saves us a huge amount of computation effort and time. By using intelligence, knowledge, and reason, we have succeeded in reducing a long search procedure, which might have made the problem practically impossible, if we didn't have the time to test all alternatives, into a few steps. We have transformed the initial state of the problem into the goal state."

```
D O N A L D  +  G E R A L D  =  R O B E R T
5 O N A L 5  +  G E R A L 5  =  R O B E R T
5 O N A L 5  +  G E R A L 5  =  R O B E R 0
5 O N A L 5  +  G 9 R A L 5  =  R O B 9 R 0
5 O N A L 5  +  G 9 7 A L 5  =  7 O B 9 7 0
5 O N 4 L 5  +  G 9 7 4 L 5  =  7 O B 9 7 0
5 O N 4 8 5  +  G 9 7 4 8 5  =  7 O B 9 7 0
5 O N 4 8 5  +  1 9 7 4 8 5  =  7 O B 9 7 0
5 O N 4 8 5  +  1 9 7 4 8 5  =  7 O 3 9 7 0
5 2 N 4 8 5  +  1 9 7 4 8 5  =  7 2 3 9 7 0
5 2 6 4 8 5  +  1 9 7 4 8 5  =  7 2 3 9 7 0
```

Nina whispered in a theatrical manner, "It's like breaking into Charles Augustus Milverton's pitch-dark house and suddenly realizing, by the sheer force of mental pruning, where you are and how the house is laid out, all without turning on the lights!"

"Wait. I'll show you now what the tree of the puzzle looks like. It's actually a summary of the tree." He touched the key board.

"A summary of the tree?"

"I mean a condensed version of its pattern. What Simon himself has used. I plan in fact to refer to it in my book. Here it is . . ."

Images flashed across the screen. A diagram appeared.

```
D=5   T=0   L=1   R=3   G<0   •
            L=2   R=5   G=0   •
            L=3   R=7   A=1   E=2   •
                        A=2   E=4   •
                        A=4   E=8   •
                        A=6   E=2   •
                        A=8   E=6   •
                        A=9   E=8   •
            L=4   R=9   A=1   E=2   •
                        A=2   E=4   •
                        A=3   E=6   •
                        A=6   E=2   •
                        A=7   E=4   •
                        A=8   E=6   •
            L=6   R=3   G<0   •
            L=7   R=5   •
            L=8   R=7   A=1   E=3   •
                        A=2   E=5   •
                        A=3   E=7   •
                        A=4   E=9   N=1   B=8   •
                                    N=2   B=9   •
                                    N=3   G=0   •
                                    N=6   O=2   G=1
```

"Perfect," she exclaimed.

He smiled. "Very satisfactory, even if it doesn't really reveal the real mechanisms of thinking."

"I see why you liked cryptanalysis so much. It's the paradigm of thinking: transforming the unknown into known."

"Don't get excited. I never said that. Solving puzzles is not the same as understanding a text or a picture or undoing a real-life knot. This involves hermeneutics. The difference is not between a bush and a tree. Hermeneutics is not just big heuristics."

"Hermeneutics? The craft of Hermes?" she asked teasingly. "But what does it involve?"

"Understanding intentions and commands."

"Then why did you spend so much time to become a master code cracker?"

He smiled once more, a brief nervous smile. "Honestly, my work has to do with many other problems. And if I don't go back to them . . ." He held his neck with his hands, imitating a hanging.

"But I don't want you . . ." she said, grabbing his hand.

He put his hand on the computer ready to type. "Don't worry, Sherlock 2000 will be operational. It'll take some time to put together the essential tools."

"Big words," Nina interrupted. "You're always trying to frustrate me." She started typing. "Don't you see?" she said. "It can work. In fact it *does* resemble deciphering. Here is how we can structure our data—take one suspect at a time just as with the cryptogram, assigning a numeral to a letter, and test the possibilities against facts and constraints. It goes like this . . ."

New lists chased away the tree Hermes had brought onto the screen.

1. No person can be in two different places the same time.
2. The person who murdered Philippos was in the same place as Philippos at the moment of the murder.
3. X is a suspect.
4. X was in Piraeus twenty minutes before the murder.
5. To go from place Y to the house of Philippos there are two ways by car or by train and then walking or taking a taxi.
6. It takes at least twenty minutes for the train to go from the station of Piraeus to Athens.
7. X was not the murderer.

She turned to Hermes triumphantly. "Sherlock 2000 will have a program to sort out all the relevant stuff and then check for consistency."

He said, shaking his head, "Not bad, not bad. Only how do you check for consistency when most of the facts you can get, if you get them at all, will probably be fuzzy?"

"What's that?"

"Words that don't *precisely* define quantities. Expressions of belief, suspicion, speculation, wishful thinking, very different kinds of facts from the one above. For example, a witness will report to you, 'I have been told something that boils down to Bob hearing that Don is rather convinced that it was Gerry who mumbled, like the Sphinx to Oedipus, that at least two guys, more or less the age of a father and son, met in the service street or it might have been the back alley, at around early dawn, saying things like someone will do something to someone soon after Christmas. Now try to test the hypothesis: "X is the murderer of Y, killed the 26th of December at 1.05 in the morning."

"Should we give up?" said Nina simply.

"Of course not. It is that problems and methods should match, not be forced upon each other. In fact . . ."

She looked at her watch and exclaimed, "My God. I'm late, I promised Eleni to be back an hour ago. She's had some bad news about a friend of hers and she wanted to talk to me. Save all we wrote in the memory and I'll arrange it later in the proper Sherlock files. You also have to tell me what happened in the Institute. I have to keep track of the smallest detail." As Hermes was turning to his machine she said, on her way to the door, "It's starting to get interesting around here."

The Lawyer

Hermes took a chair and faced his laptop. He just stared at it for a few minutes. He lifted the display panel and went through the routine of logging on. Long lists chased one another across the screen. An hour later he typed a simple paragraph:

> There is something here I do not like. Too many things that remind me of things I do not like. Of course I always try to find similarities among modes, objects, and situations and then try to systematically overturn the conclusions they lead me to. That is the case now. I need to get out of it.

He switched the machine off, shut its cover, and stood up. He walked up and down the length of the living room, again and again. He came close to the computer, nearly turned it on several times, and each time he stopped. Slowly he took a minuscule address book out of his breast pocket, leafed through it, and walked to the telephone. He dialed a number. He waited.

A deep trombone voice answered. Hermes gave his name. After some welcoming words the man on the other line said he had read about his uncle and that he was sorry. He wanted very much to meet Hermes. Yes, Hermes' affairs had been properly arranged. He would like to review his file with him though, now that Hermes was here. It could be done any time. Even later today. Although this was not a working afternoon, he would go to his office especially for Hermes. He was on his way home for lunch.

Hermes reached the building half an hour earlier than the appointed time. He hesitated at the entrance, then pushed the greasy handle and walked in. Outside the late afternoon sun was blinding, but inside the building was dark and cavernous. At the far end he discovered the elevator doors and, when his eyes became accustomed to the darkness, he could see above the elevator a large loose aluminum grid frame carrying the names of the occupants of the offices. His lawyer's office was on the top floor. He pressed the button. One of the glass doors lit up. He moved to the door.

"It doesn't work," a voice said in the darkness.

He turned in the direction of the voice.

A man was hunched behind a tiny desk, almost indistinguishable from the dark wall behind him. "Take the next one."

Hermes obeyed. The next one arrived. Hermes entered and pressed the button for the seventh floor. The elevator had no inside door. He could rub his hand on the sides of the shaft as the elevator moved. Many had done it before him. Large numbers painted on the inside of the doors indicated the floors: "1st," "2nd," "3rd," "4th—"

The elevator stopped between the fourth and fifth floors. Hermes pressed the button again. No results. He pressed another and another. He tried again. "Goddammit," he whispered loudly, "what a mess." He pushed the emergency button. No response. He shouted "Hello!" twice. Nobody reacted. He waited. He tried the top button once more.

The elevator started with a jolt. It reached the last floor smoothly without further complications. He pushed the door and emerged into an empty corridor, office doors on both sides.

He followed the numbers on the doors and arrived at the last door on the right. It was half closed. He knocked. No answer. He pushed the door and walked in. There was nobody inside the tiny room.

The room contained the usual decor of a small Mediterranean lawyer's practice: a dark wooden desk with a glass top over green felt, a globe still mostly covered with the light pink of the British Empire from India to Canada, a bronze pyramid, and next to it two long, thin black pens stuck out of a polished black marble cube. The desk was encircled by cabinets and bookcases with rows of black leather-bound volumes. A diploma hung from the wall in a funereal frame next to a colored print of a very attractive and very melancholic Christ looking toward a socket where a light bulb was conspicuously absent.

Hermes decided to take one of the four seats that, in addition to what obviously was the lawyer's own chair, surrounded the desk. He waited in total silence. At five minutes of six the silence was broken. He heard the elevator motor whir into action. Then the elevator door slammed.

The man who walked in was tiny. He wore a khaki tie and khaki jacket, army style, but he did not have a martial bearing. He stretched out a friendly hand and smiled. There was a gap between his front teeth. His voice was one of the deepest baritones Hermes had ever heard. After some polite introductions he went behind the desk and said, "In fact, after you hung up, I got your file out and went through it to save you time."

He fumbled around the papers on the desk. "Where is it now? Oh, I know! I must have put it back in its place."

He unlocked one of the cabinets. "Oh, I know! I must have thrown it in the drawer." He locked the cabinet and unlocked the drawer. "Oh, I know! I must have left it on the typewriter." He locked the drawer and uncovered the plastic cover of the typewriter.

The file was not under the cover, not under the chair, not anywhere. He stared into a void. "That's strange," he said, finally.

He started the same routine once again. "Oh, I know. I left it on the top of the desk. Now I remember." But he continued repeating the previous steps. He did it twice. Finally he eyed the ceiling and the missing light bulb in silence.

Hermes' eyes glared but his words rolled calmly. "It just occurred to me that I have another appointment," he told the lawyer, flashing his archaic smile. "Some other time."

He stood up and moved to the exit. The lawyer followed in despair. "I can't understand it. I had everything prepared, all the papers were out. And I am almost certain I had it on my desk when I went out for lunch, an hour ago. On the top of my desk."

The lawyer took him to the elevators and pressed the button for him. Hermes declined, deciding to take the stairs instead. He rushed through the ground lobby, now even dimmer. And there was no one behind the little desk.

The Philosopher of Photography: Donald

Hermes pushed open the crystal door of the bookshop. The late morning sun had already baked the handle. Inside, the air was almost wintry, and a strong smell of freshly delivered newsprint made him inhale deeply. It was a pleasant smell. The girl at the counter was the only person in the place. She was reading a fashion magazine and was lost in her fluorescent orange earphones. She flashed her teeth at Hermes as he passed her on his way to the long table at the back of the large room, where the glossy magazines lay flat. He started looking at the photography magazines.

The door opened again and a delicate Asian man walked in, accompanied by a gush of street heat and a gentle fragrance of lavender. He wore an expensive, cream-colored linen suit and a silver silk tie and seemed to be in his late twenties. His thick eyebrows were half hidden behind a pair of elegant, streamlined gold-framed glasses that were shaded by a deep green visor. Perspiration glistened on his forehead. He held nothing in his small hands.

He grinned at the girl and Hermes, then moved to the large table with the magazines. The girl continued to listen. Hermes went back to a photography magazine he had picked up. The man, his visor still on, picked up a thick issue of *Interiors* and spoke softly from across the table.

"You must be a very wise photographer." He bowed slightly.

Hermes was taken aback. "Wise?"

The man articulated a smile and worked his way with soft steps around the table, close to Hermes.

"I hope you will excuse me, but I watched you as you consulted the pages of the magazines. I noticed the advertisements that caught your attention. They all referred to the most important products, the most recent developments of technology. Only the most current and the most perfect caught your attention."

"Oh," said Hermes.

"It was very rude of me to talk to you unaddressed. But we amateurs of the great art of photography should recognize each other in public," he continued, inspecting the details of the seams of Hermes's shirt.

"You're very observant," remarked Hermes.

"Donald is my name," the man said, and bowed.

Hermes did not introduce himself.

The man raised his small hand and straightened his glasses. He glanced at Hermes' shirt again and said, "Do you agree that photography is the bridge between technology and ontology?"

"Well . . ." Hermes admitted.

"Excuse me. Excuse me for having asked you without permission such a question." The man apologized and bowed again. "I am certain you know these things, a man like you. I didn't mean to test you or to intrude. Photography and physics, to me the two are indistinguishable. Construction and reduction; they are both essays in world-making, as the philosopher put it. Or course a man like you knows all this. I apologize." He bowed. "Your great author spoke about water, oil, and quicksilver splitting, parting, and running into one another, about globular form and natural differences."

"Morphology," said Hermes.

"But there's only cartography!" said the Asian man, excited. "There are no affinities. I apologize. Only coordinates. There are no affections. Only reflections. There is *no* original. What was the appearance of your face before your ancestors were born?" He bowed once more and went on. "We think that if we see enough of what goes on around us, we will understand the world and, if we fail, we say there was not enough time. But wise men like you, I apologize, realize that it is not time that we lack. We spend our lives without ever knowing the world even a bit better. We are bent on forging tools for its decoding. But each time we are sure we have broken the code, we have just made a new world in code. Life is code making. There is no original. Everything melts into something else. Everything melts. There are no prototypes, only casts. I apologize for making such a generalization in front of you. Photography demonstrates all this. Photographs mirror the world as much as the world mirrors cameras. Photographs do not make pictures, they make enigmas possible. I apologize."

Throughout the talk and the apologies the girl at the counter had kept reading her magazine and humming quietly to a melody she was listening to through her earphones.

Hermes asked, "May I ask you what you are doing in Athens?"

"I am a student of beauty."

"Wonderful occupation. Very few people can afford it."

"Anyone can, with real commitment."

"Are you a photographer?"

"Me? No. I have never touched a camera," the Asian man said, almost in terror.

"Oh," said Hermes. "Do you write about photography?"

"One day I will," said the man with conviction. Then, still facing Hermes, he asked loudly, "Miss, two hands clapping make a . . ." He clapped his hands. "Can you please tell me what kind of sound one hand makes?"

The girl appeared not to have heard the question and continued humming her tune obliviously.

The man, content, adjusted his glasses, focused his eyes on the seams of Hermes' shirt again, and said in a lower, indifferent voice, pointing at one of the covers of a magazine at the table, "I apologize for the intrusion, but I am obliged to inform you that you are in danger. I suggest that you ask for help immediately. It will be given to you. The world moves by reciprocal complementarity. Good code breakers are good code makers."

"What are you talking about?" asked Hermes.

The man picked up a magazine and showed a page to Hermes. Hermes looked at the double spread advertisement for a new automatic camera. The girl had abandoned the counter, and with her earphones still on had walked over to the crystal door and opened it. She stared out with her back to the shop. Heat and noise poured in. The man continued.

"I have been instructed to tell you to go this afternoon to this address," the Asian man said.

He took a small piece of paper out of his pocket and gave it to Hermes. On the paper was typed:

22 Cypress Street
Psychiko

"You should go. Alone. Make sure you are not followed. Ring the bell of the house at six exactly."

Donald went to the door, bowed to the girl politely, and walked out, his visor still on. She remained in the same place, keeping her earphones on, tapping her lean right leg rhythmically. Hermes picked up a magazine and approached her.

Reducing Differences

It was already after two. The sun had entered the study room, menacingly approaching the laptop. Hermes went to the window and rolled the shutter down halfway. It took some time to adjust its height while he stared down across the street. "It's just a possibility, of course," he said. "The door was unlocked. It wouldn't have been difficult. But then, he looked kind of sloppy to me."

"He might look kind of sloppy, but Eleni's never complained about him. And she always complains about everybody."

"He insisted he had the file with my personal affairs prepared, left on the top of his desk."

Nina deliberated: "I believe him. Somebody stole it."

"Enough about it for the moment." He turned to the window again and repeated the same procedure, fixing the shutter while peering down.

Nina moved to the machine, bringing along a chair. She said: "Now that we've decided you go, how about Sherlock 2000 to plan what you do next."

"We'll use GPS," he said, sitting in front of the machine. He typed. Words flashed on the screen: "Initial state: my apartment."

"This is where I am now." He typed some more. "And this is where I have to be."

More words surfaced on the screen: "*Goal State:* 22 Cypress Street, Psychiko."

"What's GPS?"

"General Problem Solver, an early example of artificial intelligence, a rough representation of how people solve problems."

She glanced at her watch. "You have fifty-three minutes to tell me how you plan to move from your Initial State to your Goal State with your GPS and why."

"It comes in a neat procedure description, in three parts and two figures," said Hermes, craning his neck to look out of the window from where he sat. He continued, "The procedure breaks down a problem recursively, into hierarchies of subproblems. The solution of each subproblem is a means toward the final end. Each subproblem itself has an end, an intermediate end, on the road toward the final one. You focus on the intermediary end of each subproblem successively, and on the best path you can reach it by, choosing among the available means."

She thought about it. "You still talk about solving problems like moving around."

"You're right. Behind most problem-solving methods stand the metaphors, 'getting things done is a journey,' 'method,' 'way through'—the words reveal the journey metaphor. The metaphor makes us look at the process of carrying out tasks in terms of moving in space, a movement structured by local constraints characteristic of the space, a labyrinth, a thick forest, a cave, a tree with branches, a pebbled beach, a region with scattered towns. We talked about representations and how they help us solve problems. Metaphors are a way of finding a representation for a problem. They offer solutions to the problem of how to represent a problem, and the journey metaphor is the representation of problem solving. Much of our everyday thinking about carrying out tasks and discovering solutions is organized in our minds by representations drawn with the help of the journey metaphor."

She listened to Hermes talk, watching him as he stole glimpses out of the window. She too stretched to look out down along the street, saying, "This needs some more clarification. What do you mean by 'organized'?"

He smiled contentedly. "I mean extracting out of the general journey metaphor other more particular metaphors representing particular aspects of carrying out tasks. For example, we talk about how to proceed forward toward an end . . ." He peeked out and continued, ". . . step by step, going about from one point to another, controlling at each step how deeply we have *advanced* or checking out how far we still have to go, or if we have gone off in the wrong direction and we have to backtrack, if we are going around in circles or if we have to bypass an obstacle. We identify and evaluate the way to take, ask ourselves if we have *lost* our way, or if we have information on which way to choose, which ways are open or closed, how much time we have to spend going around to find our way, or if we can accelerate to arrive at our end."

Her eyes aimed far away. "It's funny," she said.

He looked at her, bewildered. "Funny?"

"Yeah. The way you talk about thinking, metaphors, and representations. Don't you think buildings, gardens, and cities must be the best means to make pictures of intelligence with?"

Hermes took a deep breath. "Do you want to be an architect now?"

"Only for theoretical buildings."

"It sounds very interesting. But keep in mind, buildings are infinitely harder to search than trees. Their corridors form loops and instead of only branching out they go up and down."

"No, I don't want to be an architect. They're the weirdest people at the Polytechnic and they all hate mathematics." She scribbled notes in the computer. "Just an idea."

He examined her face, "Actually a very interesting idea about how physical artifacts can serve as implicit representations . . ."

She interrupted him. "Not now. I won't ask you today what a metaphor is and why we picked up this particular journey metaphor to represent problem solving with. For the moment I want to see how we can plan your journey to Psychiko. Back to GPS. We've already spent ten minutes on preliminaries. We're running out of time. And can you please tell me why you've been looking out of the window?"

Hermes did not answer. He turned to the machine and typed, storing away Nina's notes. Then he smiled. "We'll make it. Don't worry. GPS will guide us."

"I can't understand how you can be so calm while . . ."

He continued: "It represents, in a very simple way, thinking as a 'goal-seeking system,' a system that on the one hand is informed about the world and on the other acts upon it after processing this information."

"Make it more real, please."

"More concretely: first we are informed. According to the system, we begin by identifying where we stand and where we have to be. Then we estimate the difference between these two states. Next, we choose a procedure to reduce this difference, how to act to overcome the distance between the two points. To choose this procedure we consult a table, the 'difference-procedure table.' The table relates differences to procedures. In our case, it tells which kinds of circulation are available as means to move between here and the villa. After consulting the table we choose one of the means, the one that is more appropriate for a distance over two kilometers and under ten, which is roughly how far 22 Cypress Street is from here. Then we act."

Hermes quickly prepared a table on the screen. He started describing it in detail and added, "Each procedure has a prerequisite to be carried out. For example the procedure 'moving in a taxi' has the prerequisite of 'getting a taxi.' This prerequisite identifies a subproblem; to get a taxi becomes our new intermediate end. We solve this new subproblem again by identifying the difference, consulting the difference-procedure table, choosing the appropriate procedure and, once more, asking if there is a prerequisite to it. Here it is: How many ways do we have of getting to a taxi? The difference-procedure table gives us several, each describing, as you can see, an alternate walking route to places from where I can get a taxi. It is obvious that taking any of these routes has no prerequisites. I have therefore arrived at the end of my means/ends analysis. I have planned completely how the task of arriving at 22 Cypress Street is implemented."

"Elementary! And boring. Next!" Nina commanded.

"Wait. It's not that simple. Imagine, for a minute . . ."

There was a big bang outside. A motorcycle engine started. A window opened across the street, then another farther down, and people started to shout. Hermes rushed and shut the window but he remained behind it, staring out.

"What is it?" she repeated.

"Just a minute," he said in a low voice.

"Are you looking at somebody? Is there somebody there? Is that why you have been looking out the last half hour?"

"There's somebody who might be called an amateur in surveillance. He's been out there for the last three hours and he was there yesterday . . ."

"What will you do about him?"

"Take him into account."

"Into the GPS? Can you do it?"

"Yes. The content changes. The form of the method doesn't."

She clapped. "Oh good, let's see. It's getting to be more exciting. Five more minutes to go."

He started making a new diagram in the machine. "My initial state is 'they know where I am.' The final state is, 'they don't know.' The alternate procedures are standard routines for throwing off your tail: for instance, entering a cinema and leaving through the fire exit, stepping out of a bus unexpectedly, or switching taxis without notice. Krypsiadis tried to give me a crash course on it." He went through many other options of getting lost, trying to explain how it fit into GPS.

Her eyes flashed every time he described another alternative. "Which one would you choose, then?"

"I believe switching taxis will do."

"You didn't mention how that works."

"It goes like this. Prerequisite to switching taxis is bringing the taxi you are in to a stop. This defines a new goal, a new difference between initial and goal state, a new procedure reducing this difference. For example, I could force or threaten the driver to stop, or . . ." He went on with more detailed alternatives on how to avoid being followed, inserting them all into GPS.

"All we need is GPS," exclaimed Nina as she looked out the window, adding absentmindedly, "Fascinating." And then, "The guy's still there." Then she turned around abruptly. "What if you come up with two procedures that are incompatible? Say you have to be in the taxi and, from another point of view, have to walk."

"That happens sometimes when you have to reduce more than one difference at the same time and you get two different conflicting answers. The system has to be extended to resolve such conflicts. GPS didn't do that originally. Newer systems that are aimed at managing plans of action for robots, for example, can resolve conflicts. We'll discuss them."

She looked at her watch. "Oh, oh. We've run out of time. How long will you need to change your means of transportation in each procedure? We didn't account for that. Your system says nothing about that."

He got up and moved to the door. "GPS originally doesn't provide ways of allocating time or any other resources among procedures."

She followed him. "Very disappointing."

"But this is only the original idea. There are other systems more advanced today. I told you. We'll get to them another day."

She was suddenly worried. "What about today? Have you really planned everything?"

"Of course."

"How can you be so sure? How do we know that this man downstairs isn't there to protect you? The people we're trying to keep from following you—are they your enemies? How do we know it won't damage you to cut them off?"

He touched the knob. "We'll see," he said, and before Nina had time to react he opened the door and slipped out of the apartment.

The Cinnamon Man: Gerald

When Hermes slipped out of his apartment, it was five o'clock. The traffic was already picking up. The little shops across the street were open, the owners casting inquisitive glances from their crepuscular interiors. He walked toward a busier street to hail a taxi.

It took more than half an hour get one. He asked to be driven toward the sea. Whenever they stopped, a small battered sports car parked behind them. They were approaching the beginning of the main boulevard that led to the coast. He asked the driver to stop and wait so that he could get out and buy a newspaper from the kiosk on the opposite side of the boulevard, next to a taxi stand. The driver began to complain. Hermes offered him the whole fare and a generous tip if he waited. The driver agreed.

Hermes crossed the boulevard and bought a newspaper from the kiosk. He watched the traffic light and, as it turned green, he jumped fast inside the first taxi in the waiting line. "Psychiko," he said. "Whew!" said the driver, and started the taxi immediately. "That's exclusive," he added, as they were heading away from the sea. Hermes' faithful follower had melted into the thick polluted air. The GPS plan was being executed impeccably.

Hermes abandoned the taxi several blocks away from his destination and continued on foot. The streets were deserted. The houses were set back, obscured by untrimmed bushes and unpruned trees. It was difficult to tell whether they were inhabited at all. The only sign of occupation was the parked cars along the curving roads, clean, new, and expensive.

At one minute before six he stopped in front of a garden gate. The address was indicated on a porcelain tile cemented to the right pilaster of the garden entrance. On the left pilaster was another tile with the name of the villa, *Euridice*. The low iron door was not latched. Hermes pushed through it and headed toward the house.

It was a low building. The setting sun projected an elongated shadow of his body on the glowing Venetian red of its front walls. It looked like a charred figure.

The entrance was through an Andalusian-looking porch. It had a low wooden roof and it was obscured by an overgrown bougainvillea. The walls of the porch were covered by painted tiles. Hermes stepped into its dark embrace. The door was slightly ajar. He rang and entered.

The whole floor appeared in full view, one very large room sunk a few steps from the entrance area. The three sides of the room, ahead of him, led directly onto the garden. They were surrounded by pergolas. The fourth, behind him, was a rough stone wall. The space was a maze of free-standing bookcases of various heights and sizes. Books were piled everywhere, on the top of tables, stools, and the piano and among vases, ash trays, and memorabilia. It smelled of old paper, leather, and jasmine. He went down the steps.

"Glad you decided to come, Hermes." The voice came from behind him. Hermes turned around. A man dressed in a perfectly pressed cinnamon suit, with thin, carefully parted cinnamon hair and cinnamon eyes, spoke politely. Hermes did not know him.

"Just call me Gerald," said the man, holding out his hand.

They shook hands. The man asked Hermes to take a seat and went back to close the door.

The sofa Hermes sat on had its back to the door and faced a low square table with a glass top. The glass top covered an old colored map of the world. The world was an island surrounded by winged figures trumpeting on the top of frothy waves.

"Have a drink?" asked the man, adding, "I am."

Hermes refused. The man disappeared behind the stone wall to what was probably the kitchen. A refrigerator door slammed and ice cubes tinkled. Hermes' eyes followed the coastline of the island of the world, shifted to the photographs in soft leather frames standing on the top of the table, most of them signed by important authors of the existentialist movement of the 1950s. His gaze settled on a newspaper clipping stuck under the glass covering the top of the low table, a funeral announcement, a month old. It referred to the deceased as a prominent publisher, a friend of many great authors, and owner of a picturesque villa in Psychiko where many literary gatherings had taken place.

Hermes raised his head. Across the room, on top of a piano, rested a small Venetian mirror. In it appeared the reflection of a striking Cycladic head. The broad forehead, the elongated isosceles-triangle face ending with a thin chin, the close-together eyes, and the short curly hair belonged to a young man who was solemnly preparing a drink.

The man called Gerald re-emerged, a ruby-colored drink in hand, and sat across from Hermes. Raising his glass he said, "To our future discussions." He left his glass on the table. "This must have been a trying experience for you."

Hermes did not react.

The man continued. "Allow me to come straight to the point. You are a very independent person with a unique and valuable mind. You need comfort and security to do your work. The latest events have shown how vulnerable you are and how much you need a base."

"I think I have plenty of base," Hermes cut in.

The man continued. "I mean more than institutional affiliations. Most of the top people around who seem unattached and freewheeling are interwoven in a dense web of power. Of course, the bonds are visible only 'through the glass darkly.'"

Hermes smiled. "I'm afraid it will take some extensive documentation to substantiate such a claim; besides I don't know what events you are referring to."

"A relative of yours has been murdered." The man looked Hermes in the eyes.

"Are you trying to sell me insurance?"

"That's very amusing. But you might say we provide security in the broadest sense of the word. We are not an insurance company. We have been of assistance to many powerful individuals and important companies around the world. Our network of contacts covers the globe."

The cinnamon man circled the outline of the world on the map with his open hand. He wore a diamond ring on his little finger. The glass with the ruby-colored drink rested on the crystal table top. The setting sun was reaching deeper inside the room. Its rays pierced through his glass, suddenly radiating myriad incarnadine circles on the world. The scent of jasmine entering the house through the open French window was strong. Nauseating.

"We are very discreet," the man continued. "Our industry is to collect and offer information; what is needed, when needed."

He took the glass in his hand and shook the ice in it.

"Information about what?" asked Hermes.

The man didn't answer. Instead he delivered a slow, disconnected speech, occasionally touching his glass and turning it slightly, never lifting it off the table. "We have been following your scientific work, and we value it. You and we have a common subject. Information processing. That interests us immensely . . . It's a pity you're in such a mess . . . Facing such a charge that is so. . . . I've been wanting to meet you for some time now but I've been very busy. Technological breakthroughs keep me very busy. Then this opportunity came up. I arrived in Athens the day after the murder. I read about it in the English-language newspaper of Athens. I saw your name before anyone else mentioned it to me. I asked people to contact you immediately."

"Why all this secrecy?" interrupted Hermes.

"I'm . . . consulting for the local government. I had to take my precautions. I didn't want to be seen with a suspect. I hope you understand."

"I'm not a suspect," said Hermes.

"I'm in a position to know that, to the contrary, you are considered one of the prime suspects. We can help you."

"But why are you so interested in me?"

"That is correct," said the man incongruously.

"What's the name of your company?" insisted Hermes.

The man shook his head condescendingly. "We are not interested in publicity, in persuading people about the value of our stock. We come under many names and none. You might find us behind all the companies of the world. You want the list? No. This is not the way to start a mutually beneficial relationship."

"Let's be creative then. Let's assume our collaboration is agreed upon," said Hermes. "What's the next step?"

"Good question. It's to get our hands on the man who really killed Professor Agrandiotis," he mispronounced, "and get hold of the archaeological treasure he stole."

"So you know about that too."

"Don't worry, Hermes. The story has gone around. No wonder. It is at the heart of the whole mess, isn't it?"

"Why?"

"Because it is obvious that whoever killed . . ."

"Agraphiotis," Hermes interjected.

"Thank you. It is obvious that whoever killed your uncle did it for no other reason but to get the treasure."

"How can you be so sure?"

"I don't doubt it; from the information we have about this killer, he is not the kind of person who would take the risk of knocking off people unless there is some very, very serious reason for it," the man said.

"And you think the instrument was worth the risk?" Hermes asked.

"I think so, knowing what we know about this person."

Hermes smiled a serene archaic smile.

"You don't seem convinced by what I'm telling you."

"Not particularly. I find the argument bizarre," Hermes admitted.

"You don't believe me?"

Hermes took a deep breath. "I just don't believe the object is worth that much."

"What makes you say that?"

"May I turn the question around and ask you how you know it's worth anything?"

"I have my sources."

"I'm not asking you to tell me who they are. I'm just asking what guarantees that this object is valuable," stated Hermes plainly.

The man was standing now. He looked down at Hermes grimly.

His left cheek trembled almost imperceptibly. "Professor . . . uh, that is, uh, your uncle, was not that discreet."

"You talked to him?"

"I didn't. It wasn't necessary," the cinnamon man snarled.

"Of course. Your people did that for you," said Hermes ironically.

"I'll be frank. Your uncle was, let us say, overheard," the man said, having recovered his calm tone.

Hermes smiled again. "And of course you immediately believed what he was saying to whomever he was talking to."

The man looked hard at Hermes with angry eyes.

"I'm sorry," said Hermes. "I didn't intend to be unpleasant but it seems to me that you people should be more careful."

"I don't mind criticism," the man cut in. "And how can you be so certain about the value of the find, or lack of it?"

"First, I've seen the object. Probably you don't know that."

The man remained unmoved by the revelation and continued looking at Hermes, his lower lip slowly protruding.

"Second, I'm an archaeologist."

The muscle tic was the only sign of life on the man's body for a few seconds.

"I have no doubt I'm correct." Hermes rose. "I hope you're not disappointed by your effort to bring me here."

"Not at all. But I'd just like to review a couple of things before we meet again. How's tomorrow afternoon? Same time. And take the same precautions on your way here."

Hermes nodded and started for the door. As he passed near the kitchen he glanced in. Nobody was inside.

The man in the cinnamon suit opened the door. He thanked him for coming.

Night was falling fast. The houses across the street appeared alive now. Most of the windows were open. There was a child in one of the balconies holding a fisherman's rod, casting about for an imaginary catch. He greeted Hermes.

It was dark by the time Hermes returned to his apartment. He rushed to answer the telephone.

"I've been trying to reach you all afternoon!"

"Robert!"

"How're you doing? Can you hear me?"

"Yes, I hear you. Where are you?"

"The line's awful."

"Sounds fine to me. I hear you clearly. Where are you?"

"I've been on a boat for three days now. They just couldn't get the phone to work. I almost sent you a cable."

"Which boat?"

"Didn't I tell you? It's for this piece I'm doing for the *New York Times*."

"No, you didn't."

"It's the expedition that's recovering a trireme near Antikythera. I'll be back in a couple of days. How's everything with you?"

"I have some news."

"News?"

"I just got back from Psychiko."

"What?"

"Psychiko. The suburb. I thought you knew . . ."

"Oh yeah, Psychiko . . ."

"From a meeting with a man who calls himself Gerald and who claims he knows . . ."

"And how's everything with the police? Are they giving you a hard time?"

"No. Everything's OK. But did you hear me? The man, Gerald, the one I met in Psychiko, claims he knows who the murderer is . . ."

"What are you trying to tell me, Herm . . ."

The line went dead. Hermes put the receiver down. He stayed close to the phone for a few minutes.

Nina had entered the room noiselessly.

Hermes turned around, saying "I didn't hear you come in."

"I *k*rept in. *K*rypsiadis' rules. I came to learn about GPS. Did it work out OK?"

Hermes said it had passed the test. Nina asked for details. Hermes recounted the meeting in Psychiko with the man in the cinnamon suit and told her about the appointment with him tomorrow. Nina was ecstatic.

"Will you collaborate with this Gerald?"

"Collaborate?"

"Sounds like an exciting offer."

"I have to find out whom he works for."

"The Mafia?"

"Maybe."

"The police? You think he has been planted in order to get you to talk?"

"That would be strange. I have to think about it."

"Let's—"

"I want to think first myself."

She bit her lower lip. "You just hung up on someone."

"Yeah. Robert. He's coming back. He just called, and we were interrupted."

"By your snoopers."

"Could be."

"Is Robert going to help out?"

"Robert? Robert is inspiring company. He's the greatest antidepressant I know. But to help . . ." He shrugged his shoulders.

"How does he make a living?"

"Freelancing. Writes pieces right and left. Very well, in fact, but he couldn't become a real writer. He has no discipline and he is completely unreliable. He never grew up."

Nina wanted to know more about Robert and the offer of the cinnamon man, but she had to rush back home. They arranged a meeting the day after the party at Villa Emma. Nina left. Hermes returned to his machine, and Robert did not call back.

The Cable

Hermes arrived at the Institute early that morning. The front door was open and the library door was open, but nobody seemed to be inside yet. He picked up his mail. There was a telegram and a letter, both from Cambridge. The telegram read,

> URGENT. CLOSED CONFERENCE ON RESEARCH PERSPECTIVES, JUNE 25 & 26. YOUR PARTICIPATION IMPERATIVE. CALL COLLECT.
> DOROTHY EVANS.

Then he opened the letter.

> Dear Hermes,
>
> I can just picture you, basking in the shadow of the Acropolis with your laptop, serenely at work decrypting those archaic inscriptions of yours. What a relief it must be to get away from the frenetic life of Cambridge—I really do envy you. I hope you got my card congratulating you for the Guggenheim. Sorry I didn't get a chance to say goodbye. I meant to call to ask you if you needed a ride to the airport, but Paul wanted to go away for the weekend and we had left for Mount Desert Island.
>
> Concerning our plan for the book for the Press based on your dissertation, I have not yet received your outline. We are very eager to send you a contract, but we do need a clear proposal. I have been thinking about this project the last few days and think you should look at it as more than just a bound edition of your thesis aimed at archaeologists only. Let's get these ideas out from under your notes, appendixes, and piles of references, and make them more accessible.

Looking forward to hearing from you soon. Bob sends greetings.

Love,

Esther

P.S. I just talked to Sis. She says she's writing to you tomorrow.

He tore up telegram and letter and threw the shreds into the wastebasket. He went out of the building and headed toward the center of Athens. It was still too early to be hot. A breeze from the north had cleared the pollution somewhat. He could see the sea far off on the horizon, a pale outline that could have been Salamis. A car passed him and stopped a few yards ahead. The football-athlete driver got out, came up, greeted him and said, "Do you mind coming with me to the office? I'll drive you back afterward."

Hermes shrugged his shoulders in annoyance.

"I'm sorry," said the driver. "They told me it would only take a few minutes of your time."

Hermes looked into the car. Nobody in the back seat. He stepped in.

A Second Interview

Karras waited behind the same desk. He was wearing the same displeased face. Hermes sat down on the same chair.

This time Karras asked his questions explicitly.

"When did you inform Professor Agraphiotis that you were coming?"

"A month before my arrival."

"When was the Institute notified?"

"About the same time."

"Your department?"

"Same."

"Was any other person informed?"

"A couple of colleagues, neighbors, my landlord, my cousin here. That's all."

"Would you object if I asked you to put down these names, with addresses?"

"Why should I object?"

Karras wrote down by hand the dozen names Hermes dictated to him. Then he said, "It seems you don't have a wide circle of acquaintances."

"My research leaves me very little free time."

"And what research are you working on now?" asked Karras when he had finished.

"Not as much as I'd wanted."

"Were you planning to decipher the inscriptions you mentioned seeing on that object?"

"No."

"Were you interested after you saw the object?"

"It wasn't part of the research I had planned to do here."

"Could you describe it?" Karras ran his fingers over his chin.

"I can't say. I just looked at the piece for a few seconds."

"How does the work of an archaeologist deciphering an archaic tablet compare with that of a professional cryptanalyst?" Karras removed his fingers from his chin and stared at them.

"Very much and not at all."

"Let me put it this way. I'm a lawyer." Karras looked at Hermes. "But I'm also a kind of policeman. I have a good background in cryptology. Do you think I could sit down and find my way through such archaeological inscriptions?"

Hermes knit his eyebrows. "Theoretically, archaeologists and cryptanalysts *appear* to do the same kind of work."

"That's what I thought," Karras said quietly.

"But that's only theory. Very abstract theory," added Hermes.

"Archaeologists lie back and contemplate while cryptanalysts engage in battle and trickery. Is that what you are saying?" Karras asked.

Hermes said, "Well, archaeologists have to be active and resourceful too. They have to fight time, and that's a real struggle. Time obscures, decomposes, transforms."

"And what about competing archaeologists, racing to decode an important inscription. Couldn't this lead to violence and murder?"

"In a detective story." Hermes smiled.

"I see. You don't think Professor Agraphiotis was murdered for reasons of professional antagonism," said Karras without moving a muscle.

Hermes laughed. "I believe it's a little far out. You must think we're a wild lot."

Karras went on, "You said theoretically archaeologists and cryptanalysts do the same kind of work. Where's this theory based?"

"There were efforts to create a General Theory of Information, as it was called. It was supposed to cover encoding, electronic transmission, text understanding, pattern recognition, translation from one language to another, and, certainly, cryptanalysis," Hermes said with a sad smile.

"You don't seem to be happy about it."

"It didn't work."

"Why?"

"Because general theories, made to fit everything, tend to fit nothing in the end."

"I always thought the power of a theory depended on how much it could explain," Karras ventured, genuinely serious.

Hermes shook his head. "Good theories and good methods for solving problems come from the study of particular contexts, specific constraints. Universal theories are prestigious, and they give an illusion of power. In fact, very often they're weak and ineffective."

Karras looked at Hermes with a strange expression. "So, general methods of decoding don't exist, and this disqualifies me from deciphering archaeological inscriptions."

"That's not the issue. What I'm trying to say is that general methods are not enough for people to jump from one problem domain to another. You need to understand the particular constraints of the domain, the background."

Karras asked: "How will this improve deciphering?"

"It helps you find what they call a 'handle' in the cryptogram, a 'crib,' anything that can indicate the probable presence of a certain message in the cryptogram."

Karras nodded.

"A crib," Hermes continued. "I'm sure you know it under a different name. It's the standard piece of information that military cryptograms include routinely, with references to place and date, the identity of the sender and receiver, and relevant data on an ongoing operation, soldiers, weapons, equipment. Handles and cribs suggest what to look for and where in a cryptogram. Their presence constrains search computations, making deciphering easier. You must have some idea about how it works. In this respect it's not very different in archaeology."

Karras nodded again.

Hermes continued, "But then archaeological deciphering can be more complex. The contemporary military cryptanalyst and cryptographer may belong to enemy camps, but they are part of the same universe. They share the same 'horizon,' to quote Husserl. This makes discovering handles and cribs easier. The first assumption of a decipherer is that the cryptogram is not written by a madman, a Martian, a complete alien. It's different with an archaeologist and the author of the unintelligible inscription. They're not adversaries but they might have very, very different ways of thinking, different interests, desires."

"Do these mental interests supply the 'cribs' of archaeological deciphering, like motives in a police investigation give clues?" asked Karras.

"They're even stronger constraints than cribs. They're presuppositions that structure representations of reality. They proscribe communication, thinking, and action."

"I want to know where archaeologists find these world views."

"They have to reconstruct them."

"Is this reconstruction of world views what you've been busy with?"

"Something like that."

"And without this work?"

"Some texts would be sealed off from the interpreter. They would be completely invisible."

"Invisible? That opens the door to an interesting enciphering method," Karras said casually.

"I'm an archaeologist," said Hermes stubbornly.

"Good," Karras replied. He looked at Hermes in a displeased way once more and added, "When I need more information I'll send for you." And after a short hesitation, "And let me know if you plan to leave Athens."

Hermes stood up.

Once more it took Hermes several minutes to find his way out of the building. Once he had reached the bottom of the stairs, he recognized the football-athlete driver waiting casually. He came up to Hermes and said, "You dropped your address book. I'll drive you home if you like."

Return to Psychiko: Euridice Deserted

Hermes left his apartment an hour after being dropped off. An hour and a half later, taking every precaution, he returned to Cypress Street. The garden gate was unlocked, the porch darker. He rang the bell several times but there was no sound and nobody came to the door. A student was practicing the scales on the piano next door, ascending, descending, ascending, descending. Hermes left the porch and walked along the side of the house. The shutters were open. He peered in. He could see the whole room. It was totally bare. Even the bulbs of the wall lights were gone. He turned around. A bronze-colored cat was passing through the neglected flowers. The sound of the piano stopped short and a lone cicada took its place somewhere high up. The cat vanished into the shadows of the early evening.

Hermes started toward the street. Every few steps he stopped to look back. A dry branch cracked under him, and he grabbed at the slim shaky trunk he found waving on his right for support. A shower of jasmine blossoms poured down onto his head and his shoulders. He shook them off brusquely. The fragrance lingered. He approached the old Cadillac parked inside the garden under the eucalyptus trees, among the overgrown weeds.

The occupant of the back seat wore the same carefully ironed cinnamon suit. His thin cinnamon hair was parted carefully to the side and it appeared more colorful because the face under it was ashen gray, and the small round hole in the middle of the forehead was black. It was impossible to say if the eyes had preserved their cinnamon tone.

Out of the garden across the street a car was just pulling up, full of people. It stopped in front of him. A ball came out of the vehicle first.

Three children followed, then a leashed dog pulling a woman who was holding a large basket in one arm. They all went into the house across the street. Two men stayed behind. It looked as if they were putting the car in order. Hermes continued to the end of the narrow street. As he turned toward the noisy avenue, the car doors slammed shut.

The Medium

The trolley started from the heart of Athens. It moved with difficulty through crowded, narrow streets, lurched around sharp corners, crawled laboriously up small but steep hills, and finally arrived in Piraeus. Hermes stepped out at one of the last stops on the line. Tall apartments formed a continuous wall on both sides, following the ascent and descent of the street. Diffused bright light and a strong salty smell suggested that the sea was close by. He climbed to the top of the hill and then turned left into a quiet narrow passage. At its end the apartments framed the setting sun reflected on the sea.

He walked toward the opening and arrived at a flat area, four hundred meters long, a hundred meters wide, covered with patches of dried, burnt grass. It extended to the edge of the plateau, to the steep drop to the water. In the middle there was an enclosure and inside it an old villa with sealed windows.

He moved into the empty space, away from the apartments with their shutters closed against the western sun, toward the enclosure. Behind the stone wall, higher than a tall person, rose the building, almost a perfect cube if one discounted the propped-up pediment breaking the skyline and the few decorations sticking out of the walls. It was difficult to determine what color it was. The plaster was peeling off in layers of strawberry, ochre, lime, and cerulean blue.

A small iron door was ensconced in the massive wall. On the door, protected behind glass, a visiting card had printed on it:

MELANIA
MEDIUM—CONSULTING
BY APPOINTMENT ONLY

The well-oiled door opened before he rang the bell, and a short, obese, almost pyramidal, woman asked him to enter. Hermes stepped inside the precinct.

The high walls fenced in only three sides of the lot, leaving the fourth open toward the sea, a gap, yawning wide over the deep slant. A cock walked nervously along the edge.

Pistachio trees grew at regular intervals, and judging from the scent, there must have been an acacia somewhere close by. In the center of the space stood the house, stark and austere. The entrance was in the middle of the wall facing away from the sea, reached by a terrace, raised six steps above the ground that projected from the block. The steps that led to the terrace were flanked by two terracotta sphinxes. Each face was young, round, content. Between puffed cheeks was a small, straight Grecian nose and underneath, between the nose and a delicate, protruding chin, a small mouth, half-open, in a frozen, unuttered whisper.

Behind the entrance opened a long hall that divided the floor into two equal parts and led to a huge glass door at the other end. Halfway down the hall to one side a staircase rose. A series of doors ran down both sides of the hallway.

"Yes. My sister has been expecting you," the woman pointed toward the last door to the right. He walked in.

The room was plain and small.

"Thank you, Elpis!" said the woman, who was sitting behind an oversized desk loaded with pieces of paper of different sizes and colors. Elpis shut the door behind Hermes. Her steps faded down the corridor.

The woman's face was covered almost completely by a pair of oversized dark glasses rarely worn by women but frequently used by members of the military with overt political aspirations. Her head was topped by an impressive mass of ink-black hair. Her body seemed to be short, squat, almost a cube. Hermes sat in front of the woman on a low couch.

"Krypsiadis has spoken to me and to you. There is nothing else to add. He who talks too much lives to regret it. You don't need to know more, I don't want to know more. Just tell me what you want me to pass on and it will be done. No written messages. Human memory is the best means for recording the world." The dark glasses were turned toward Hermes' face.

Hermes started with the encounter in the bookshop, the meeting with the cinnamon man. He finished with the description of his second visit to the house in Psychiko, the car in the garden, the corpse. Throughout the talk the dark glasses did not change position.

"I hope I've been clear," he said in the end.

The woman remarked, "The message will be received by tomorrow morning."

The dark glasses shifted, reflecting the horizontal stripes of the shutters. Melania rose from her seat. Hermes rose too. She opened the door and stepped out of the room first. She was agile. There was something in the way she handled her body, despite her mass, that reminded him of Krypsiadis, stocky but well exercised, military bearing.

"One day I want you to tell me about your own work," she said, removing her glasses. She had beautiful eyes.

"Archaeology is rich and can reveal much . . ." said Hermes.

"Yes, yes. I know all about that. But what I'm more interested in is your artificial intelligence side . . . I have to be updated. Professor Votris gave me a few lessons about cosmology and optimization. The brigadier always used to keep me informed about the latest developments. He hasn't been keeping up with his reading recently, although since his retirement he's had more free time. I'm very concerned. I thought I might subscribe to a computer magazine. I don't usually ask for favors from my clients but I will ask you. Which of the publications would you recommend?"

"I'll think about it," said Hermes. "You know, there are some programs written recently that compute horoscopes. They are very fast, but you need a machine."

She shook her head. "I'm not limited to horoscopes. My vocation is intelligence, my craft decision making, my specialty difficulty. Theory of the occult and complexity theory are difficulty's two sisters. I have been studying them for years, the structure of guessing in chaos. Goodbye, Hermes."

Elpis reappeared in the hall. Melania returned to her room. Elpis led Hermes out of the house to the garden.

The wind had died down. Just above the waves a flock of sea gulls swirled around an invisible locus searching.

"The summer will be very hot and very brief this year," she said as she let him through the garden gate.

Out in the opening a radio was turned on somewhere in the apartments and a song descended over the water where the birds continued their quest.

"Heard the news?" asked the driver of the taxi on the way back to Hermes' apartment.

"What news?" said Hermes.

"Record heat tomorrow."

"Oh," said Hermes "I'm sorry."

"Did you go for a swim?" asked the driver, familiarly.

"No. I wish I had," said Hermes.

"Hmm. Working all day," The driver mumbled. "Hmm. Trying to see into the future backward. Sagittarius is late entering into orbit. It won't work. Just lie back and enjoy the rest of the sunset. Night will be here soon," and he kept to the wheel.

Hermes did not respond. The rest of the trip was silent.

Accident on the Highway

It was ten at night when Hermes jumped into a taxi once more. He shouted the address to the driver. Loud music was coming out of at least four speakers, strident noise of cars racing by through the windows, all wide open. The taxi driver said something. Hermes did not understand. He leaned over the front seat, asked the driver to repeat, asked again, and got the same answer: "I never enter Psychiko."

"What does that mean?"

"I always get lost on my way in and I can never find my way out. You want to go to Psychiko, you drive yourself."

Hermes did not argue. He paid and stepped out of the taxi on the shoulder of the highway. Psychiko lay on the other side of the busy six-lane road. There was no pedestrian cross-over. He waited for the moment when the traffic would abate that, according to queuing theory, he knew would come. He waited patiently. The road was very dark. Cars were flashing their high beams. A man farther up the road was getting out of his car. He wore a Panama hat. It shone strangely as the high beams hit it, on and off.

There were fewer cars now. Hermes stepped onto the pavement. He crossed the first lane. He let a truck pass that was coming slowly up the second lane with its high beams on. Then he dashed over to the third lane. A speeding car that he had not seen behind the truck caressed his back as he reached the middle division of the highway. The screech of car brakes followed as the car switched abruptly to the second lane and passed the truck. The truck started to honk like an alarmed animal, howling. A hundred meters away from Hermes a man was crawling onto the middle division. His Panama hat had been blown off by the wind. A car coming up from the opposite direction crushed it. Hermes rushed to the man's help. He was just approaching him when the man stood up. He glared at Hermes and then, limping, started to run away along the middle division. Hermes turned and hurried to cross the other half of the highway, leaving the man behind.

The street on the top of the hill was cluttered with cars, breaking every parking regulation in existence. A din mixed with frequent tinkling of glasses and the cool scent of a freshly watered garden rose above the garden wall he had reached. It was a meter high, white-washed and glowing like a neon light in the dark. Above the wall there was a tall iron fence with flat sheets of metal attached to it. On its top, at regular intervals, spotlights bent their long necks over the street like ferocious animals made of steel. He came up to the gate.

An Interesting Party

A small, narrow-chested, impeccably liveried dark man examined Hermes maliciously. A large, broad-shouldered man, equally impeccable, grinned at him amiably. "Good evening, sir. Your name, sir, is . . ."

Hermes gave his name. The small man stood attentively and whispered the name into his lapel where a tiny but noticeable microphone clung. The small man nodded to the large man and he, as if canceling out the annoyance that the small man had caused, volunteered to lead Hermes inside the compound.

Hermes was ushered among powerful spotlights placed no more than a half meter above the ground. They left everything above them in the dark and illuminated everyone's shoes, shins, and ankles brilliantly.

The host, a friendly middle-aged person, stood in the middle of a circle of laughing men. He greeted Hermes cordially, guided him to the bar, and promptly abandoned him.

The bar, set up in the garden, was made up of a U-shaped group of long tables covered with Oriental appetizers, desserts, and glasses of various sizes. Hermes asked for a glass of orange juice and a waiter handed him the drink. Hermes looked at the face. It had a familiar Cycladic look, but the hair was short, crew-cut. The eyes, close together, were smiling.

"Dr. Steganos?" a woman's voiced asked. She was petite, with a short, platinum crew-cut. She wore a strange-shaped dress. It had been cut, assembled, and hinged by either a genius or a schizophrenic. The woman, despite the deconstructed, expressionistic dress, appeared calm and cheerful. She was the hostess.

"There are many archaeologists here tonight," she said, "many scientists and many artists you will enjoy meeting."

A man was passing close by.

"Dr. Patouhas!" she cried. "Dr. Patouhas teaches at the university here. Archaeology," she explained to Hermes.

Dr. Patouhas crept toward them with a jerking step at an oddly oblique angle. He smiled at the hostess very fast, then turned and riveted a severe face in Hermes' direction. Bits of potato chip were stuck to his thin, tightly pursed lips. Hermes stretched out his hand, but the thoughtful-looking man just stared ahead.

"Dr. Steganos will be at the Institute for a year, Dr. Patouhas," she said.

"Excellent," the man said to the hostess, enthusiastically. Then with equal enthusiasm he asked, "Is Michael coming tonight?" The bits of potato chip were still there.

"No, he decided to spend one more week in Corfu."

"Pity," Dr. Patouhas said, pressing a paper napkin to his mouth, instantly uninterested.

One of the young men who worked behind the bar came toward them. He whispered to the young hostess. The woman turned to them, apologized, and ran toward the house.

"Auf Wiedersehen," said Dr. Patouhas to the general region of Hermes' forehead and jerked away, still clutching the paper napkin to his mouth.

In the distance the librarian appeared. She was talking to the wife of the director of the Institute. Hermes turned in another direction.

"No one can be sure whether Victor learned anything from the episode," a man said in an irritated voice behind him. "How could the lie detectors have gone so far off?"

Two men passed him.

"The counterargument by those who advocate this use of the polygraph," the other answered pompously, "is that it works."

They turned and disappeared in the darkness, still arguing. Hermes moved toward an area soft music was coming from. Two young couples seated on a stone bench were listening to a person standing before them, lecturing to them in German.

The speaker was excited. "The sun was setting and I was ready to go when there, in front of me, on the western wall of the Temple of Didyma, the same wall I had looked at so many times for weeks, in front of me stood illuminated in the shadows the very diagram which revealed the workings of the entasis, the geometrical construction that was used to calculate the curvature of the columns of ancient temples. It was like a present from the sun."

Hermes continued toward the music. He could not see the orchestra but found the place where people danced. A middle-aged couple was trying to keep pace with the tempo of the music. The man was flabby and shorter than the wiry woman. The music changed to a faster pace. The couple stopped dancing. They started walking toward Hermes.

"Pat," a female voice cried. The couple responded. "Hermes," it shouted next. It was the hostess. "So sorry to have abandoned you—you should meet Pat and Kate." Pat and Kate came out of the dark. The hostess continued, "Pat knows all the famous archaeologists of the world but you."

Pat smiled. "That's an overstatement," he said. "I only run a yacht-renting business."

"That's an understatement, too. He owns a fleet."

Pat beamed with the pride of a schoolboy. His hair was carefully Brylcreemed above a round, glistening face. He was generous with brief smiles, but his forehead had a permanent crease that gave him a sad look. His eyes were fast, eager, and worried. His chin and neck seemed soldered onto his broad fat shoulders.

"He is also an amateur archaeologist," added Kate, his wife.

The hostess disappeared once more. Pat proposed a drink. Hermes said he was happy with his juice. Pat started for the bar. Kate smiled at Hermes, a smile different from her husband's. It lasted longer. It seemed to pull with it all the muscles of the long, bony face and with it the long neck, the long angular limbs.

"I'm Greek," she said, waving her long, dark hair, "although I was born in Tulsa. My husband was born in Tulsa, too. From the time he was a child, he dreamed of becoming an archaeologist and moving to Greece. Well, he married a Greek girl, settled in Greece, and collects archaeologists. Not bad."

"Are you an archaeologist?" asked Hermes.

"No, no, only an amateur," she said.

Hermes looked away.

"A friend of my husband's from the Institute told us of your arrival," she said pleasantly. "Will you stay the whole summer?"

"Maybe a year," said Hermes with some hesitation.

"You should," said the woman. She turned around to see if her husband was coming. He appeared, holding a glass in each hand.

"Pat," she said, "Hermes is spending a year in Greece."

"Well, well," said Pat, offering Kate the wine glass and keeping the martini for himself. "To your stay."

"What will you be working on?" she asked.

"I'll be writing a book."

"A book," said Kate with admiration.

"A book," repeated Pat. "Interesting. Do you have plans to go to the islands?"

"Not for the moment," said Hermes.

"We'd be delighted to have you as our guest for a few days in Santorini."

"Santorini?" said Hermes in surprise.

"Yes, Santorini," said Kate. "It's very simple. My husband invites authors on his cruises and to stay in the small houses he owns. It looks very good in his brochures."

"I see," said Hermes.

"Santorini is unique, as you know," said Pat. Then, dropping his jovial tone, he said, "I'm very sorry about your uncle. It was a real loss."

"We knew him," said Kate sorrowfully.

"You must join us," said Pat.

"Thank you very much. I don't even . . ."

"There's no rush to commit yourself," interrupted Kate, "and I've exaggerated the public-relations side. I might have scared you."

"Not at all," said Hermes affably. "Only . . . you might be interested in inviting somebody whose book is close to completion. Mine doesn't have an outline yet."

"Then come write your outline on our boat," she said seriously.

Pat got a small leather folder out of the breast pocket of his polo shirt and handed a card to Hermes. "Here are my telephone numbers."

"Let me give you my coordinates," said Hermes.

"Where did you learn that, Hermes? That is a Russian expression." asked Kate.

"Kate!" trumpeted a short woman in dark glasses and a long gypsy dress, who stumbled over the garden steps with her dress tangled between her legs.

"She's an avant-garde film director," Pat explained quietly as the woman embraced and kissed Kate, ignoring him. Pat said, "I'll give you a ring, Hermes," and slipped away to the bar from whence a group of tall men now approached. The women exchanged fast glances. The group came closer. Pushing through his friends, one of the men went straight to Hermes. "Wind," the man said introducing himself, "Aby Wind." He stooped over Hermes shaking his abundant, shaggy white hair, stretching his protruding white eyebrows, inhaling deeply through his prominent, broken, eagle nose. The rest of the group shook hands with Kate and the director.

"We'll be meeting soon in Cambridge," Wind said to Hermes. "I know you've been invited to the conference."

Kate said, "He'll be joining us in Santorini before your conference, I hope."

"Santorini?" said Wind, taking a deep breath.

"Why don't you join us?" said Kate.

"Why not?" repeated, as if in chorus, the men.

"We fly back in seven hours," replied Wind matter-of-factly. He turned to Hermes and said, "I'm looking forward to hearing what you have to say about cognitive science and archaeology. I believe the two fields have been kept apart for too long."

"I'll be happy to see you in Cambridge," said Hermes politely, as the group started toward the gate.

"I'd heard about his collection," said Kate, "and about his funding of restoration projects, but I'd never met him in person."

The avant-garde director cast a hateful eye onto the backs of the men, uniformly tall, uniformly shaped, uniformly dressed, with only the rebellious white hair tossing in the night to distinguish Wind from the rest.

A new group was walking toward them now.

Hermes smiled at Kate and slipped smoothly away in the direction of the illuminated swimming pool and the tall cypress trees that marked the end of the lot. Between the trees he caught a glimpse of a man standing dressed in a cinnamon-colored, carefully pressed double-breasted suit. The man paid no attention to him. Hermes came close to the man, who continued to ignore him while staring attentively at the swimming pool, as if waiting for somebody to surface. A shadow moved behind the trees coming toward the light. One could see he was wearing an earphone. Hermes turned away toward the gate.

At the gate people were still arriving. A few were already leaving.

"Hermes," somebody whispered. Robert looked apologetic.

"This is a surprise," said Hermes, his face brightening. "Where have you been hiding, Robert? How do you know these people?"

"Everybody knows these people. I mean, you don't have to be prominent to be invited here. How's everything with you?"

Hermes shrugged indifferently. "Who are these people, anyhow?"

"Oh, ship owners—New York, London, and Athens."

"And why all this security?"

"If you ask me, they're in the antique smuggling business too."

"I get the picture," said Hermes.

"Hermes," said Robert. "How *are* you, what's happening?"

"Not too bad," said Hermes. "It's rather boring here."

"Good. Let's get the hell out of here. You have to tell me your news."

"But you just arrived."

"So what."

"Did you speak to the host?"

"Hermes, you're archaic. They don't give a damn. If you want to be proper, send them a thank-you note tomorrow."

They went through the gate.

Hermes asked "How do we get back to the center of town from here?"

"I kept a cab," said Robert. "It's around the corner."

"Mine didn't even want to drive this far."

"You don't know how to talk to taxi drivers."

They came to the cab. The driver was leaning against the car looking up at the sky, whispering a melody. He jumped as they came closer and opened the door for them.

"To the sea," said Robert in ungrammatical Greek. "To the Zephyros."

Hermes looked at his watch. It was almost one in the morning.

A Late Dinner at the Zephyros

It was almost two by the time the obedient driver brought them to a bay not far from Melania's mansion. Robert told him to wait. A row of restaurants bordered the coastline. Some were closing. A few seemed to be going strong. The brightest and busiest had a big gaudy illuminated sign that read *Zephyros.* They walked toward it.

They sat at a table just a step away from the waves. The first dishes arrived quickly. Robert's hand plunged into the olive-laden plate. Hermes picked up a small pickled pepper.

"Peace and quiet at last. Have the police contacted you? And what about this famous Psychiko contact of yours who says he knows who the murderer is? Was that for real?" Robert asked as soon as the waiters left them alone.

"My contact, as you put it, has unexpectedly vanished into thin air." Hermes' eyes had a disappointed look.

"Are you sure this man wasn't a disguised policeman?"

"Might well have been. The police officially . . ." Hermes described his two interviews with Karras. As Robert listened, gloom spread over his face.

"Now you have the whole picture," Hermes said when he finished.

Robert said, "Are you getting any professional advice? I don't like your story."

"I tried a lawyer. Totally incompetent."

"People to help you? Anyone connected with your family?"

"I have almost nobody here. But don't worry about it, Robert. Of course I have nobody here. You know that. A very distant cousin and her daughter who is an undergraduate engineering student. I've seen a friend of my father's, a retired professor, and a pensioned general."

Hermes raised both hands and let them drop on the table. "And I visit an unconventional counsel."

"What do you mean? Are you trying to be mysterious again?"

"I visit a medium."

"I knew this would happen some day," said Robert. "Back to the cabala. Deep at heart you're a traditionalist and a mystic."

"Not that bad," said Hermes. "I'm doing it out of personal need."

"Everything is a personal need, Hermes. That's no excuse for your escapism, especially now that you need to be so close to reality. It reminds me of your senior thesis. Remember? You panicked and said you had either to run away to Yellowstone Park or become religious. Fortunately you opted for the first and everything turned out OK."

"She actually . . ." Hermes hesitated. "She helps me come close to things I want to hold on to."

"Amazing," Robert sighed. "Is there anything I can do for you? I mean in the practical realm?"

"I just want to be able to work."

"I know. I know. What do we do in the meantime, though? We have to be pragmatic. You might be heading for real trouble."

"What kind?"

"Don't you understand what this magistrate is aiming at?"

"That I shot my uncle to get his fortune?"

"Or this treasure that's disappeared."

"Why hasn't he locked me up, then?"

"Because obviously he hasn't got enough evidence. Because he's waiting for something."

"You mean he's playing cat and mouse with me?"

"Something like that. That is why I'm asking you again. Can I do something to help?"

"Thanks, Robert. Unless you have something special to suggest." Hermes smiled.

"Well, not for the moment. I'm just a part-time journalist, Hermes. But I'll try. Tell me, when do you see the police again?"

"I don't have regular appointments. They just pick me up on the sidewalk when I'm not expecting them."

"And the medium?"

"Oh, it all depends on how I feel."

"And me?"

"That depends on you. When's your next expedition?"

"OK, don't rub it in. I know. I've been busy."

Robert had paid the bill. "Let's blast off," he said and looked at his watch, irritated. "I've got to go and earn some bread."

They started off toward the taxi.

"What's your assignment here?" Hermes asked.

"Just an excuse, can't you see?" answered Robert.

"See what? I'm sorry," said Hermes apologetically. "I haven't asked you about your trip. We've only talked about my business."

"Why not? First, your affairs are always more urgent," said Robert, grumbling. Then his expression changed and he added confidentially, "Second, what's the use of speaking about me? I don't give anything away. You told me I was a zero-knowledge proof a long time ago. And that's what I am. After a billion observations you still know as much about me as the first time we met."

Hermes moved his head sadly. "That's because you never give away more than half a piece of information and then never pick up that piece again. So one never manages to know the whole or even the whole half."

"And what about you? I don't think you're any better in making yourself known. You never reveal your motivations. If you ever enter into this detective story as a hero, you won't interact, either with the author or the reader." Robert laughed stridently. The laugh resounded over the motionless bay.

"You're underestimating me. How humiliating," said Hermes simply.

They reached the taxi. The driver was sleeping in the back seat. The day was slowly dawning.

Preparations for Departure

There was a message on the screen. Nina could not come this morning (her reading, her mother, etc.) and she was reporting: "Ultimately GPS is proving as frustrating as everything else." Could he comment? Could he type it in the computer? The message ended with, "What now?"

Hermes typed immediately: "Representation of commonsense knowledge coming up." Then he added: "Medium turned out to be a methodologist too. Had a very interesting party. Good news: Robert is back."

The clock on the screen indicated it was midday. A message appeared next to it: "Dorothy Evans!" and a number. Hermes walked to the telephone and dialed the number.

"I was on my way to the swimming pool. No, you did't wake me up." The voice was brusque, the sentences curt. Yes, everything had been paid for. Hermes would have a business-class ticket. The conference would be very informal. Sponsors appeared to be interested in supporting more theoretical projects now. They wanted to know about long-term research ideas in archaeology that would enhance the understanding of human cognition. "It is imperative that you be there," she said, "and I quote."

Then Hermes dialed a second number.

"Apollo Navigations," said a woman's voice.

"I have a message for Mr. Sloan."

"I'll have to switch you to his secretary. The line is busy. Could you hold the line, please."

She put him on hold. Music played on the line. The level of the music lowered every so often and the sound of sea waves followed.

"Good afternoon. Can I help you?" said another voice.

"Yes" said Hermes. "This is Dr. Steganos. Could you tell Mr. Sloan that I'll be delighted to join the excursion. Tell him I'll be in the airport at the agreed time."

The telephone rang as soon as he put down the receiver.

"Jesus, Hermes. I've been trying to get you for hours."

"I was here all morning, Robert," said Hermes. "The telephone's only been busy for the last thirty minutes."

"That's right. I didn't try to call you before twelve. I was busy sending telexes. I have to make a living. I'm not on leave of absence from a prestigious institution."

"Neither am I, not any more that is," said Hermes.

There was a moment of silence. Then Robert said faintly, "Are you quitting?"

"No. I'm going back to Cambridge. Only for a few days, though."

"So soon? Anything serious?"

"No, just an unexpected meeting for long-term research financing."

"I never realized archaeology was getting so businesslike. Why didn't you tell me anything the other night? Hermes, hermetic as usual."

"I just heard about it myself. I was just talking to my chairperson."

"Well. Are we still meeting tonight, now that you are part of the jet set?"

"I stick to my agreements."

"At the Rio at six."

"Six," said Hermes. Then he added, "Before that I have to ask my parole officer for permission to travel."

"Good luck."

Finally Hermes called the number Karras had given him. Karras answered himself. He could see Hermes at five.

A Third Interview

Karras was behind the same desk. He immediately began to inspect the empty top of his desk, but briefly. Then he raised his eyes to Hermes, appearing less displeased to see him this time.

Hermes said, "I'd like to travel."

"When?"

"Tomorrow."

Karras' face remained unmoved.

"And I have to make another trip in ten days," Hermes added.

"In ten days." Karras resumed his inspection of his desk, flicking some imaginary dust from its surface.

"Yes. I have to go to Cambridge for a meeting," Hermes continued.

Finally Karras looked at Hermes with contempt. He articulated his words slowly. "You have to attend a meeting in Cambridge."

"I have to deliver a paper."

"On . . ."

"Does it concern you?"

"A paper that . . ." Karras was almost talking to himself but Hermes responded anyway.

"A proposal for a comparative study on a large number of antique objects."

"A large number of antique objects," Karras echoed. The echo made Hermes's phrase sound incomplete.

Hermes continued. "Objects that carry inscriptions or even better, shapes that aren't suspected of being anything but superfluous decorations now, as being there merely for the pleasure of the eye, as they say."

"Like the inscriptions on the Golden Thinking Machine," Karras interrupted.

"Maybe. I didn't have time to study them very carefully. I told you that."

"So these objects carry data."

"Not only. My proposal refers to objects holding more complex information than just data."

"More complex?"

"They document inferences . . ."

Karras looked at Hermes out of the corner of his eye.

". . . of a certain kind," Hermes completed.

"Geometrical inferences?" Karras asked.

Hermes clarified. "Inferences about space, you might say, with inference and space being conceived in a very different way from the way they are today."

"With different categories?"

"Radically different categories, and a different kind of thinking."

"An alternate logic?"

Hermes lifted his head in surprise. "You might call it that, although it could be misleading. What they call alternate logic most of the time today isn't exactly what I mean. I mean a logic that's different."

"You mean nonsense then?"

"You might call it that, but that wouldn't be correct either. It isn't nonsense for those who live in it."

"In our previous interview," said Karras, "you talked about ways of life that may lead to 'cribs' for deciphering. Now you are talking about 'inferences,' 'categories,' 'logic.' Can these be related to 'cribs' too?"

"Yes. Ways of thinking and ways of life are closely interwoven. One can support or destroy the other, and for this reason we can understand many things about one from the other. As far as 'cribs' go, everything is very speculative."

"What about this project? Does it deal with 'cribs'?" Karras pressed on.

"I don't understand what you mean."

Karras' voice took on a more relaxed tone and changed the subject. "What would another way of thinking be like, for instance?"

"It would permit many interrelations between facts that aren't possible through the logical operations we use today, and link data and conclusions in ways that are not permissible in our frame of mind."

"Are you talking about changing conventions of thinking in history?"

"Yes. And maybe about more fundamental changes that occurred during human evolution, constitutional rather than conventional—changes in the wiring of our thinking apparatus, so to speak."

"And what happens to the old thinking paths when such changes occur?"

"Give me an example of a new kind of path."

"One that permits self-reference, self-analysis, self-awareness."

"What about causal inference, logical deductions, or the *tertium non datur,* the law of the excluded middle? I always thought these were the most advanced ways in which thinking is organized. Actually I know of people even today who are not very developed in this respect. Some of my colleagues . . ." Karras said, still finding absorbing spots on his impeccable desk top.

Hermes went on, "The emergence of self-awareness, of awareness of belief as distinct from knowledge, is the most important transformation in the evolution of human cognition. And we still know very, very little about how it happened and how it works."

Karras hesitated. Then he asked, "Is that why, as far as I know, there is so little of it in computer engineering?"

Hermes answered, "Yes."

"Is your archaeology going to shed light on this problem?"

"I hope so."

"What about analyzing skulls?" asked Karras.

"There's work done on prehistoric endocasts of hominids that tries to determine the size of the brain and reconstruct the blood supply structure and the area organization."

Karras turned his head away from his desk top abruptly. "Seems very promising."

"Maybe because you've spent too many hours with homicide specialists," Hermes said casually.

"Actually," said Karras, fixing his eyes on Hermes, "I've spent more time with deciphering specialists, but that is beside the point.

In principle I hesitate to derive conclusions about the design of an engine on the basis of its output alone. I wonder what the engineers think."

"I wouldn't know, I'm just an archaeologist."

"And how long will it take you to explain all this to your colleagues in Cambridge?" asked Karras in a slightly changed tone.

"I'll be away five days. I can be reached through the Department of Archaeology at Harvard," answered Hermes as if he had not heard the question.

"All right." Karras stared at him abstractly.

"Well," said Hermes, "that's it," and looked toward the door.

"Goodbye," rejoined Karras, impenetrable again.

The meeting had lasted half an hour. Hermes found his way out of the building without much difficulty this time.

At the Rio

The Rio was a café, or what one might more accurately call an expresso bar, common in other Mediterranean cities but unique in Athens. Located at the corner of a canopied sidewalk and a covered passageway, it was a unique urban observation post and a privileged, temperate city seat in the midst of hotels, airline agencies, and restaurants. Hermes entered the bar ahead of the agreed time. His forehead was drenched with sweat. He had walked from the police station for half an hour under the sweltering sun in the midst of demolition and construction, noise and dust.

The place was cool and empty. A young woman stood behind the counter while an older, somber woman stood behind the water fountain. Brass gleamed. The air was pungent with the smell of fresh coffee and strong detergent.

"Rio is famous for its coffees and fresh fruit juices," Robert had said to Hermes the other night. "It's notorious for its eccentric service carried out by semiretired waitresses or young university dropouts. Its claim to fame, though, is the clientele that it attracted immediately before and after the Second World War, when it was a hangout for informers and a nest of spies—a pool of disinformation."

The somber woman ignored Hermes, but the young woman smiled and said, "Would you like a nice hot chocolate?"

Hermes said, "No reasonable person would in this weather. I'll have an orange juice."

"Reason doesn't make us act. It only regulates our actions. Two hundred drachmas please," she said.

Hermes smiled, paid, and proceeded to pick up the tall glass from the somber woman. The glass was chilled and foggy. It almost slipped through his fingers. He nearly slipped on the freshly polished marble floor. He moved to the front of the shop. Along the window ran a long, narrow, varnished ledge. He set his juice down. He watched it slide lightly down the width of the ledge. It rested next to a cup of coffee painted on the window. Out of this cup rose a cloud of steam painted on a blue background. The cloud was shaped like South America. The spot where Rio should have been was a hole left out of the map at eye level. Hermes stared out through the glass and through the hole. Images rippled up off the hot pavement of the road.

A crowd of boys and girls was being unloaded from a bus farther up. They paraded along the other side of the street and down toward the square, carrying bags, sacks, folding furniture, sun umbrellas, even flags.

Then he thought he saw the Asian philosopher of photography. He was partially hidden by the crowd. Hermes was not sure if the man, now wearing a white short-sleeved shirt and baggy khaki pants, walking at the same pace as the rest of the milling crowd, was he. The man turned his face. He appeared to look at Hermes and to recognize him. The man seemed to hesitate for a moment. Hermes found the face with the green sun visor he looked for.

By the time Hermes had rushed out of the café, another bus had pulled up. Its roaring engine released a warm, asphyxiating cloud of gas that shimmered as it rose. More crowds were unloaded. Hermes walked through the group. A young woman offered him a straw hat. Everyone was friendly. None of them resembled the man he believed he had seen.

There were many paths the philosopher of photography could have taken to get out of sight: an undersized arcade, an oversized entrance to a building, the steps of a large hotel, a small bar, a black Morris Minor that had just turned the corner. Or it could have been nothing but a mirage in the glare of an Athenian afternoon after all.

The incident reminded Hermes of a malfunctioning computer-vision program that he had seen once. The program could recognize images even if they were fuzzy and fragmented. The competence of the program derived from the prior knowledge it had of the stereotypical descriptions of objects and from the way it made use of them.

When the data received by the system just approximated one of the prototypes, the program would begin to generate what one might call controlled hallucinations. Information would be pulled from the prototype, and the program would create hypotheses or expectations of what a complete image would be. The program generated projections of the absent parts and indicated where they might be found. It made suggestions about the presence of additional lines within suspect areas and subsequently activated a line tester that searched for evidence of what might match the stereotypical description.

The specific case of malfunctioning concerned an application of the program to identify fighter aircraft. The system knew the description of fighter aircraft, and it was made even more intelligent by being given the capability to take into account contextual aspects, the probability of encountering the enemy in the surrounding area. Based on gathered military intelligence, appropriate thresholds of hypothesis generation and testing were established. From radar operators the system had received fuzzy, fragmented data originating from some civilian airliner. Other information confirmed that an attack by hostile forces was imminent. The system was put on high alert. The expectations of encountering enemy aircraft were raised. The mechanisms of generating image fragments were activated while those of testing were hampered. The system became prone to a kind of paranoia.

Hermes walked back to the café. Robert was peering out at him. The sun was setting in front of his face but he seemed not to mind. He was holding a *Wall Street Journal*. As Hermes advanced, Robert put on a pair of round, purple-rimmed glasses with dark iridescent, mirroring lenses.

"What an amazing story. He was one of the biggest egos in the United States. One forty three and a half," he said abstractly. "The market is crazy. Something's got to happen," he added. Then he turned soberly to Hermes. "You're late. Where have you been?"

"Out. Having a hallucination," said Hermes.

"You told me no new knowledge is possible without some hallucination. Do you feel wiser?"

"Just fine," said Hermes, sweating.

The girl at the counter smiled again at Hermes, then turned to Robert. "Have you decided what you want for you and your friend who's always late?"

"The best," Robert said.

"Capuccino is better than Greek coffee, Greek coffee is better than orange juice, and orange juice is better than capuccino," the girl said.

"Incommeasurable!" exclaimed Hermes.

"Is this the way to keep us imprisoned for ever, Sphinx?" asked Robert. "But I can get around it. I'll have a capuccino for myself, and a Greek coffee and an orange juice for my friend."

"My name is Tina. You pick up your drinks at the bar. Six hundred drachmas, please," she said.

"Sphinx is not interested in us anymore. She let me break up the vicious circle."

"Where do we go from here, Robert?" asked Hermes in a defeated voice as they were having their drinks.

"Going to an outdoor movie is better than going to a taverna in the mountains, and going to a taverna in the mountains is better than going to an evening concert in the ancient theater, and going to an evening concert in the ancient theater is better than going to an outdoor movie."

"Be more original, Robert."

"OK. The night's still young. I thought of proposing a party first."

"Another one?" exclaimed Hermes, glancing out. The bus had gone.

"You seem worried. You shouldn't be," said Robert. "You know I never reveal any real plans till it's too late. Do you want to go back to the same restaurant we were at the other night?"

Zephyros Revisited

They were back at the same restaurant by the sea. It was empty this time. A waiter and two young helpers were moving around, slowly setting up the tables. Robert and Hermes sat by the water again. For a few minutes they gazed at the waves without uttering a word.

"Well, we need a vacation," said Robert, taking a deep breath.

"I'm on leave of absence. I don't qualify," said Hermes.

"Of course you do, and I'll tell you why. I think we should take a trip to the Bosporus."

"The Bosporus? But you realize I have to go to Santorini and to Cambridge."

"I see you're taking vacations inside your vacations pretending to write a book," said Robert. "You should continue this practice."

"Both trips are for business. You know that."

They were interrupted by one of the two young waiters who had approached noiselessly. They ordered grilled octopus, tsiri, eggplant salad, ouzo, and orange juice for Hermes.

Robert continued, "So. Santorini and then Cambridge, on business. God, you're compulsive."

"So are you," Hermes said. "You've been running around day and night. You must be getting rich fast. What are you going to do with all that money? Or are you just trying to make your first million before thirty?"

"I'm running away from myself," Robert murmured with a mock-tragic raising of the eyebrows.

"We all are."

"Some of us make money in the process, some of us don't," added Robert defensively. Then, as if deep in thought, he continued, "You and I should pool our talents one day."

"I thought you wanted to go on vacation."

Robert roared, "You're right. I'm always recanting what I've just said."

"It looks like it."

"Things are more obvious than they look." The aggravated tone came back. "The difference between you and me is that, although we've both learned that inconsistency is the essence of life, you have chosen not to know that you know it and I haven't. You keep trying to save the rational reputation of the universe. I, on the contrary, have given up."

"You're beginning to sound like a literature major," Hermes said.

"What would you prefer me to sound like? A medium?" Robert retaliated.

"That's nonsense," said Hermes angrily.

"So are your insinuations about literature. I'll tell you, it has inoculated me against the illusion of truth and logic. I wish the same had happened to you. Laboratories are a different experience. Even archaeology laboratories," he continued in a somber mood. "Once you've sat in front of a text in order to find its meaning, as happens routinely in literature classes, you realize how fatal and hypocritical it is to search for the one unique, correct interpretation, not only of a poem or a phrase but of anything in the world. Interpretation can never be anything but a monologue by the interpreter about himself."

"How many times are we going to go over that? You're ignoring the recent developments in theory of interpretation. Contemporary research has moved away from the single-minded problem-solving approach. We recognize now that a previously existing structure guides the understanding of any new information. Preknowledge is indispensable for new knowledge. Every reading of a text is by necessity a merging of at least two points of view, the reader's and the author's, the beholder's and the designer's. This isn't relativism. It is a transactional view. Multiple interpretations are completely legitimate. The aim is to explain them rather than to exclude them. They are the center of concern. Subjectivism and relativism have been an easy way out. They ended up as an alibi for limiting the work of the interpreter. They didn't enrich interpretation, they did away with it," Hermes said calmly.

"You people think that if you present multiple interpretations, each one of which provides a different perspective of the same story, you can achieve objectivity," Robert responded, irritated. "You don't realize, or you don't want to admit, that one more analysis doesn't improve your knowledge. It just brings you back where you started from."

"You mean I've spent my whole life decoding scripts in vain?"

"Not exactly. You've made a living and a reputation out of it. But you've only been making convincing pronouncements without really generating new knowledge."

"That's quite a compliment coming from you. Relativism leads unavoidably to nihilism," said Hermes epigrammatically.

"Hermes, you know I speak in allegories. Even when I speak about you. There is nothing personal. You are my *dramatis persona*. You are what civilization is about; not only is nobody capable of producing truth, everybody is frantically busy fabricating deception under the cover of disinterested explication."

"How do people talk to each other then?"

"People don't communicate. That is the thing. They never did. They never will. They just pass messages on to each other in order to recognize their own existence and to violate each other's will."

"Is this the reason you want us to get rich?"

"I knew you were going to ask that."

"What do you want me to do, Robert, deconstruct the universe? Or make more of those zero-knowledge games that you call literature, and drive everybody crazy? Or should I just drop out?"

"You'd have been much better off taking an unproductive vacation. Drop the idea of your business trips."

"Impossible," said Hermes.

"Hmm. Well what about doing research in Istanbul with me to write a novel?"

"A novel? That's a novel suggestion."

"I don't mean just any novel. I mean a detective story."

"Everybody seems to be interested in detective stories recently."

"Of course. They're the closest thing to a true study of human nature."

Hermes smiled. "Back to nihilism, I see."

"Not yet. What I want to say is that detective stories are difficult and that they are about difficulty. Now, there's a task for you."

"Sure. Crime's great. That's because it's about recognition, inference, explanation, interpretation. The hardest things intelligence is used in. But I wouldn't say detective stories are the most difficult kind of literature. Their language is so superficial . . ."

"We're talking about a different kind of difficulty," Robert interrupted. "Plot. To begin with, you have to write, with detective stories anyway, at least five plots. Not just one, as you do with other kinds of stories and scientific narration. And not just two, as Chandler claimed. The first is the plot supposed to be constructed by the criminal out of his actions. Then the criminal, again, by withholding information, destroying evidence, disguising facts, and spreading misinformation, creates his own, second plot. The third is the plot the detective writes, so to speak, while he is decoding the mystery. The fourth plot is written by the author herself or himself, and it is the greatest secret. This plot is all about how the author indulges in reticence, reverses and mixes events, creates an aura of equivocation, evades and prolongs. The fifth plot is all about how the author offers hints, connects seemingly unrelated events that weave the other four plots together. As you can see, the story contributes nothing to knowledge. It has nothing to do with recognition, inference, explanation, interpretation and all that humanistic, scientistic stuff you're so fond of."

"Scientistic?"

"Yeah. Scientistic."

"I'm sorry, Robert, but the only point you've succeeded in making is that detective stories try to make explicit representations of processes of information that are more complex than simple recognition and inference and so on. They are about making patterns out of motifs and, out of patterns, levels for the patterns to grow in and structures to keep track of all these expanding levels that anticipate, compare, and correct all at once."

"And what about domination and torture, the game the author plays with the reader, cast in the struggle between the criminal and the detective, or the game the reader plays with the author, with the author struggling to predict and obey the reader's desires? And if you want my opinion, this is what you should do in your lecture in Cambridge—tell them a detective story. They'll love it."

"Fascinating," said Hermes. "I might just do that. But for very private reasons. The more I think of it, the more the detective story is a simple and expressive way of demonstrating this idea of levels of human reasoning. If I could develop a geology of reasoning that would go well with my archaeology—the antagonistic as well as cooperative-forum nature of reasoning. I'm sure music, poetry, architecture, painting, and cinema are all to some degree about the same idea, the representation of intelligence, but detective stories with their spare style are more explicit."

"You're doing it again, the wrong way 'round. You start from human reasoning, then you go to the detective story. You should turn things upside down. First there's . . ."

But the waiter had arrived again noiselessly with the drinks and the appetizers. They ordered broiled mullet.

"You are very influenced by the surroundings," said Hermes later on, sipping orange juice after a bite of mullet. Robert shut his eyes silently in horror at the sight. "You really are obsessed with detective stories and you want me either to write one or be in one. I wonder. Is it the mess this murder has created or is it the general climate of this country? You know, they've been obsessed with plots and plotting for the last two thousand years. Take the myth of Hermes or *Oedipus Rex.* Great detective stories."

"You oversimplify. The Hermes myth is about thieves and only implicitly about detectives and you don't qualify for it. You're much too dull for either role. I've told you that. *Oedipus Rex* is a story of detection. But not your kind of detection: problem solving, pattern recognition, deciphering. It isn't a story *about* detection so much as about problem solving. It's about the self-defeating nature of detection and interpretation. The hubris of it all. It's too depressing for you. I don't advise you to be part of it, even though you have just accused me of being nihilistic."

Imperceptibly the waiter had approached once more. The sun had set. There were more people around. The long festive garlands of small electric light bulbs that surrounded the restaurant platform had been turned on. The air smelled strongly of grilled fish. A group of children and adults had just appeared. The children were quiet, taken in by the view. The adults were shouting and pointing in the direction of the sunset, at the blood-red color of the sky. "I've never seen children behaving like that in front of a sunset," said Robert.

A person came to shore slowly in a small boat from nowhere, moored it, leapt onto the platform, and passed among the tables. He met another person who had come between the tables from the other side. The other man had arrived with a dusty, dilapidated, tired bicycle that now rested against a light pole next to the road. The bicycle seemed to have come from a long way off. The two people did not appear to exchange a word. They crossed the street and moved uphill, away from the sea and the road. The boat and the bicycle stayed behind.

Hermes and Robert went on with their eating and talking.

"I don't see why I couldn't travel under the circumstances. The examining magistrate seemed rather content the last time."

"You don't know those bastards. I've had more experience with the police than you. They lie. You're very vulnerable. You were at your uncle's just before the shooting. Why not during? You've seen the treasure. You're enough of an expert to understand its value, to know how to dump it. You could make use of the money. Why not do it? See now?"

"What would you suggest?"

"I would avoid traveling. The moment you set foot on the plane, they'll claim you tried to escape, and arrest you."

"But you were just suggesting a trip!"

"That was a metaphor," said Robert, and laughed. "I meant you need some rest. You're overstressed."

"We've known each other for such a long time. I never realized you're such an overly cautious person."

"You've been in your cocoon all these years. I've been hustling. I assure you it wasn't easy, Hermes. So, do you have to go?"

"I have to."

The young waiter arrived with a tray full of desserts.

The Medium Once More

The old villa at the edge of the plateau appeared starker, darker, and more cubical as the moon hung above it in the full light of day. Next to a small garden gate was a dark gray car with no one in it. When Hermes rang, Elpis came to the gate as she had the previous time. The cock was standing at the gate. At the steps the sphinxes looked on.

Elpis took Hermes to Melania's office. Melania received him wearing the same oversized dark glasses.

"I have some things to report and I'm going on two trips," he said.

Noiselessly Elpis closed the heavy door.

"The message will be received by tomorrow morning," said Melania after Hermes had finished. She stood up. "Have very good trips," she said.

Out in the large hall she said, "I promised you I would tell you about the work I do. I keep my promises. Next time I would like to show you the House of Esoteric Knowledge. And of course I still expect you to tell me about your research." Hermes agreed and she led him to the door.

The breeze had changed direction and a lone cicada droned.

Santorini

Hermes and Pat were sitting in the front deck pit. The helmsman, a young, sickly looking Irishman, was the only other person in sight. With all its sails flying, the yacht was gliding over the deep waters.

Pat held a chrome cocktail shaker in his left hand and a cigarette in his right. The hands were plump and trembled very slightly. Hermes picked white cherries from a fake Byzantine turquoise bowl. The discussion was hovering aimlessly.

"Your uncle," Pat let the words hang in the air briefly, "he worked for years on the island."

"Did you know him well?" Hermes said, looking over the waves.

"Impossible not to. Santorini is a small island and a major part of my business is here . . ." He glanced at Hermes with nostalgic eyes. "I used to meet with Philippos often. There's someone who really knew how to live." He took a sip out of the shaker, inhaled, and added, "What a shame. Did you have a chance to see him after you came back?"

"The day I arrived. A few hours before he was killed."

"We'll be visiting the site he was working at," Pat said softly. "Tomorrow."

"It's very kind of you to have arranged it."

"Do you know his work?"

"Not really. He didn't publish much."

"He didn't. I knew that. Archaeologists gossip a lot about each others' work, and I see too many of them."

"He was mostly a field researcher and an administrator."

"He was self-content. A great guy. He was excited about something he had come across in his excavation just before he died."

"He was a very enthusiastic man in general, I think."

"I remember he mentioned something about some success he'd had with proto-Hellenic instruments."

"That would be hard to imagine on such a site."

"He'd even told me that such findings could confirm many of your famous conjectures."

"He was very flattering about my work. I wonder who'll take over the excavation now."

"Did you come to Greece to work on a specific archaeological site?"

"No. My subject is more theoretical."

"So I heard. And what's your topic?"

"The archaic way of thinking and, by implication, the nature of thinking itself. It's in part archaeological, the archaeology of mentality, one might say, and in part about cognition."

"Fascinating," said Pat, clearly confused.

Hermes picked up a few more cherries from the bowl and looked into Pat's blue eyes, their tiny rivulets of scarlet arteries. Cigarette smoke glided over the eyes. The slant of the sun fell on the eyes. The eyes closed. There was silence for a couple of minutes. The yacht was heading into the end of the day.

Pat said, "I have some plans that might interest you, Hermes. I'm planning to retire soon."

"Retire?"

"Well, not completely. I've been in this part of the world, the same business, for twenty years."

"Twenty years!" Hermes echoed politely.

"The time has come for something more challenging." He smiled, sipped, and inhaled again. The smoke cast a shadow across his lips. The shadow curled over the contours of his jaw and nose, then dissipated as it neared his forehead. It was a low forehead. "Doing business here is so petty. Everybody is so narrow-minded. I'm ready to move on to new things."

Suddenly a darkness fell on both of them. Pat raised his head and looked up. Hermes turned around. Santorini rose right ahead of the bow, two thousand feet high. The boat was rounding the edge of the island. A crescent-shaped bay opened up before them, white houses gleaming high up in the sun, forming a precarious white edge along the fall line of the cliff.

"We're now sailing over what used to be the center of the island of Thera before the big eruption," said Pat. "Awesome, isn't it? You can sense what power can do. A whole island split in two. Whap!" He brought down his hand with force as in a karate blow on the table. "One half sank under two thousand feet of water and the other was covered under mountains of dust." Then he turned to Hermes and added, "Philippos had spoken about the machine he had found in the context of the big disaster. Did he mention anything to you?"

"Not a word," said Hermes.

"The eruption was like a manmade occurrence. Like somebody did it with an explosion. I used to be excited by technology when I was young—big engineering projects. I worked in Pakistan in the 'fifties. That was my other passion, next to archaeology." Through the narrow slits of his eyes Hermes caught a swift glimpse of the deep blue water. Pat took another sip out of the shaker. "I still have lots of ideas, some of them very pragmatic."

"You seem to have many interests."

"I simply had to do a lot in my life that I was not really much interested in."

"You mean your hobbies are your real interests?"

"You might say that. But I don't regret it because this way I have both the money and the friends to support projects. Projects I would like to see happen."

"Archaeological?"

"Mostly. But also broader culture. I'm very worried. I think the end of culture is imminent. This is something I want to talk to you about. It concerns me very much. We've got to do something about it. I see it everywhere around the globe. I see it in this island."

"When did you first come to Santorini?" asked Hermes, devouring the last cherries.

"Ten years ago. I bought a house on the first day and I met Professor Agraphiotis as well. It was a busy day."

A strong wind was carrying them swiftly to the dock in the middle of the inner rim of the crescent.

"We'll have a busy program. You'll see," Pat announced loudly and stood up.

The deck was coming back to life. The Maltese captain commanded the horizon. The crew, Manolo the cook and Daphne the stewardess, were taking down the sails and starting the motor. The helmsman steered intently. Kate and Mrs. Mitchell, her friend, were also there.

"So thrilled you're here, Hermes," Kate hollered from the other side of the boat, as the cook cheerfully tossed the rope toward a man waiting on the jetty. The man started to tie it around a rusty mooring pole.

An hour later Hermes was inside one of those tiny white houses perched on the abyss, one of the thirty owned by Pat, that overlooked the crater. He was trying to shave. It was not easy. The blinding rays of a bronze western sun hit his face through the bathroom's narrow arched window. The left side of his face was submerged in darkness. The bare light bulb did not work. Not everything in Pat's small empire was in order.

Out of the window Hermes could see two cruise boats that had entered the crescent of the bay. A woman's voice reverberated from the loudspeakers of one of the boats. She was lecturing about the island.

"The volcano erupted about 4500 years ago. Huge tsunamis reached the coast as far as Africa. Earthquakes followed; masses of hot ashes fell from the sky. They buried the entire island and the town of Akrotiri, and reached as far as Crete. The strange thing is that not one skeleton, not one piece of jewelry, not one bit of precious metal, not one weapon was found on the site. It appears that all the inhabitants took everything valuable they could carry when they left, even domestic animals, a few months before the eruption. It is still not known how the people were informed of the imminent catastrophe. Still unknown also . . ."

A green bottle crashed through the window, smashed the mirror, and shattered in the middle of the sink, sending splinters of glass all over the bathroom. Some were in Hermes' hair. A second missile hit the edge of the window frame and was deflected without entering the room. Hermes rushed out of the house, wiping the glass out of his hair with a towel.

A hundred meters away Pat was coming down the road in a white linen suit turned shocking pink, reflecting the sunset against a cobalt-blue sky.

"Great sunset," shouted Hermes. "It's really relaxing to be here," he added, as Pat approached, puffing.

Polar Star

Night had fallen. "I'm glad you like the place you're staying in. I think you'll like this restaurant, too," said Pat to Hermes as they parked in front of a blank wall. It was punctured by a humble black door under a neon sign that read, "Polar Star." "Last year it was called 'Nebula.' Let's go on in fast, before it turns into 'The Forbidden Planet,'" he said, as he pushed open the door.

They were on a small platform, barely three feet square, at the top of a steep, brilliantly lit, whitewashed amphitheater. They descended a long stair. At the center where the stage would have been were a few tables surrounding a slightly raised dance floor. Stairs radiated on all sides leading to other platforms with more tables. The whole thing overlooked the starry archipelago.

"Breathtaking, but a hell of a layout for the waiters," Pat said to Hermes, raising his chubby hand to greet Kate and Mrs. Mitchell. They were seated at a table on the first platform with two other people. Pat was immediately welcomed with servile cordiality by the director of the restaurant.

"Hermes," said Kate when they reached the table. "I'd like to introduce you to the Baron and Baroness de Vouët-Vuillard." Nods and smiles were exchanged all around. Pat and Hermes took their seats. Drinks were rushed over, compliments of the establishment.

The baron picked up where he had left off before the interruption. "Oui, oui. On a beau dire que c'est le proletariat qui a tout détruit. Mais non! Je vous assure. C'est la classe moyenne! Elle est encore pire! C'est elle qui a détruit Santorini! Ma foi! Mais enfin! Pauvre Santorin."

The baroness, who spoke only French, continued with a description of their voyage on the Aegean just before the Second World War.

She recounted the death by drowning of a Hungarian spy during a moonlight excursion. Kate responded sympathetically in a mixture of English and German, sprinkled with a few Spanish words, and Mrs. Mitchell nodded approvingly.

Pat turned to Hermes. "Kate invited them on behalf of Aegean Tours. The baron claims he's a descendant of Charlemagne."

Appetizers arrived in dozens of small dishes.

As the evening progressed, the place became more animated. Waiters rushed about, climbing and descending in all directions. People danced to recorded music blaring from loudspeakers.

"Have you ever heard of the Fissiparons Club?" Pat asked Hermes, clearing his throat.

"I don't think so," Hermes answered.

"The name comes from the word fission. It means reproducing by breaking into parts with great release of energy. As the title suggests, it is dedicated to . . ." Pat seemed suddenly uplifted. He was about to continue. But just then a waiter came up to the table and apologized.

"Something the matter, Spyro?" asked Pat.

The waiter bent over and said something into Pat's ear.

"Sorry, Hermes, an urgent long-distance call," said Pat as he picked up his drink and followed the waiter.

Someone approached the microphone and made a loud blast with an old accordion. The dancers were confused. He mumbled, "I will now play a fox trot for you. You all know the story of the farmer, the goose, the grain, and the fox, don't you? They all tried to cross a river in a little boat. You must have spent quite some time trying to work out the ending, right? However, it shouldn't take more than a couple of minutes if you describe it the right way. Listen to me and you won't regret it. It goes like this." He caressed his accordion, stretched it out, and started to sing:

> Fox, goose, farmer, and grain
> Desperately await, to cross a river,
> A tiny boat which only two can contain:
> The sole means for passing they consider.

Some people tried to dance as the song jerked along.

If alone, with no farmer's restraint,
The fox eats the goose, and the goose the grain.
He must invent an intelligent scheme
For safely shipping the rapacious team.
He has to search for the big constraints
That the problem undoubtedly self-contains.
To do this smartly, the farmer thinks,
I must represent the problem through nodes and links.

Links describe the allowable crossing,
Nodes, an arrangement that he'll be bossing.
A fox, a goose, a farmer, and some grain,
To one solution committed remain.

Farmer and boat, the goose deliver
While fox and grain stand by the river.
Farmer, fox, and grain, across the river,
Observe with envy the goose, that free-liver.
Farmer, goose, and grain with patience refrain
And watch the fox alone, the misgiver.
When fox, farmer, and goose their seat obtain,
They look at the grain, their lips aquiver.

Farmer, fox, and grain together remain
On the opposite bank of the river.
"Beautiful boat bring the goose," they blither.
A fox, a goose, a farmer, and some grain
Finally succeed in crossing the river.
Now they are all gladly willing to testify
To the great potentials of AI
Singing *en masse* on a cantilever.

Swift solutions you only elicit
If you consider what remains implicit.
And alternately cast, novel descriptions
Are totally outlawed by strong circumscriptions.

The plot is ending, as it began.
They all ate each other, in spite of the plan.
But who is the farmer, the fox, and the grain
Is hardly for me to you to explain.

The singer gave his accordion a violent squeeze, left the musical phrase suspended, and walked angrily toward the bar. Hermes followed the singer with his eyes. A few minutes later he asked to be excused. Pat had not yet returned from his call. He went in the direction of the rest rooms, then changed course and stepped into the darkness of the bar.

The room, or rather the dug-out cave, could have been a church or a warehouse. It was impossible to tell where the space ended, what its size or shape was. Tiny light bulbs attached to what appeared to be a vast fisherman's net hanging from indeterminant walls gave an astral effect. Small reading lamps like those that illuminate the lecterns in lecture rooms helped two bustling women behind the bar find their way among glasses, bottles, and mixers.

Hermes discovered the singer alone next to the beer tap, boozing. A small man in his late twenties, he had a bony, tortured, sparsely bearded face; he looked like an Alabama sharecropper out of Walker Evans's photographs of the Depression. When he spoke, he sounded Californian and drunk.

Hermes asked, "Did you write that song?"

"Yep."

"Great music."

"Yep."

"Great words."

"Uh-huh."

"An allegory?"

"Maybe."

"What did you have in mind when you wrote it?"

"No computation without representation."

"It's such a sad song. Why?"

"Are you a kind of AI character?"

"Sort of. Why the gloom?"

"It's over."

"What's over?"

"Natural symbol computation."

"Do you believe what they say?"

"Look at the facts, man."

"The facts don't say much. Yet."

"If you wait too long, it will be too late."

"But you've already dropped out."

"There was nothing else left for me to do. I couldn't become a turncoat. Besides, I hate statistics."

"Have you written other songs like that?"

"Sure. 'Waltz's Procedure.' It's a waltz but that's just a cheap coincidence. It goes like this." He hummed:

I took a stroll on a sunny day
I followed a line across the bay
Lines convex and lines concave
Minus and plus I had to save.

"Incredible."

"Now watch what I tell you."

"What now?"

"D.M.D."

"What do you mean?"

"Don't make deals. Get it?"

"Nooo . . ."

"So long."

"Nice meeting you."

"We'll always meet, again and again."

The singer bent over his glass and looked at Hermes sideways. "Those people. What are you doing with them? They're going to destroy each other. Don't you see? They're programmed for it. And then, it will be love," the singer said dreamily. Switching to a more pragmatic tone, he said, "I'll catch up with you later tonight. Better go back to your table now. And don't forget. D.M.D."

Hermes got lost in the crowd that had just left the dance floor and was pouring into the bar as the sound system started to exude taped electronic stellar music.

When he returned to the table, Pat was already there. "I thought you were lost," Pat said.

"We thought you'd been carried away," said Kate.

"By the metaphysics of the place," added Pat.

"By the punks," smiled Kate.

"It's getting late," said Pat. "What about a little Santorini by night?"

"Mais les grecs sont tous des escrocs!" the baroness was saying in an abrasive voice.

The baron's light green eyes were focused on something far away beyond the sea crater into the night. "Mais oui," he agreed, "mais oui . . .", then, suddenly grating his teeth he muttered, "avec des mitraillettes!" The sailor's shirt he wore over his frail body was too large and sagged on the sides as he tried to imitate holding a rifle.

"Let's go," said Mrs. Mitchell. It was the only thing she had said all night.

They left the Polar Star around midnight. The street they went to next, five minutes away from the restaurant, was narrow and crowded. A long line of minibars were on both sides of it, some with entrances on two streets.

Most people had brought their drinks out in the open. A stereo produced a constant beat like the heart of a great giant somewhere nearby. A dipsomaniac, heavy-boned man with a heavy sagging mouth moved from group to group volunteering comments in a heavy, loud slur.

"Oh God," said Pat, "there's that welfare state bum, Lekkerkerkerkerker, again. He collects unemployment from back home and spends it all here. He's been in Santorini for years. Lots of free-lunchers around like him."

Manolo appeared. More people were arriving every minute now.

"Donald," a man shouted. "Where's your visor? The moon is still bright." Hermes turned to where the voice came from. Two black men were shaking hands.

"Anybody want a drink?" Pat vanished into the bar to pick up another ouzo. Mrs. Sloan proposed a disco. Mrs. Mitchell smiled. Hermes looked into the crowd and searched. At the back of the bar was a little man who resembled an Alabama sharecropper of the Depression years, very drunk, moving his lips. He was with Pat who, with a worried look on his face, appeared to be listening.

In the car Pat said, "Hermes, I'm afraid we have a change of plan. We have to leave by ten tomorrow. There's some urgent business I have to attend to in Piraeus. We'll visit the ancient site very briefly in the morning and sail immediately for Paros." He dropped Hermes off and drove on.

Hermes woke up with a start, his whole body wet with sweat. The sound was coming from the cliff below the house, perhaps two hundred feet below his window. It could have been steps. He listened carefully to the dark. There was a rattle, then a brief interruption, as if the person was resting, hesitating, or exploring alternative paths. Then again a soft rasping and the sound of feet on gravel. Then silence. The climbing had no end, or so it appeared to Hermes.

The next time he woke it was to the roar of jet engines and the sun shining in his room. He leaned out of the window and caught a glimpse of two silver fighter planes diving into the bay. Their twin shadows ran ahead of them on the water, then soared toward the horizon, where they vanished.

It was quiet. But only for a few minutes. He heard the steps again. He stretched his head. Down the slope a lean, lonely donkey was circling a cactus, relentlessly biting at the air in its attempt to yank out a few stems, failing, retreating, encroaching again.

There was a knock at the door. It was Mrs. Mitchell.

"Coffee's ready, Hermes."

The Cook Vanishes

It was late morning when Hermes and Pat arrived at the boat. It was anchored at Akrotiri now, close to the southern end of the island, near the excavation site.

"I'm sorry we had so little time," Pat apologized to Hermes.

Daphne took them back to the boat in a Zodiac. Kate and Mrs. Mitchell were already on board. Manolo had created two large plates of sandwiches of crabmeat and small Santorini tomatoes. The captain and the helmsman were preparing for immediate departure. Daphne and Manolo joined them.

The plan was to sail from Akrotiri westward to the tip of the island, then turn northward, skirt the crater, and continue on to Paros. They would use the motor instead of the sails because of time constraints, the captain said. Catching the late evening plane from Paros to Athens would be no problem. Manolo agreed. Daphne bared her teeth in agreement. Only the helmsman did not join in, passing a look over the horizon.

Soon Mrs. Mitchell withdrew to her cabin. Mrs. Sloan did the same.

Pat and Hermes were left alone. "Let's have a drink," Pat said. They walked to the bow and sat facing each other on two very low canvas chairs. From somewhere Pat produced a flask and two glasses. He filled one and offered it to Hermes. Hermes refused and Pat kept it for himself. "Hermes," he said, "our trip came to an end earlier than I expected. Earlier than I had hoped. We'll make up for it with another trip to Santorini. But before that we'll meet in Athens."

Pat seemed eager to go on. Hermes did not interrupt.

"We've got to complete the discussion we started the other day on this boat on our way to the island," Pat continued.

Hermes stretched his legs and changed the position of his head to catch less of the sun.

"A very strange thing has happened to me," Pat started, then took a deep sip. He put his glass on the deck and searched for his cigarettes. "A very strange coincidence. The day after we met at the party, are you following me?"

"All ears," said Hermes. He rearranged his body in an even more comfortable position.

"By now you've seen how much I prize archaeology and archaeologists. Some people even think I'm a sucker for archaeology." Pat took a gulp. His hand shook.

"In what way?" asked Hermes.

"Well, people have taken advantage of the tours I organize, of the houses I rent. People try to sell me antiquities."

"I see," said Hermes, and pushed back the hair the wind had blown in his eyes.

Pat checked the deck right and left. Only the helmsman was there, at the stern, too absorbed in his job to notice the sea gulls who, just over his head, were keeping up with the boat.

"Well. Last week I was offered an archaeological treasure for purchase. A newly found object of tremendous value," Pat said.

"Happens a lot in Greece and southern Italy," Hermes commented casually, scratching his Adam's apple.

Pat blew out smoke that, carried by the wind, passed with great speed over Hermes' head up toward the sky. "An object whose origin, I am afraid, I know all too well."

Hermes nodded.

"And I bought it," Pat said, and stared at Hermes motionless.

Hermes nodded, still looking at Pat without much conviction.

"Don't ask me for the moment who the person is."

"I won't."

"I'm also returning the treasure to the authorities."

"You must be very happy," said Hermes simply.

"Oh, I am. I am. But before I do, I'd like you to have a look at it too."

"What for?"

"It isn't an object outside your interests."

"Still, that doesn't make it less strange. You have to return it first and then, I assure you, the authorities, or whoever its legal owner is, will let us have as many looks as we want at it," Hermes said.

"This is a very exceptional case."

"You are talking about the find of Professor Agraphiotis that probably cost him his life," said Hermes simply.

"I am," said Pat. He blinked. "How did you . . . ?"

"You've been hinting at it."

Pat's blue eyes blinked once more. "I know. I'm no good at concealing things. Anyhow, sooner or later I'd have told you. I hope it doesn't upset you that . . ."

"This is an unsettled situation, and there are many reasons for me to feel uncomfortable about the whole thing, to say the least," said Hermes sternly.

"I know that."

"But looking at your invitation," Hermes continued, now sitting upright, "from an objective point of view, as long as you have already informed the authorities that you are in possession of the treasure and that you are in the process of delivering it to them, I can have a look at it with you."

"That's exactly how I saw it," said Pat.

"You know, I've already seen this treasure once," Hermes went on. His eyebrows were raised.

At this, Pat's face turned into an expressionless blob.

"It was when I visited my uncle briefly, just a few hours before the murder," Hermes said.

"I'd heard rumors," Pat whispered.

"I had a glimpse of it for not more than a couple of minutes, and then I left."

"How could you have?" Pat opened his wondering eyes.

"I wasn't very well, I guess. It was right after my flight to Athens from Boston."

"You mean you just walked away from such a find? God."

"I never imagined, of course, what would happen afterward."

"Of course . . . But it's all different now. I wish we had Professor Agraphiotis with us. I want you to know, Hermes," Pat hastened to add, "my interest in the object is not just a question of fancy. It's very deep. You agree with me that the object is not just an antiquarian curiosity."

"Not at all. It's an extremely important find."

"That's why I'd like you to examine it in relation to the institute I'm planning to found," said Pat, stretching out both palms as if he were holding the institute. He threw his cigarette into the sea and said, "Until we meet again I'll ask you . . ."

"Don't worry. I'll keep strict confidence about this," Hermes said, completing his phrase. "But you realize it will be a few days till we meet again."

Pat scanned the deck very quickly once more. "I was planning to ask you for tomorrow," he said nervously.

"Impossible. I'm leaving for the States."

"Not even for a couple of hours?"

"Afraid not."

"Then the day you come back. I've got your dates."

"I'll be back around noon."

"How about that evening? That evening at my house. It's in Psychiko. I'll give you the address.

Hermes agreed and Pat's sweating face brightened.

"Think I'll have a short nap," Pat said as he rose. "I'll be back in a quarter of an hour. We'll have a drink."

Hermes prepared to doze in the front deck pit. He stretched out and gazed at the heavens. Two white sea gulls were circling overhead. He was soon one of them, under a golden dome among many other birds, shiny chrome birds, squawking in a code that was hard to break.

When he caught sight of the blue sky once again, people were rushing on deck, yelling and cursing. He jumped up. The engine was dead. The captain was shouting at the helmsman. Daphne was bent over the starboard side. Pat was standing on the top of the deck table holding a pair of binoculars. He looked panicked. Kate and Mrs. Mitchell came up from below deck, disheveled.

"What's going on, Pat?" Kate asked. Pat was scanning the sea with his binoculars now and did not answer. "Pat!" she demanded.

"It's Manolo, Mrs. Sloan," said the captain calmly.

"What about him?" she asked. "What's he done now?"

"We can't find him."

"Is he hiding?"

"He's not on the boat."

"Did he fall overboard?"

"We don't know, Kate," said Pat. "We just don't know."

"I'll call the port authority," said the captain soberly. He ran down through the trap door. The helmsman continued steering and surveying the horizon. Hermes drew up to him. He noticed the yacht was circling now.

"You didn't see him, did you?" Hermes asked him.

"Honest to God. I didn't see or hear anyone jump into the sea. Why on earth would he do such a thing?"

"An accident," said Hermes.

"Must be," rejoined Pat, jumping down from the table and joining them.

"But what kind of accident?" Mrs. Mitchell interrupted.

Pat did not answer. He went to the end of the boat and turned his back to the others, leaving the binoculars behind him. Kate picked them up and started searching for herself.

They were between the crater and the crescent of the island. The archipelago was bustling. Three cruisers rested in the middle of the bay, each blaring a different tune. Two ferries were trumpeting their arrival, bringing new hordes of tourists, tons of vehicles, and drinks. Small motorboats ran in all directions and at different speeds, producing different levels of sound.

The captain was back on deck. "They're sending a warning to all boats in the area," he said.

Pat took him by the arm and they went to the back of the boat. They talked. The engine noise and the wind scattered their anxious words. The sun calmly begun its downward turn. The sea gulls were still close by. Hermes looked back at the broken reflections on the water.

They returned to Athens with half a day's delay and without news of Manolo. As they were leaving the airplane, Pat, who had sat silent next to Hermes throughout the flight, smiled regretfully. "Well, Hermes," he said, "it's been an exceptional trip with an unexpected ending. We've failed to show you how relaxing an Aegean cruise can be. But there will be other opportunities I hope, and we have an appointment when you return from Cambridge."

Cars of Aegean Tours were waiting for them. One took Hermes directly home. It was about noon when he arrived. A note from Eleni announced that they had left for Corfu to visit a friend who had just fallen ill. There was also a short postscript by Nina, in code, which, it turned out, Hermes was unable to decipher.

Nets, Frames, Stardust

The laptop rested on the dining room table, Hermes meditating in front of it.

Nina moved in noiselessly and stood behind him. He continued to be absorbed by the screen.

"I'm back," she announced.

He typed a few symbols.

"After what you told me," she said, "I thought a lot about the meeting in Psychiko. It's a good thing you didn't contact them. Robert was correct. They were probably police agents bluffing. Robert's not bad."

He nodded and continued typing.

She leaned toward his ear and whispered, "The problem remains unsolved. What are you going to do about it?"

He focused harder on the screen.

She made a face behind his back. "I think they're spying on you from across the street. I've seen the retired colonel bending over the railing and minding his geraniums in his pajamas several times a day."

"What's wrong about that?" he said finally, but continued at the keyboard.

"He's never done that before. He usually reads newspapers inside."

"Maybe he decided to change his lifestyle. You're becoming too curious about the way others live."

She spoke fast. "I'm only curious about knowledge representation, about people who are curious about us, and about you and why you don't do anything drastic instead of theorizing and taking trips."

He stopped typing. "Like Robert you don't want me to travel. You don't want me to work, either. What do you want me to do? Wear my powder-blue suit with a dark blue shirt, and display handkerchief, and start driving around the boulevards of Psychiko?"

She said softly, "No, Marlowe. I only wish I knew how to represent commonsense reasoning and come to conclusions using that data of yours. Eleni has already left. You're taking the plane in a few hours. I'll be alone. I can work undisturbed. Facts have accumulated. They seem unconnected and random. But there must be connections between them. I have to follow these connections scientifically. I have to be able to deduce. I need a good inference engine."

Hermes scratched his head and started, "Commonsense knowledge can be represented by semantic and net frames," then murmuring, "or at least some aspects it."

"Wait." She drew up a chair and sat at his side. "This already sounds intriguing. Like catching a suspect off guard. What does one do with semantic nets?"

"Nothing that adventurous—you just capture information. They're called nets because they're made up of nodes and links."

"Nodes and links. Again?"

"Nodes and links, that is, graphs. They're a standard way of representing problems that deal with sets of discrete objects and two-part relations, like search trees, or," he smiled, "organic chemistry molecules. They help us think about thought as a physical, coherent organization. They implement physical symbol systems in a computer, make us capable of carrying out many humanlike functions such as remembering ordinary life facts, extracting out of single cases general commonsense ideas and carrying out conclusions in a natural manner."

"How?"

"In very broad terms nodes stand for objects and links for relations. It goes like this." He typed:

```
COMPUTER                          ((ISA MACHINE))
NINA'S-LAPTOP                     ((ISA COMPUTER))
                                   (COLOR BLACK)
                                   (MATERIAL STEEL)
                                   (BELONGS NINA)
```

```
NINA                    (ISA WOMAN)
CHIPS                   (ISPART COMPUTER)
STEEL                   (ISA METAL)
```

He continued, "This is a very simple semantic net describing, a few facts about a small number of objects: 'Nina,' 'laptop,' 'chips,' 'steel,' or 'relationships,' 'Nina's laptop' . . ."

"Not true," she cut in. "The laptop unfortunately is not mine."

"Wait. That's pragmatics. We're only talking about the semantics of these representations."

"Sorry. What's on the left?"

"On the left side you have a number of object-atoms. On the right a property list."

"But where are the nodes and links? I only see words and parentheses. That looks like LISP to me."

"It is. It's a LISP representation of a semantic net. This is how data are represented in the program. You can do it visually too. It's easier for humans to grasp it graphically but takes me a little bit more time and effort to demonstrate it in my machine." He started to draw a diagram on the screen:

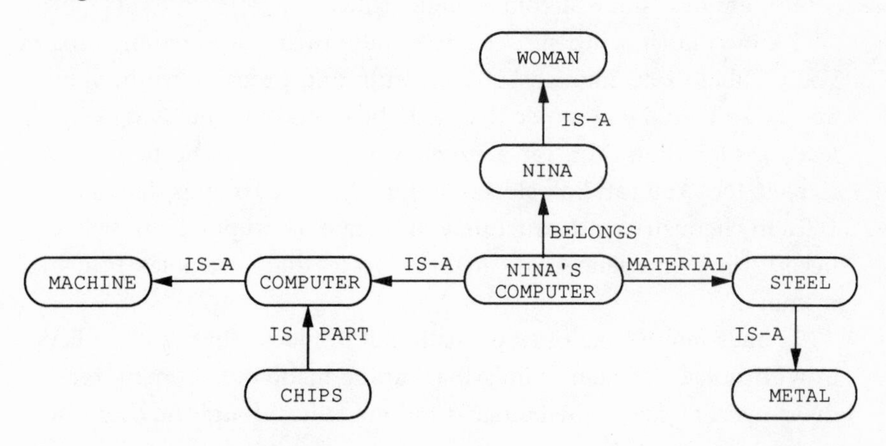

"But you mentioned frames too. What about them. What do they catch? Aren't nets enough?"

"You can do more things with them. Process information more economically and closer to the way people do it. This is what they look like:"

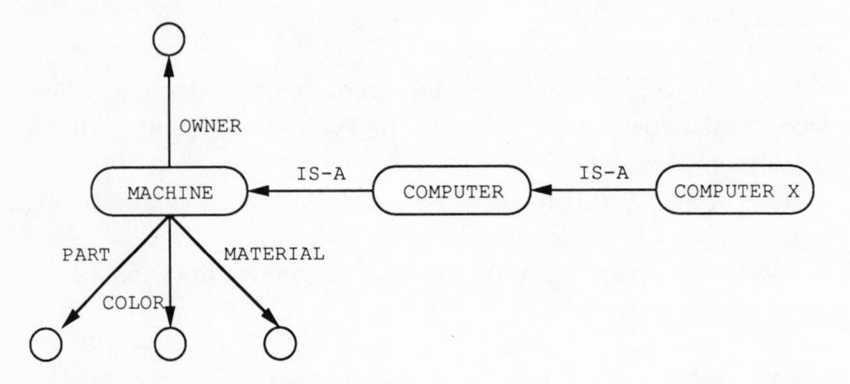

"Like semantic networks."

"In their nodes and links structure. But instead of representing only specific, isolated facts, they represent stereotypical situations, generic classes of objects. Unlike semantic nets, frames are made up of *slots,* which contain no specifics, where values, *facets* of values, can be entered to describe a specific object or event. Through them you can represent many shadows of reality within the machine in a human-like manner."

"But I'm only interested in a single truth."

"I know. But tracing suspects who hide their traces requires that you be able to distinguish between truth and probable truth, value and default. And you can do that with the facets of frames and exploit leads in detection. You can identify vast webs of connections with frames, too. You can link slots of a frame to other frames, like molecules in chemistry, and structure your data in conceptual bundles reflecting life experiences, in an open form that resembles human memory."

"Frames remind me of cities made out of blocks that can be filled in with houses of many kinds that can be made out of many room divisions that can be instantiated individually through many furniture arrangements."

"You really do like architecture more than you like chemistry. Well, let us look at one of these houses. It can be represented in a frame as a structural system but also in frames as a sequence of spaces adhering to certain proportional rules, and as a mechanism of micro-environments, three different frames of the same object whose slots occasionally are joined."

"Frames are so natural."

"And very economical. They allow you, instead of attaching values to an object automatically, to compute them only if and when you need them by using demons."

"What an empire! I can just see it. Sherlock 2000 meets the demons in Psychiko!"

"Demons are actually very kind and a kind of ordinary control device. They're a process in suspension, they just sit and watch information come in. When new data arrive, they are activated. Once the condition asked for has been met, the demons let in the data. Then they go back to rest."

She frowned.

Hermes went on, "Your Sherlock needs frames. They deal with change, with data in flux. They can also be used to generalize, to condense facts, and you'll need to condense your facts soon. You're getting too many of them."

She said, "I get the idea. But it seems so arbitrary. Do we really have such nets and frames inside our heads? Isn't our best chance to reproduce thinking through the use of representations that are like the ones our brains use? I can't believe brains hold such symbols so explicitly close to words. Don't you think they ought to look more like . . . stardust?"

"What? What do you mean by 'they'?"

"Thoughts. That's how I always pictured the stuff they're made of in reality. Stardust. Much, much smaller and finer than symbols. What do you think?"

Hermes protested, "That's not the issue here."

She pulled Hermes' hand impatiently. "Let's go on with the nets. Where's the knowledge here?" She pointed to the screen. "These are just lists. What can you do with them?"

"You can answer questions. Using not only the facts that are explicitly stored but also those that dwell implicitly inside the facts you have in hand."

Nina moved her head dissatisfied. "But how can you ask questions and answer them through such nodes and links only? Don't you need grammar and syntax? I don't see them here. Grammar and syntax are big bores, next to organic chemistry, but I can't see how you can have a system answering questions without grammar and syntax."

Hermes looked at her in wonder. "You are demanding. *And* correct. But semantic nets and frames don't represent the organization of words in natural language texts, nor the way things are organized in the world. They represent the structure of our beliefs in our thoughts. Nodes stand for concepts."

"I see. You mentioned something like that before, when you were talking about representations and using them to reason about things that may not exist. I can have Sherlock think about 'Manolo's murderer' even if the murderer doesn't exist because Manolo might have committed suicide, and about the Agraphiotis' murderer as distinct from the thief of the Golden Thinking Machine even if in reality they are the same person."

His face darkened. "What made you think it could be a different person?"

"It just occurred to me to use it as an example. Intentionally." She smiled. His somber mood continued. She went on arguing. "You see, the murderer and the thief might resemble each other and thus be taken for the same person. We must be able to distinguish them."

He stared at her as she talked.

"What's wrong?"

"Nothing. I'm thinking."

"That I know," she snapped. "Now tell me, how do I make something out of my data, nets, and frames. How do I infer?"

"By using the right computational procedures, IF-THEN rules, running forward, as it is called, from known facts to new deductions, or from hypothetical conclusions to known facts. Whatever fits your data."

"Deductions," she jumped up. "What I need urgently is something logical and simple: Sherlock meets Euclid."

"But Euclid can be a straitjacket on your poor Sherlock. You can use Euclid for theorems but not for stories."

"Stop worrying about it. Sherlock himself recommended Euclid to Watson. Besides, I'm dealing with detection and Sherlock, not with stories and Conan Doyle."

He smiled. "I'm curious about what you'll produce."

"Only curious? Watch out! The man across the street is snooping again. And you don't care. Of course you're leaving and America will keep you away from these troubles for some time while I'm working hard to solve the problem." She hesitated. "Now, will you tell me what your talk will be about? I wish I could come and listen to it."

Moneybags Wind

"Wonderful talk," said Wind, shaking his hair and stretching a hand out to Hermes. "You have a book on the subject, I understand."

"I'm working on one."

"And when will we see it?"

"In a year, I hope."

Aby Wind was one of the main sponsors of the meeting. Among archaeologists he was known as a patron who subsidized the restoration of ancient vases and a major Etruscan mosaic in Italy. Recently he had made news by proposing to save the 3,200-year-old burial chamber of Nefertari that was peeling and being eaten by dampness in Egypt.

"I was wondering if you would like to see my collection before you leave," asked Wind with an imperious tone. "What about tomorrow night?" he added, without waiting for an answer. "I know you have a dinner appointment with Dorothy. She told me it could be switched."

"If Dorothy changes her mind so easily, I find no reason why I shouldn't," Hermes responded.

Wind chortled and walked away.

A complex of barnlike, red wooden buildings at the edge of the vast, black northern Vermont forest ran past the airplane window. Then the plane touched down and they were gliding smoothly between tall dark pine trees. On and off the sun penetrated through the branches and came in through the porthole. Wind seemed to be pondering, his big body embraced by the custom-tailored brown leather armchair. His right eye gleamed hazel in the sun. His left eye, shadowed by the prominent aquiline nose, was shut. The airplane bore them quietly inside a large hangar and came to a stop.

Wind jumped out of the plane first. Hermes followed the pilot who carried Hermes' knapsack and Wind's briefcase. A Doberman pinscher broke away from the men who waited and rushed up to Wind. Wind closed his long arms around the animal's shoulders. An assistant came and took their luggage. Wind addressed the group, pulling the dog's ear. "Good afternoon to you all. We will be visiting the curator's quarters right away. Dinner at seven." He grinned, released the dog, motioned his head toward Hermes, and headed toward the exit. Hermes followed.

The hangar door gave directly onto an elevator cabin. They went down and came out into a long, lighted corridor. "We built an underground network so as not to disturb the forest," said Wind. "Follow me."

A system of stoas led to an arrangement of spacious, windowless atria. "The compluvia," said Wind, referring to the light shafts, "are designed to look like small barns from the outside." A stark, functional light came down from above ground discreetly onto arrays of identical cases that were either free-standing or attached to the walls from floor to ceiling.

"Nobody will disturb us. Everybody's away on vacation," said Wind. "Pull out any of the drawers you'd like."

Hermes pored over epigraphs on fragments of stone, pottery, and glass commemorating events, citing famous passages, inciting people to action, or simply recalling the passage of a person on earth. There were medals, cameos, seals. There were segments of figures of the ordinary real world: torsos, trunks, limbs. These were often in unexpected combinations: an eye staring through a cloud, a swan kissing a young girl, a snake biting its tail, a winged helmet. There were objects with no apparent meaning, suggesting the structure of texture, of rhythm, of pattern: concave next to convex, curved after flat, straight below angular.

Hermes and Wind improvised interpretations. It was almost by agreement that their exegeses led to no agreement. It was as if they were demonstrating the equivocalness of the hieroglyphs, emblems, and configurations next to their competence to unriddle.

"This is what gives interpretation a bad name," said Hermes jokingly.

"On the contrary, this is what makes interpretation and iconology a profitable enterprise," Wind roared.

Hermes said, "But the real money was kept for writing the iconographic programs, not for embroidered emblems or iconological exegeses."

"Code making is more expensive than code breaking," Wind said, "but, of course, it depends on the message."

"Certainly less remuneration for conceiving allegorical medallia than hiding military data," added Hermes.

"You're behind the times, Hermes. Today war is waged through concealed ideological instructions in seemingly innocent cultural messages. These are indeed expensive secrets encrypted by very highly paid specialists. Haven't you heard?"

Hermes shrugged. "I'm more interested in the secrets of the mind, the information inaccessible to consciousness."

"How does it become inaccessible?" asked Wind, apparently not minding the shift in the subject.

"Because of the compartmentalized structure of the mind."

"And how did that come about?"

"Through evolution."

"Now, that is a fascinating topic. You mean you believe that information is suppressed by some blind ruling oligarchy in the mind and not by the control of information exercised by the modularity of society acquired through history?"

"My undergraduates have asked me the same thing many times—why cognitive studies are not more concerned with the social control of information."

"I thought this was what you were driving at in your lecture when you talked about the need for bringing together historical and cognitive studies."

"I see how you interpreted me," said Hermes. "But what I am interested in is not so much what changes in the content of thinking. I'm more fascinated in structure, what doesn't change, or what changes very radically, but very rarely. I try not to mix conceptual structures with, let us call them, cognitive ones. They operate at different levels and develop at different rates of change."

"That's exactly what I found exciting about your speech."

"The separation of levels?"

"The total approach, the focus on change, your interest in the origin of consciousness, anthropogenesis."

They continued down another underground passage and emerged into a long space formed by two consecutive atria. In each one desks were arranged under square light shafts. Wind led Hermes past the computer terminals, piles of neatly arranged notes, and stacks of assorted books. They stood under one of the light wells.

"The project you propose," Wind was saying, "you might call psychopaleontology."

"Well, I wouldn't put it quite so ambitiously."

Hermes had just noticed the floor. Strewn over it were fish bones, eggshells, melon rinds, pea pods, broken dishes, and dried leaves. In the midst of the desks, the chairs, and the blank computer screens, these remains of a meal appeared carnal, sinister, almost real. The breaks between the tesserae of the mosaic they were pictured on were becoming indistinguishable in the dimming light of the early summer evening.

"The unswept home," said Hermes.

"Yes. *Asarotos oikos,*" echoed Wind. "Quite a picture."

"The vanity of representation as resemblance," said Hermes.

"The banality of affluence," added Wind.

"Northern African?"

"Possibly Carthage."

"A perfect decoy," said Hermes.

"I bet you'd rather have grapes by Apelles," said Wind.

"They'd only attract birds."

"If you're worried about animals being drawn by the unswept food, you should keep in mind that we are very well organized around here. No moles." He motioned with his head. "None. Let's go before you commit yourself to any more conclusions. There's more to see."

They moved to a similar arrangement under the other light well. The tesserae were even finer and more compactly laid out than in the previous mosaic, but they were only black and white. They formed stark patterns with the exactitude of projective geometry and the clarity of India ink drawn on silk paper by a meticulous draftsman.

"Fine restoration," said Hermes.

Wind beamed. "They both arrived here cut in parts with canvas glued over them to keep them from falling apart. It was like putting them together from the beginning."

"Hellenistic?" asked Hermes.

"Probably. Though nobody really knows anything precise about them."

The mosaic was bordered by a wide band of inlaid rhomboid parallelograms. They could be perceived as forming a two-dimensional representation of cubes stacked in space. Looking more closely at the picture, its meaning changed. Now the cubes projected from the floor, now the image reversed itself and the cubes seemed to recede into the floor. Now three rhomboids made one cube's three sides, now they were attached to three different, adjacent cubes, each one implying a different vantage point on the part of the spectator. Inside the band there was a broader band. It was filled in with crosses with rhomboids attached to their sides in such a way that the cross and rhomboids would appear as representing an object in space. But each side of the cross showed the object seen from a different side, each interpretation precluding the acceptability of the other's, making one single image impossible.

"Quite a collection of paradoxes and impossibilities," said Hermes. In the center of the mosaic was a square with a two-dimensional representation of a transparent cube.

"The Necker cube!" Hermes exclaimed.

"It is unique," said Wind. He touched a button at the edge of a desk, and a myriad of tiny hewn stones seemed to vibrate as the light brightened gradually with the smooth warmth of an early morning sun. The edges of lines, and planes, glittered harder and sharper. The cube appeared now to have collapsed inside the pavement, now to have leaped above its polished surface.

The cube, along with the circumjacent black and white images, all seemed to crouch, spring, flicker. As if in an orchestrated order, they flipped, flopped, folded in, and burst forth. Arrays and surfaces turned and returned in endless reversals, a landscape of peripeteias and puzzles.

"Don't you think the Necker cube should be the symbol of equivocalness?" said Wind. "'Depth reversing,' as they call it—two contradicting inferences produced by the same data."

"An interesting metaphor for switching truth and temporal and situational logic maybe," murmured Hermes.

"What fascinates me about this cube," said Wind, "is that no matter how much I have read about it, talked to scholars about it, and looked at it, I have never tired of its effect. It always appears fresh. It is like some melodies that, no matter how many times you hear them, never stop surprising you at a certain moment."

"This might reveal something about the way the mind is built in independent components that I was talking about."

They had slowly walked out of the second atrium to the corridor. They came to a copper-plated door. The door slid open noiselessly and an elevator cabin waited behind it.

"My personal study," said Wind as they came up into a large space. The furniture, with the exception of a large seventeenth-century painted globe, was modern: a small secretarial desk with a voluminous computer terminal and a green-gray metal desk, the type that entered offices immediately after the Second World War, which was crowded with papers, books, and wooden, tin, and cardboard boxes. A torn tape measure, a small camera, and a pair of camouflage-painted field glasses looked conspicuously at odds with the rest of the objects. Equally incongruous among these objects, upright in a soft black leather covering, elegantly proportioned, was a flat rectangular case. Hermes took a glance at the case. It could have been an object that he had thought he would never see again.

"A drink?" asked Wind.

"Orange juice," said Hermes.

Between an Eames armchair and a Breuer couch stood a low Mies table holding drinks ready to be served. "Birthday presents from their designers," explained Wind. Next to the drinks rested the Doberman pinscher. "He's old and senile. Like me. He couldn't hurt a fly." The dog, still in repose, tilted his head to the side and looked furtively at Wind as if annoyed by the remark.

Wind offered a glass of orange juice to Hermes and prepared a large martini for himself. He shook the mixer several times, opened the top of the container, and gave the drink a last stir with his finger. He held out his finger to the dog in a routine manner. The dog licked it.

Wind turned to Hermes and raised his glass. "To hermeneutics," he toasted.

"To secrets," Hermes responded.

"Without them nothing is possible." Wind shook his head at Hermes.

They drank standing.

"How did you come to the idea of an anti-heroic art collection?" Hermes asked. "It's so . . ."

"Unglamorous for a tycoon," Wind completed. "I'll tell you. But first, what about some food?"

"Good idea," said Hermes. They moved to the room next to the library.

Throughout dinner Wind talked. "My idea came slowly, out of a dismay at seeing museums and private collectors obsessed with masterpieces that they don't hesitate to declassify and relocate in the basement from one day to the next."

"Was it just a reaction?"

"My father's influence, too."

"Was he an art historian?"

"Only the owner of a small financing business. An immigrant from Latvia."

"And how did he influence you? Was he a collector?"

"No. He was just a minor moneylender conducting his moneylending affairs in the Lower East Side of New York in a tedious, painstaking way. I hated it. I dreamt of being a true tycoon with worldwide concerns. You will ask how this came to shape my art collection interests. It happened this way. One evening I was reading a book about the Vanderbilts in my room. I was only fifteen. My father walked in and found me with the book. He didn't say anything. The next day he told me we were to spend the weekend together in his office. For two solid days we were locked up in the vault, sitting across from each other. My father went through box after box, bundle after bundle, pack after pack, reading me every document and every record of transaction. Slowly it was clear what he was trying to tell me about his business, and about every successful operation in the world. Each of these meager dealings, meticulously registered in the piles of stored cheap paper, patiently chronicled longhand in the books, shrewdly tabulated, led to real persons, individuals struggling for a handful of goods. But eventually each of the humble acts added up to enormous accumulations. It was a great lesson about history. But I also learned something beside history in this meeting. That my father, contrary to what I thought, was already a millionaire."

"And your collection?"

"I started it in the late twenties. But it was only after the Second World War that I got a clear idea of what I wanted. After I served in Europe. In France."

"Did the ideas of the then-young French historians influence you?"

"Yes. I met many historians there. They talked about almost everything, they had a 'total' view, and were concerned about a unifying method."

"Did you ever meet Marc Bloch?"

"No, I didn't. Marc Bloch. My son had been preparing to study under him. Neither of them survived the war." Wind smiled. "But tell me about yourself, Hermes. What are your plans? They're more interesting than my memoirs."

A voice from the library behind Hermes asked, "Will you have coffee in the library?" Hermes turned so abruptly to the sound of that voice that he pulled a neck muscle. He could have sworn it was Manolo's voice.

They returned to the library but nobody was there to receive them. A tray with coffee ready to be served was left on the low table. The dog, in the same place, did not bother to look at them as they entered.

Wind served coffee. "I've already told you I was very impressed by your lecture," he said, sipping, his eyes closed, leaning back on his armchair, and pressing his head back hard on the headrest. "It points to a direction completely opposed to that of the studies I've been supporting. You're proposing a top-down approach. We've been working bottom-up. Both types of study aspire to the same results, in a complementary way. They both try to identify what is in the mind of the maker of the artifacts in hand. My collections are not worth very much to me. I collect to understand the mind. Shapes and attributes are cues toward its detection. But we've been too concerned with attributes and discrete features, while you've been making leaps, studying the architecture of the mechanism that produces them. I have shied away from that. That was my materialist predisposition. I detested idealism. Now I see that I was too one-sided, an idealist of another kind. That's why I'm so fascinated by the kinds of studies you've been initiating. You might bring me close to grasping what produces world views." Wind projected his fist, as if holding within it an object long sought after.

Suddenly Wind's face looked drained. The dog lifted his brows, peered at him, then dropped them again. Wind went on, but in a lower, slower voice. "Listening to you the other day, I kept thinking of Hercules at the crossroads. A fascinating humanistic topos. You know the paper by Panofsky?" The dog turned his eyes to Hermes as if following the discussion carefully.

"What made you think of the youth of Hercules? I thought I'd passed that age."

"Structural parallels," Wind answered. "You're receiving offers from all directions. You have to make a choice."

"Choice? What choice?"

"Do you want to remain ambiguous, like the Necker cube?" Wind tried to laugh. "It seems Necker's spirit is with us tonight."

"A pregnant paradigm."

"A loaded allegory," added Wind, raising his hawklike nose as he raised his coffee cup, ". . . allegory," repeated Wind grimly. "But you're not a loaded allegory, Hermes. People don't last as long as loaded allegories do. You won't be migrating from continent to continent for ever. You won't be translated and reinterpreted over the centuries. Human life is short, shorter than the life of symbols. They can afford to be ambiguous and to be interpreted many times in many different ways. People have to make commitments. You want to remain free of commitments?"

"I find the idea of freedom very appealing, but I don't see what you're driving at."

"I thought freedom might not be outside the vocabulary of an archaeologist interested in cognitive psychology and artificial intelligence. Freedom is like the zero sign—an empty character, but still very useful to think with."

"To me freedom is less metaphysical. Its reality is almost biological. Definitely tangible and measurable. It is the degree of independence of an organism from environmental factors."

"But how can *you* say that. Freedom is a social concept like a person's worth. And a person's freedom or worth is valued only in reference to the Other. A person derives his knowledge of freedom or success as it is mirrored in the eyes of the Other."

At the word *other,* the Doberman lifted his head, yawned, then let it fall again.

Wind bent over, looked intensely at Hermes and said: "Hermes. It seems to me you've been drifting far too long. You need a place where you're not an alien anymore, where ethics and methodology aren't incompatible."

There were a few seconds of pause. Wind took a deep breath, bent toward Hermes again. "Where you won't be deceived and blackmailed anymore," he said quietly. Wind leaned back and closed his eyes. The last words hung in the room like a menace.

"Is anyone threatening me?" Hermes asked.

"Of course. You know very well they are. We know it too. We also know who stole the treasure."

"How do you know?"

"We have the greatest detectives in the world working for us. That's not an interesting question."

"Will you answer the interesting one?"

"The person is an acquaintance of yours."

Hermes followed every detail of Wind's face.

"Pat Sloan," said Wind.

"Pat Sloan?"

"I see you're surprised but not shocked. You're a very intelligent man."

"Did he also shoot—"

"He did," cut in Wind. "He killed your uncle, probably accidentally, trying to get at the treasure."

"And how is he going about blackmailing me?"

"You don't have to work hard to find that out, Hermes. You know Sloan knows about your cryptanalytic discoveries, and we know you know."

"But what proof do you have for all this?"

"The Greek police has found fingerprints and the bullets, but they have no idea whose they are. The police have no idea that they match Sloan's and that we know that and that the bullets match a gun with Sloan's fingerprints in our possession."

"Why don't you report it?"

"It would jeopardize our success. It would also be very difficult to prove anything without linking Sloan with the treasure directly."

"What do you propose?"

"You are the only one who can do it."

"Me?"

"Yes. Don't try and convince me you are incapable of doing anything devious. We all are."

"You mean I should pretend to agree to collaborate with him and . . ."

"Precisely. The rest is a question of tactics."

"Right."

"Now, I've got something to ask you. Once you have the thinking machine in your hands, before turning it over to the police, try to make it possible for you and me to spend twenty-four hours with it." The color was coming back to his cheeks and a light shone in his eyes.

"I suppose it would be possible."

Then Wind said abruptly, "Would you like some more coffee?" Without waiting for an answer, he poured some coffee into Hermes' cup and tried to force it into his hands. Hermes remained impassive. Wind grinned and returned the cup to the table. The dog stood up and walked to the corner of the library. He looked back over his shoulder at Hermes and Wind, as if to check that everything was in order before retiring.

"It's late," said Wind. He looked strangely disconcerted. "We'd better let you have some rest. I'll stay here." He rubbed his chest and smiled. "I have more work to do. I hope, as I said, this is only the beginning. I plan to fly to Greece myself the end of this summer on my way to Egypt. I have to check the program of the restoration of the Nefertari frescoes. My people will contact you in Athens the day after you arrive. We're expecting a lot from you. Why don't you see yourself out? The guest house is right across from that window over there."

Hermes walked unaccompanied toward the guest house. Mist was rising slowly. The air was cold and smelled of evergreen. Between the trees the modest silhouettes of the cabins emerged, telling very little about the huge spaces dug beneath them. Of all the windows of the compound only one was lighted, the one in the library.

When Hermes woke up, the sun was shining directly on his face. He noticed a typed note next to his bed. "Please dial 88 when you want breakfast to be served."

He was served breakfast in the guest house by an unsmiling man. "Mr. Wind has already left for New York," he said. Hermes was to be flown back after his breakfast.

An hour later Hermes was airborne for Boston, on his way to the other side of the Atlantic.

Athenian Heat

Hermes was among the first to disembark.

"Forty degrees today," screamed a sweaty attendant enthusiastically from the ground. "Jesus! That's over a hundred degrees Fahrenheit," someone grumbled behind Hermes.

As he descended the burning steps of the air terminal, a limousine pulled up and a plump hand and a worried forehead leaned through the door.

"Get in the other side, Hermes, I'll give you a lift." It was Pat.

Hermes jumped into the car.

"How was Cambridge?" asked Pat, racing out of the airport.

"Much cooler," said Hermes.

Large drops of sweat were dripping down Pat's face, despite the air conditioning. "You saw our friend Wind," he said.

"I did. I stayed at his estate."

"Did you! It's a great place, they say. Fascinating character."

"A great friend of archaeology."

"Of course. Very erudite."

"An eloquent speaker also. He gave an excellent short speech at the conference."

Pat glanced at the rear-view mirror. Hermes looked out of the window.

A group of young boys were climbing on each others' shoulders on the beach, forming a huge pyramid. The sun was setting behind their athletic bodies. As the car turned from the coastal road toward the center of the city, the pyramid toppled.

"An excellent speech," Pat repeated, returning to the rear-view mirror. "Did he speak about deep-water archaeology?"

"Not this time. Is it supposed to be a favorite topic of his?"

Once more Pat switched his eyes to the rear-view mirror. "It is," he said. "Whenever I meet him he talks about it—eloquently, indeed. But it smells of caviar. Although," he added between his teeth, "very few people would agree with me."

"Caviar?"

A station wagon raced by them, caressing the side of Pat's car. Its windows were tinted. Pat swerved to the right. Seconds later the car slowed down. Pat found the opportunity to accelerate, leaving it behind at a stop light. "Could we meet later tonight?" he said. "About eight?"

"Fine," said Hermes.

For the rest of the ride they hardly exchanged another word. As they parted in front of Hermes' apartment, Pat said, "I'm glad you can make it tonight," and left it at that.

When Hermes turned on the computer, there was a message for him. Nina had scribbled that Eleni was still away and that she was on the way to a great discovery.

Hermes slept five hours. When he woke up, it was time to leave. On his way out the telephone rang.

"Yes?" answered Hermes. "Robert! . . . Very well, thank you . . . Of course I presented everything the way you told me to . . . You wonder why I don't write a mystery story myself? . . . What? You take it back because you don't think I'd be happy until the novel looked like a mathematical proof? Listen, a proof is just like a novel. And, not only that, both are like war . . . Sure, I'll tell you what I mean. Wars end when the will of the enemy is bent. Proofs are accepted when the will of the community of scholars to criticize is exhausted. As for novels, they end when the will of the author to keep on improving it is finally broken. See now? . . . No, I *don't* think I'm beginning to sound like you. In fact, familiarity breeds defamiliarization . . . Maybe you're right. Maybe polemical metaphors of mine are being overly influenced by the times we're living through. Listen, I have to go. I have an appointment . . . I *know* I ought to be grateful to you! . . . All right, I'll invite you to dinner . . . Not enough? . . . OK, I'll pay for the taxi too . . . Tonight? Impossible . . . I can't change it . . . Sorry . . . *Yes,* it's a serious appointment. I can't tell you about it now. Tell you about it tomorrow . . . Sure. Lunch . . . At the Rio . . . Fine . . . Half past twelve at the Rio."

He paid a call to the medium in the early evening and stayed for a short time. As he walked away from the villa, he glanced back. The sky looked like it was on fire; the cube was an immense block of charcoal against it. After a chain of linking trolleys and buses, he got into a taxi and asked to be driven to Psychiko.

Everything he touched in the cab was warmer than his hand. Hot air blew in from everywhere. He leaned forward to avoid resting his back on the seat.

He arrived at Pat's street twenty minutes early. It was a narrow, dim street. Oleanders bloomed on both sides, thickly covering the hot night with a bitter aroma and blocking most of the view into the gardens. No light came from the small subdued villas. A giant rosebush grew over a fence, its faint fragrance an overlay for the bitterness of the oleanders. A vine climbing from behind the bush had gotten entangled in a wild olive tree; the struggling plants fell onto the sidewalk, threw each other against the wall, and sprang up again, sending branches gesturing above the road and seizing the weak streetlamp. Down toward the end of the next block a floodlight cut a white guard's booth out of the darkness in front of what was probably the residence of a diplomat. The floodlight reached the mass of growth, weakly pointing out a few silver spots on the tips of the leaves and outlining a vague, still, humanlike figure behind them. The rest was hidden in darkness.

The street was deserted as Hermes walked down its center at a leisurely pace, the hot asphalt pavement burning under his feet, its heat radiating onto his face. A car, parked a few yards from Pat's, with its windows rolled down, served as a nest for two young people passionately locked in each other's arms. Behind a low iron fence Pat's well-trimmed garden stood in great contrast to the overgrown disordered lots that surrounded it. The house was a vast, one-story ranch. None of the windows was lit, and no car was parked in the driveway. Hermes continued his walk. A little farther up the street, inside what appeared through branches to be a more luxurious car, the shady shapes of another couple embraced in their air-conditioned environment, windows rolled up, engine purring.

Hermes reached the guard's booth. It was deserted, and the house behind it showed no sign of being occupied. A brightly colored beach ball gleamed in the pool of light just behind the locked gate. Hermes' lean shadow crossed over the ball.

He went around that block and continued onto the next, continued full circle, and re-entered Pat's street. He walked slowly on the sidewalk this time, behind the thick oleander bushes, avoiding the hot asphalt pavement. A car rolled down the quiet street, stopped five hundred feet ahead of him, in front of Pat's house, and veered toward the right side of the street. The car door was opened. Someone stepped out. She walked toward the gate lit up by the front beams. It was Kate.

There were two sharp flashes of light. The woman jerked forward, then backward. The body dropped. The other door opened and someone seemed to move to get out. More sharp flashes. The second body dropped. It was like a movie with the sound turned off. At least four people were running around. One entered the car and came out with what clearly, in front of the headlights, was an attaché case. The headlights were switched off. Two cars pulled into the road and left in different directions. There was no more movement, there were no more parked cars, and no lovers. The floodlight farther down the street was turned off.

Hermes came out into the middle of the street. Without looking back, he walked rapidly away. Sirens were heard as he crossed the highway and headed toward a multilevel shopping center. It was festively illuminated, beaming a quarter of a mile away like an ocean liner at dock. He hastened his step under the bright lights between the parked cars. More sirens screamed from up the hill.

The automatic doors swooshed open for him. Inside cool winds and party music whirled around as he picked up a basket. He loaded it randomly. Everyone around appeared to be in beach clothes. The music stopped suddenly. The loudspeaker announced that it would be making an announcement. Then it announced a Christmas in the Alps event and a special sale of Swiss cheese on the top floor.

The top floor was arranged as a café, with wrought-iron seats and round tables. It was cold and windy. Bells continued clanging and pictures of snowed-in mountain tops flashed. In the back of the room Hermes turned to the bar, which was displaying cheese in front of a huge image of Mont Blanc. Hermes added some cheese to his basket. Then the voice came back. It was closing time.

Hermes paid and carried two large, full shopping bags to the exit, walked down to the end of the parking lot and entered a taxi. The taxi moved with difficulty through the crowds. It finally entered the highway and turned toward the center as, over the hill, sirens streaked through the distance.

Hermes emptied the bags onto the kitchen table. Tomatoes and peaches, cans of vegetables and preserves, paper napkins, paper towels, toothpicks, matches, coffee, sugar, several types of yogurt, and Swiss cheese rolled out. He stared at his purchases. Then he threw away the toothpicks and the sugar. He hesitated with a can of tomato paste, then put it back on the table. He placed the yogurt and cheese in the refrigerator. He left the rest as it was on the table. He took a tomato out of the refrigerator and cut it on a plate. The pulp was red against the white porcelain. He stared at the plate. He threw the tomatoes away. He drank some water and moved to the study.

He switched on his laptop. Symbols ran down the screen.

Circumscription

A tap on the door. It was past midnight. He went silently to the entrance and waited.

"Even Pinkertons have to sleep." It was Nina. He unlocked the door. She walked in holding a huge shopping bag full of tomatoes. "Welcome back," she shouted. "I thought I'd bring you some midnight dinner. I got you some tomatoes. There's cheese in the refrigerator." She walked to the kitchen and saw the groceries on the table. "You have been doing a lot of shopping. What are you up to? Hoarding for World War Three?"

He didn't answer.

She left her bag on the table. "You don't seem to be enjoying being back. When do we start working again? I have a lot of questions to ask you."

He walked to the study without answering her and she followed him.

"It's so hot," she said. "It was forty-five degrees this afternoon." She moved to the balcony. He followed her. "What's the matter with you?"

"The Sloans have been shot," he murmured.

She turned around and shoved him back to the room.

"What? Stop screaming!" she said incongruously. "When did you hear about it?"

"I was there."

"Where?"

"Psychiko."

"At his house?"

"Just in front of it."

"When?"

"Early this evening."

"What were you doing there?" Without waiting for his response she rushed back to the balcony. "Be quiet," she said as he came after her. She crossed her lips with her index finger. "Listen."

In the apartment across the street, a floor lower, out on the balcony, a television set was broadcasting the late evening news. The volume was turned up. It was an older couple, he in shorts and undershirt, she in a loose nightgown. He was eating out of a bowl with one hand and fanning himself with the other. She was peeling some kind of vegetable. The broadcaster's voice was stern and restrained as it reported the assassination. Hermes and Nina listened.

"Communists!" shouted the woman.

The man answered something inaudible.

"Communists!" repeated the woman.

"I can't believe it. You were there?" whispered Nina.

"The investigations are proceeding," the television voice was saying.

"Let's go in," Hermes murmured. They went back to the study. It was stifling inside. Hermes wiped the sweat from his forehead with the back of his hand.

Nina asked. "Could it have been political?"

"How would I know?"

"What were the Sloans in the end? And why were they interested in you?"

"I never figured it out."

"What do we do now?"

"I have to visit Melania. I'll call Robert, too."

"Will you tell Melania? I don't trust her for a second."

"Tell her what?"

"That you were there. That Pat wanted to see you urgently for some reason. Will you tell Karras?"

"I haven't made up my mind yet."

"Is there a connection with Philippos' murder?"

"Maybe."

"Two murders in a row . . ."

"It could be a coincidence."

"Think so? Where's Manolo then? That makes it three."

"Don't let paranoia destroy your thought processes, Nina."

"And what do you want me to do? Be the next in line?"

"When everyone is a suspect, nobody is a serious suspect. Completely useless. Self-destructive."

"I know. Stalin was killed by a combinatorial explosion, trying to find suspects. You've already explained that. But it's already too late, Hermes. You can't help it. You'd better put your paranoia to use." Suddenly anger surfaced on her face. "Our tools are inadequate. They are stupid. A tiny bit of a new fact, and everything has to be rethought in this detection system."

Hermes looked at her, surprised. Anger rose in his voice. "You call murder a tiny bit of fact?"

"Oh, sorry," she said. "What I meant was the 'avalanche effect,' a single entry and a mass of changes follow. And there are even more facts to come whose impact we can't anticipate. How can I continue with such a system?"

His tone was low, calming. "That's how it is." He smiled. "Gods don't reveal everything to us mortals at once. Mortals discover and improve only after long searchings."

"Sounds like a quotation."

"It is."

"Who said it?"

"Somebody ninety-five years old who lived 2,500 years ago. Xenophanes."

"Ancient and impressive. You think he invented the Golden Thinking Machine?"

"He might have seen it. He traveled a lot. But he's a lot younger than the machine's inscriptions."

"I hope he was happy."

"What does that have to do with anything? As a matter of fact, he claimed he was rather miserable."

"He deserved it. And what'll happen to us?"

"To you and me?"

"No, to Sherlock 2000. Do you realize I have to make my deductions all over again? And just when—I hadn't the time to tell you this before—I finally replaced semantic networks with frames—you were correct, I needed them—and started tracing the movements and interactions of the suspects. Everything started to be so easy, especially with the help of the demons. I succeeded in fitting everybody into microworlds and condensing the data so neatly. No use showing it to you now, in the light of the new facts."

"Why don't you try to restart integrating the new facts?"

"You know it won't be that simple. It's not just backtracking in the search tree. It means redoing the whole data base, the whole search structure."

"I thought you'd enjoy it," he said.

She looked at him, furious. "How did you reach that conclusion?"

He shrugged. "I thought you wanted to become a superdetective, bringing in facts, turning around conclusions, backtracking all the time. Isn't that what detectives do in all those crime stories you like to read so much? In fact, this is what people have said they have been enjoying in detective plots since antiquity. They call it *peripeteia*. Halfway through the book, when readers have already made up their minds about who did what, in comes a messenger with a new fact, or maybe an old fact that had never registered as a fact before. Then all the guessing constructs get blown away in the wind and the readers applaud."

"Sure. That's fun. It's like a game. But what I have to do with my data base now is just drudgery, dragging myself from file to file, updating and deducing all over again. It's stupid."

"Maybe what you need is to change your system, too. Maybe it's not intelligent enough to cope with constantly changing facts in everyday life."

"You dare say that? *You* suggested this system."

"I thought it was you who had asked for a detective-inference engine. 'Euclid,' you said, quoting Sherlock Holmes. That's what you got. Sherlock Holmes, of course, did not confine himself to Euclidean deductions, despite his declarations. The problem with Holmes is that there is much more to his thinking than the simple explanations Conan Doyle's text suggests."

"I must say I believed his confessions. I also said I was only interested in this simple model, but of course I didn't mean it."

"What do you mean you didn't mean it? Did you say you were interested in anything else?"

"I took it for granted you understood what I wanted the system to do. Should we always say what we mean? Should I have gone through all my requirements exhaustively? Nobody else does. You don't."

"I believe I always state clearly what I think."

"You don't. In your discussion about problem representation, when you spoke about the farmer trying to cross the river in a boat, you didn't tell me why we had to go through that back-and-forth by boat instead of using the bridge, or how he could leave a fox alone to wait without risking the fox's disappearance. You didn't say anything like that. As a matter of fact, now that I think of it, you said that the fox could stay unwatched by the sack. It contradicts the fact that foxes never behave like that. Your algorithm is false," she accused him.

"It's not false. It's just invalid in the light of the new facts you brought in as part of the problem."

She wasn't satisfied. "What difference does it make, false or invalid? Your solution is just plain unacceptable."

He smiled. "My algorithm wasn't unacceptable with respect to the ways the problem was initially circumscribed."

"Circumscribed?"

He explained. "What is presupposed before starting to solve the problem."

Her eyes flashed. "You never talked about that when you spoke about representation."

"I know. I took it for granted. So did you, of course. That's why you didn't ask for the list of what was presupposed. In fact, most of the time we presuppose things through some tacit unspoken convention, without spelling them out."

"So we don't have to draw circumscribing lines all the time."

"Fortunately not, but we have to be ready to confront them. You are not. You defined your Sherlock as a closed, deductive inference engine. Even with the frames you used, I don't think you exploited all their potential. You just used them to make some good summaries of your data, efficient storage. You haven't applied them as a device to keep track of what stays the same, which beliefs are maintained, and what has to be rearranged as new events come in. You see, detectives can't afford to work with a closed mind. They never say this is the problem, these are the facts, this is how I solve it. Instead they define a problem only tentatively, and they are committed to this definition *unless* the view of the world within which the problem was defined changes. Detectives identify a way to solve the problem and hold to it—*unless* something prevents them from using it as anticipated and they accept being bound to a set of facts, *unless* more facts arrive."

"I see. So I should have said this is Sherlock, *unless* somebody identifies him as somebody else. He uses deductions, *unless* somebody prevents him. He believes in certain facts, *unless* some other facts arrive. It sounds ridiculous. But I see your point. Good theory. What do we do now, Hermes?"

"Replace your system. Recast your data."

"All right," she said. She typed fast and cheerfully. On the screen appeared a new file name: "Sherlock 2000, Version II."

"It's way past midnight," said Hermes.

Nina continued to type. She said, "I'm ready." The screen read: "Morning Notes."

It was Hermes' turn now. He typed: "Monotonic Systems."

"It sounds like a type of depression," said Nina.

From the half-open window, a black shiny bug darted straight onto the lamp, hit it full force, fell onto the tablecloth on its back, turned over, slowly walked to the other end of the table, and climbed under it.

Hermes went on, "Traditional systems of reasoning, called monotonic, are closed systems. They appeal to our sense of order, simplicity, stability, security. They are like *temene,* temples of purity in a world of wilderness, beyond and above the pains of indeterminacy and change. You've been generating deductions within such a system, what you called the Sherlock-Euclid system, using a small set of facts, represented as logical propositions like . . ." He typed as he talked:

Robert is a friend of Hermès'.
Pat is a rich man.
Pat is married to Kate.
Rich people have rich people as friends.
No friends murder friends.
Everyone is a friend of someone.

He continued, ". . . these closed systems lead you happily to simple proofs by chaining backward from the conclusions you want to establish, like 'Kate is not a suspect,' to that set of facts that you hold onto as assumptions, or by *refutation*. They show that the negation of the conclusion you wanted to prove, such as 'It is not true Kate is not a suspect,' contradicts your assumptions. As most of us do when we first come into contact with inference engines, you fall for timelessness and perfection, the smiling chimeras of artificial cognitive systems. But suddenly you realize the limits of this kind of reasoning. You find you have been adding new facts to the system you adopted without worrying what this adding could lead to. You are now confronted with a set of contradictory facts and cannot eliminate the contradiction by adding new facts to the system. You can only exorcise it by diverting attention from it, by adding some distracting statements to your list of facts. But this is psychology and not rigorous problem solving. You realize the world you are dealing with is not a serene stone temple after all. It's 'a blooming buzz,' and a cunning one . . ."

The bug had returned to the top of the table. It was hurrying, as if late for an appointment. Hermes and Nina watched it. In mid-path, the bug's polished back split open. Luminous, delicate wings unfolded from its body, and the bug flew away as unexpectedly as it had come. They laughed.

"Good lecture," she said, "but where does this lead us?"

Hermes typed, and on the screen appeared: "Nonmonotonic Systems."

"Aha. The therapy," she whispered, opening her eyes wide.

"Nonmonotonic reasoning systems," he said, "are made to cope with insecurity, instability, indeterminacy, contrived thinking, and uncertain beliefs. They are more fit for real-world problems faced by anxious doctors dealing with incomplete diagnostics, nervous consultants with unreliable stock markets, agonizing architects with chaotic cities and lunatic clients . . ."

Nina added, ". . . and robbers, detectives, spies and spycatchers, skeptics, cynics, opportunists, pessimists, and deceivers. I've thought of all that. What do I do now?"

"You have to start linking conclusions to conditional assumptions and following up the implications of your revisions. It's all in the tutorial."

"You realize how much I have to rewrite? Are you sure this is the ultimate method?"

"On the contrary. I'm sure it's not the ultimate method."

"You have a way of diminishing my expectations. Still, it's getting exciting at last."

He said, "It's getting late."

She responded. "Hey. You stole my line. That's what I always say."

The signature tune of the radio from across the street announced the end of the day's broadcasting.

Old Friends

Hermes hung up. He went to the kitchen, poured himself some orange juice, and ate a carrot. He left his apartment at about eight-thirty. It was already oppressively hot in the streets. He walked straight to the Institute, where he was greeted by the librarian.

"There was a call for you. I told them you'd left the country," she said indifferently.

"I told you I'd be back today."

"I wasn't sure when you were going to return."

At the exit the receptionist leapt in front of him in a state of excitement.

"You're wanted on the telephone. You can talk from here." She pointed to the room to the left with one hand, and with the other she cupped Hermes's elbow.

"Yes. He's here. He just arrived," she said into the receiver. "Right away."

"You're always flying, Mr. Hermes," she said, handing him the receiver. She smiled at him. Then she whispered, "The head librarian sticks her nose into everything. She's been asking me to monitor your hours in the Institute. Here's a letter for you. I didn't give it to her. I held on to it for you."

It was Karras on the phone.

He had to wait in the magistrate's antechamber in an ovenlike atmosphere. The magistrate was on his way, the perspiring assistant apologized. He took the envelope the receptionist had given him at the Institute out of his pocket. The letter inside said:

Dear Hermes,

A rushed note. I hear you are coming to Cambridge for a meeting. As things stand, I might not be here. Please leave your outline on my desk. I'll explain another time.

Love,

Esther

An hour later he was still gently baking in the same chair watching somber, sweating civil servants rushing in and out of the adjacent offices. There was much commotion. At a quarter to twelve the assistant returned. He was uneasy. "The magistrate just called, Professor. He'll be delayed one more hour. He's in meeting."

"I have an appointment at noon," Hermes said sternly.

The assistant held opened his mouth, embarrassed, and moved his head meaningfully.

"I'm leaving for my meeting," Hermes stood up. "I'll be back at two sharp."

"Three will be fine," said the assistant relieved.

The Rio was packed. Its clients had overflowed onto the sidewalk with their drinks, standing under the covered passage. The strong smell of coffee and perfume—mostly pine and lavender—seemed to be keeping people animated. One person near the middle of the sidewalk held a tabloid close to his nose. On the front page was a photograph of the bodies of a man and a woman. Their white clothing was blotched with dark stains. The headline read, "Terrorists strike again? Forty-eight bullets kill couple."

With difficulty Hermes moved through the crowd trying to enter the shop and reach the counter. A tall woman with long, bare limbs, wide shoulders, and big, prewar-tango-dancer's sad eyes blocked the way. She was trying to talk to two men at the same time, the one old and balding, the other a very tall, bearded young person moving his legs and arms nervously and leaning over her in various postures.

"He was the head of their intelligence service station," said the bald man.

"It was a commando group," snorted the bearded one, "they've-ve-ve already escaped," he stuttered.

"It was a settling of accounts," she concluded confidently.

Behind the trio an intense-looking scholar with lacquered-down hair and a dry smile was explaining to a female teenager of ravishing beauty, "My theory is that it is due to the chaos phenomenon combined with the greenhouse effect, a condition caused by an increase in carbon dioxide in the atmosphere resulting from the burning of fossil fuels. The temperatures may soon hover between 42 to 45 degrees. It's deterministic chaos."

The girl was watching in amazement. Her tousled, curly, dark locks were getting into her green eyes and half-closed lips. She blew the hair away. It bounced back. Dark ripples ran over her smooth skin and her eyes flickered. "And the dollar?"

"The same effect. Oscillating turbulence. It soared the first half of the decade like the high atmospheric pressure about a third of the way across the Atlantic . . ."

"And the assassinations?"

"An identical crisis, typical of bifurcation and chaotic regimes."

"What a philosopher," she gushed.

Beyond the couple Robert came into view.

"I started worrying," said Robert, taking off sunglasses with lettuce-green frames.

"The authorities."

"Trouble?"

"No idea. Nobody showed up."

"I'll get you something." Robert turned around and spoke to the young woman behind the counter.

"What do you recommend today, Sphinx?"

A woman with a mournful face, wearing a loud dress, pushed through, bumping against Hermes violently and Robert lightly before docking herself at the counter. She ordered. The girl ignored Robert and served the woman first. Then she turned to Robert.

Robert spoke: "It's nice and cool."

The girl argued: "It's hot and crowded."

"People are always polite," Robert continued.

"My name is Doxa," she said.

"Everything you say is true," added Robert.

"People are rude sometimes," she whispered.

"My name is Donald," he rejoined.

She blushed. "At most only one thing you have said is true."

"Something you have said is not true," Robert concluded as another lady approached.

"What a scandal!" shouted the lady.

"No. Just a paradox," said Robert.

"What made you tell her your name was Donald?" Hermes asked Robert.

"I try to remain anonymous. You've invited me for lunch."

"I have to be back at three," said Hermes.

"Let's blast off. So long, Circe," said Robert to the woman at the bar and to Hermes. "I have to start working at three."

The girl behind the counter looked at them, disappointed. Then she said confidentially to both, "Too late. There's no way out, Sam."

Robert left a tip and they walked out.

They chose an outdoor restaurant under a blue tent in the middle of a court surrounded by two antique shops (one specializing in engravings, the other in coins), a boutique for ties, and another for bathing suits.

"How was Cambridge?"

"The same."

"That bad, huh?"

"Too much to do."

"Get any offers?"

"In my field, Robert, we apply for grants and wait a year. We don't get offers. You're confusing me with somebody else."

"I confuse you with Hermes. Very often in fact. It's because of your mercurial nature, your constant identity crisis. How's the plot coming along?"

"Getting thicker all the time."

"Oh. How?"

"The cast is assembled. More numerous by the minute."

"You've got it wrong again. Stories aren't about heroes. There's always only one hero, the author. The characters are the ways in which the author gets to talk about himself."

"And Madame Bovary in fact was Flaubert, and Tolstoy at least six characters. Any more platitudes?"

"We're all authors, Hermes, all parallel, distributed, and processed, as you would say, in many, many heroes." Robert looked melodramatic once more.

"Robert, you read too much pulp psychology. Why don't you read some Minsky for a change?"

"Hermes, will you ever stop being so damn fixated on father figures?"

Hermes rested his eyes on Robert and did not speak.

Robert looked away. Then he turned back. Their eyes locked. He said amiably, "You seem to specialize in being the last to see people before they get murdered." There was silence. "One thing is a fact," he continued. "Sloan's murder doesn't make your position in the Agraphiotis case any easier."

"No. It doesn't," Hermes said at last. He took a deep breath, his eyes still fixed on Robert without expression. "It definitely makes investigators more paranoid about me. I'm sure they know by now that I knew the Sloans." He brought both hands to his temples slowly. "And that I spent some time with them in their compound in Santorini and on their yacht."

"At the police headquarters they'll be tempted to try and associate the two murders. Watch your next interview."

"Did you know the Sloans were friends of Agraphiotis'?" Hermes asked.

"Doesn't surprise me. It's a small world. Although I'm certain the Sloan murder had to do strictly with politics, and not with archaeological treasures. I might be very wrong, of course. The Sloans were too multifunctional. You know what I mean. The point is whether the investigators will find patterns and links where none exist just because it's convenient for them."

"I'm so tired of playing the detective, honestly," said Hermes.

"Well, let's change the subject temporarily."

Hermes smiled. "You promised me a vacation. Don't tell me you're copping out."

"Will they let you go this time?"

"I have a feeling they won't object. Do you suppose I can find a professional reason to leave again, just one week after two other trips during a period in which I'm supposed to be writing a book?"

"Of course. Your book. You can always say you've got urgent research to do. That you'd like to visit the Auerbach library."

"Auerbach? The author of *Mimesis*?"

"Yeah. I never paid much attention to the book since I don't believe in the possibility of representation. I leave such things to you. But what's always fascinated me is his library."

"Never heard of it."

"The story of the library begins when Auerbach, escaping from Germany during the war, was offered the job of chief librarian in Istanbul by the Turkish government. When he asked to be taken to his quarters, they brought him to a totally empty palace. Throughout all the years Auerbach held this post, until he went to Princeton, that is, the library never acquired a single book. The same noble tradition has continued ever since. I want to pay tribute to that library."

Robert frowned in thought and continued, "What about leaving three days from now? There's a flight at noon. I'll make the reservations."

"When do we come back?"

"How about four days later?"

"Good. Perfect. I have to go, otherwise I'll be late. You said you had to do some work, too." Hermes got up.

Robert remained seated. He took his sunglasses out of his pocket and put them on.

"You amaze me! You're so compulsive. I just have to answer a telex. I can do it right around the corner. Call you at nine."

"Nine," and Hermes was gone.

A Fourth Interview

Hermes was back in the magistrate's antechamber. Again he was asked to wait; a few minutes had passed when the door of the magistrate's office opened. About a dozen young men in short sleeves, with long, somber faces in various degrees of unshavenness, poured out. Tobacco clouds rolled behind them. The assistant came last. "Please come in," he said holding the door invitingly. Hermes walked in.

Karras sat in exactly the same position as always. But his few wrinkles were deep as scars now. His eyes were bloodshot and less indifferent. He wore a white shirt that stuck to his chest with sweat. He faced Hermes directly.

"There's been an assassination," he announced before Hermes had time to sit down.

Hermes did not respond. He stared at the magistrate.

"A friend of yours," said the magistrate almost viciously.

"I know. It's on the front pages of today's papers."

"What's your opinion?"

"What do you expect?"

"You spent some time with the couple before you left for the States."

"I've already told you everything about the trip."

"Repeat it."

"It was a cruise to Santorini."

"What kind of cruise?"

"I don't know much about different kinds of cruises."

"Do you recall anything special about it?"

"Of course. The cook disappeared."

"What do you think about that?"

"Bizarre."

"How did it happen?"

Hermes went over the whole event.

"Whom did Sloan speak to during the trip?"

Hermes recited the list. The magistrate took no notes. He listened to the names, the familiar disinterested expression gradually returning to his face.

"Where did you go during your excursion?"

Hermes went through the details of the trip once more.

"How did you meet the Sloans?"

"I've already told you that, too," Hermes said. Then he went ahead and made a quick sketch of their first encounter.

"He knew many archaeologists. Did he mention he had met Professor Agraphiotis?"

"Yes. He said they had met several times. It would have been strange if they hadn't."

"Did he know you were his nephew?"

"He did."

"The Sloans seemed to be very well informed about everything."

"They seemed to have been everywhere."

The magistrate shook his head in slow motion. "Sloan's fingerprints were found in Professor Agraphiotis' house."

"So?"

"You're not surprised?" asked the magistrate with what seemed genuine surprise.

"What's strange about that?"

"You haven't asked *where* they were found."

"Where?" asked Hermes.

"You met the Sloans by chance," said the magistrate in his monotonous style, ignoring the question.

"I told you how we met," said Hermes, with some impatience.

"Did Sloan ever mention names of art dealers he knew?" the magistrate insisted.

Hermes named a few.

"I assume you know some of them?"

"Only by name."

"Why?"

"I'm not involved with the art market."

"And how did you become interested in artificial intelligence?" Karras changed the subject suddenly.

Hermes bunched up his shoulders. "I read an essay."

"By whom?"

"Somebody called Turing."

"Turing who?"

"Alan Turing."

"The one who worked at Bletchley Park during the Second World War and broke German secret messages enciphered with the Enigma machines?"

"Yes."

"Then I don't see the connection."

"What I read was an article in *Mind,* a British journal of philosophy, on intelligence and computing machines."

"And what's Turing doing now?"

"He's dead. Supposed to have committed suicide."

"Suicide?"

"The circumstances are still unresolved."

But the magistrate was not interested in the rest. He said, "What impressed you about this article?"

"He stated some very significant ideas about computers as thinking machines. Of course he wasn't the only one at the time."

"Who else?"

"Claude Shannon, for example."

"Another cryptologist."

"Well, he researched information and encoding in general but also chess and other games, always from the problem-solving point of view. He wasn't a professional cryptologist. You seem to know a lot about the field," Hermes said.

"I told you. In my job it is necessary to have some knowledge of cryptography. I'm not an exception."

"I'm not exceptional either, considering how many archaeologists there are who specialize in deciphering inscriptions," Hermes said.

"But you *are* an exception. Your knowledge of cryptanalysis goes deep. Talking to you, it's obvious you've been thinking very hard and very systematically about information encoding and decoding."

"That's true of you, too," said Hermes. "Your questions and comments aren't those of a person who has knowledge of cryptology for instrumental purposes only. Your real interests appear to go beyond professional security problems."

"And what about *your* real interests?" asked Karras.

"I'm an archaeologist. The rest of my interests are incidental."

"They all say that," replied Karras with malice. Then he added, "You're too multidisciplinary, your friends have too many interests, you travel too much, and there are too many loose ends. Let me know when you plan on leaving the city again."

"As a matter of fact, I'm planning to very soon."

The magistrate looked at Hermes with astonishment. "When do you work, if I may ask?"

"When I'm not being bothered."

The magistrate pretended not to hear or see. "I suppose you still have my phone number. If I were you, I would always have it accessible wherever I go." Then he concluded, "Dates and places."

Hermes gave him the information while the magistrate seemed to be making mental calculations.

He looked at his watch and said no more.

As Hermes turned to leave the room, he caught a last glance of the magistrate's head, slightly dropped toward his chest, at the drawn eyes, the stretched lips, the knot of wrinkles, the skin shrunk and contracted over the face.

This time Hermes went briskly through the corridors of the building. Very fast. Very easily. There was no backtracking, no returning to a previous choice node, no trifurcating link routes inside the dingy guts of the headquarters, no need to try different paths, no dead ends, no stops.

Too easy, he thought. Then he felt a light touch on his back.

A Conscientious Driver

"Not that way," a voice ordered. "Follow me." They went down to the ground floor and zigzagged through several corridors. The man, short, fast, broad-shouldered, led the way. They reached the side exit. The man stopped, turned around, and waited politely for Hermes to step out. A parking lot spread out in front of them.

The man said, "Stavros is busy. They asked me to drive you."

"Who's Stavros?"

"The magistrate's driver. I'm parked right over here." He pointed to a small car, indistinguishable from the ones Hermes had ridden in with the magistrate before.

"I'm going a long way," Hermes remarked.

"That's what I'm here for. Take a seat." The driver opened the front door. "Unless you prefer to sit in the back."

"I'll sit up front." Hermes got in.

In a few minutes they reached the main road.

The driver said, "You didn't tell me where to take you."

Hermes gave the address of his apartment.

"Back home," he said.

"You're well informed."

"It's part of my job," the driver said.

"Have you lived in the States?" Hermes asked.

"How did you know?"

"The way you drive. Different from Stavros."

"Yes. For two years. After the navy. I worked for two years and quit."

"What kind of job did you do?"

"I worked as a guard in New York. Very tough, tougher than the navy."

"What did you do in the navy?"

"I was an M.P. I had to round up all the drunk sailors every night."

"I can imagine."

"You lived in the States too."

"I still do. I'm only spending a year here."

"I know. You're a genius."

"I'm an academic. Is that what you mean?"

"Not really. I heard people referring to you as a genius with my own ears. You're an archaeologist."

"That's correct."

"Great job. I also worked in a museum in the States, but only for a month."

"In a museum? What did you do there?"

"I was in the security branch."

"Which museum?"

"The . . . Metropolitan."

"The Metropolitan. Did you . . ."

"I was only a temporary, though."

"It wasn't that tough, was it?"

"No, it wasn't. Wonderful people. What I admired most was the scientific spirit of the archaeologists. It made me feel proud to work in that place."

"How long have you been in this work?"

"Ten years now. Enough time to know the difference between a criminal and an honest man."

"I thought it took a long time to investigate a crime."

"A long time to establish proof, maybe. But to have a gut feeling is different."

"You speak like a detective."

"I'm not a detective. I'm a police driver. An outsider."

"You mean you're not part of the outfit."

"I am not part of the racket."

"The racket?"

"You wouldn't believe what goes on here."

They were taking back streets that did not lead toward Hermes' apartment. Hermes appeared not to notice. The driver kept on driving carefully, as if searching for something, and continued to talk.

"You see, for me, being a policeman is more than a profession. I've thought a lot about it for the last twelve years, the idea of justice, and I'm disgusted with the business of enforcing it."

"What don't you like about it?"

"I don't like how much is covered up and how they decide to nail a good man."

"Does it happen often?"

"All the time. Take your case."

"What about my case?"

"They want to frame you."

"Over the case of Professor Agraphiotis."

"That and much more. Don't kid yourself."

"What else could they want to frame me for?"

"Now they're dragging you into the Sloan thing."

"But the two cases have nothing to do with each other."

"That's what you think."

"But how can they be connected?"

"They're talking about networks, conspiracies, international agencies."

"And where am I supposed to fit in?"

"That's what they're working out."

They were driving through an area of small yards, empty warehouses, deserted workshops, and houses that were either abandoned or never finished being built, it was difficult to tell which.

"Look how they've ruined this country. They've turned it into a garbage dump. Everywhere. Not only here. Everywhere. It's a rotten place. A kingdom of rag men. The best for you would be to get out of here."

Hermes looked at the driver in amazement. The driver went on calmly, as if talking to himself.

"When I heard you'd left for the States, I thought you'd never come back. They let you go because they weren't ready yet. They gambled and won. They got you back."

"Of course I came back. I have work here. Anyhow, why should I try to escape? Escape what?"

"I know, I know. You don't know anything. Look. It's all rotten. Take Agraphiotis. He was a prominent man, a relative of yours, OK, good family. But this is a rotten world—you don't have any idea. Agraphiotis and Sloan were two sides of the same coin."

"What do you mean?"

"They were smugglers who worked together and worked against each other for a long time. Each had his own part of the police collaborating with him. It was a kind of balancing act that lasted for years. Then one day this treasure, the Golden Thinking Machine, was dug up, and they were at each other's throats as never before. Agraphiotis was the first casualty. The cook followed."

"Which cook?"

"Sloan's cook, on the yacht. You met him. You must have."

"Was he murdered?"

"Of course he was. He was doing work for us."

"You mean he was a double agent, working for the police and Sloan?"

"No. He only worked for us."

"And he managed to get hired by Sloan?"

"Not bad, eh? He didn't have fun for long though. Sloan turned him into food for the sharks. But then it was Sloan's own turn. You see, there's a secret war dragging on inside the services between the supporters of each faction. A dirty war."

"I gather."

"You're surrounded. Even this medium is one of them."

"Melania?"

"The woman is a well-known spy. Ever wonder who would need her and why?"

"Not all people have the same needs."

"You mean you need people you miss. I'm a little surprised, Professor. You have no idea whom you're dealing with. A nest of British spies. The father, the founder of the 'establishment,' came from Smyrni. He picked up the clients of another famous medium to whom he was introduced by the British. During the First World War this other medium had almost all the wives of Greek government ministers and of the ambassadors as clients. He'd also been a good friend of a British writer. When the war ended, this writer returned to his country and wrote his memoirs. In the book he revealed that he'd been the chief spy of the British in the area and that this medium had been one of his major collaborators. A major scandal. You never heard of the book? Its pretty well known."

Hermes shook his head.

"The book was confiscated and the writer was brought to court, but the damage was done. The medium was ruined. Then this other medium from Smyrni appeared and picked up all these clients. He was also set up by the British, although probably without his knowledge—at least in the beginning. A few months before the Second World War the man died and his eldest daughter inherited the practice and the clients. The Intelligence Service approached her about carrying on the same kind of clandestine business. She agreed and she was trained secretly as a commando. She became part of a great team. The head was a famous professor. During the war she did very important work. She was even decorated for it. Secretly, of course. But she's never stopped being an informer. This is your medium."

"And you think she's still working for the British Secret Service? You are talking about events that happened almost half a century ago."

The driver coughed and coughed. His eyes became bloodshot. "The pollution," he said. "It's possible. History never ends. Or she might just be selling information to any other parties concerned. Once a spy always a spy."

"But what use am I to her?"

"They want to know your moves ahead of time and your intentions. It's easier to trap you that way."

"How do you know all this?"

"We have our own people everywhere."

"But what is this 'we'?"

"Just honest people."

"Are you an organization?"

"Just honest people. But we can deliver."

"And what do your people think about me?"

"That you have to get out of here, and fast."

"You believe what you are doing now is moral?"

"It is the most honest thing I have done for a long time."

"Aren't you afraid?"

"Afraid of what?" he laughed. "You reporting on me? Why should you? If you're a criminal, you won't. You have nothing to gain. If you're honest why should you? I'm not undermining justice. All I'm doing is helping undo something that's breaking every law in this country. There are many of us who feel the same way. We can help you get out of the country."

"Aren't you interfering with due process?"

"What's due process? What's the purpose of discovering whether Agraphiotis shot Sloan first or vice versa? There are so many things in the world that haven't been cleared up—let mysteries be mysteries. We're interested in justice, not explanations."

The sea was in view.

"What happened to the scientific archaeology you valued so much? Now you are reasoning like the enemy you criticized," Hermes said.

"They're the ones who have started it all. But they won't last for ever. In the meantime they might hurt you. That's why we want to help you get out of here."

"Where to?"

"There are places. You could become head of a whole research organization."

"I thought you just wanted me out of the country."

"You have to be careful about where you go. They might ask for your extradition. You're linked with a double murder, possibly a triple murder."

"What?"

"Yes. There's a theory circulating about your contacts with the Mafia, though not many subscribe to it."

"The Mafia! This is getting fantastic. Nobody can believe in anything like that, I assure you."

"Still. They claim there's a connection between you and a head Mafia person who was found dead after you visited him. Shot in the forehead," he stuck his finger against his forehead and pretended to pull a trigger with his thumb.

"No!"

"Yes! You should look at their reports. You want to see the instructions I have to tail you?"

With his left hand he took a piece of paper out of his pocket and unfolded it. He gave it to Hermes. The text was typed, had a serial number, and was labeled "strictly confidential." Hermes read the text. It had the form of a near-algorithm and referred to a man to be followed under the code name of Ram.

"Why Ram?" Hermes asked.

"Simple. The ram was an animal associated with Hermes in mythology. There's a former archaeologist working in the office. He thought of it."

"That's quite a document," said Hermes, returning the paper. Then he inquired casually, "When you were in the States, did you meet a collector called Wind?"

"Look. I was only a guard." He looked at Hermes out of the corners of his eyes. "I knew no collectors." Changing his tone, he whispered, "We can get you out of the country in three days."

"But that's the day I'm flying to Istanbul anyway."

"I know. They're planning to trap you that very day. We have a plan of our own, though."

They were driving away from the sea now, in the direction of Hermes' apartment.

"What plan?"

"Get the *Athens Gazette* tomorrow. Go to the classified announcements. There'll be an announcement concerning a garage sale. The time will be correct. The address you should add three hundred to. Go to this address. There will be a green Fiat waiting. You will get into the car. From that moment on, your worries will be over."

Hermes looked at the driver. "Why risk so much for me?"

"It isn't for you. It's what you stand for. Will you be there?"

"If there's no other alternative."

"There isn't!"

They reached Hermes' apartment. The driver said, "They might ask you why we took the sea route. Tell them you asked me to drive you that way because you planned to do something and then you changed your mind. Don't forget. The classified announcements. Tomorrow."

Sherlock 2000 II Uses Ariadne's Thread

Hermes went to the kitchen, picked up his laptop, and took it to the dining room. The telephone rang. He listened to the receiver. He answered,"Just a few minutes ago . . . Of course you can come downstairs for a few minutes . . . We don't have to talk on the telephone . . . OK."

Soon after there was a brisk knock at the door. He got up, went over, and opened it. Nina walked in. Her short hair was even more spiky than usual.

Hermes asked, "Is Eleni back?"

"No. She called. She's been delayed. She'll be back in four days," she said. "I have a feeling they're closing in. Do we still need more facts to start acting? Is that what you're busy doing?"

"I'm just working to keep my mind going, and you should get some rest."

"I can't. What are you working on?"

"Something technical. Complexity theory."

"Complexity theory? You never told me anything about that."

"I doubt it would calm you down."

"But what about my education? Complexity theory, please." Her eyes were restless and pleading.

"You're always in such a hurry," he objected, but started. "Complexity theory investigates the resources we need to solve a problem, resources such as time for computation and memory for storage in solving problems."

"You mean what algorithms and machines to choose."

"Not at all. In fact a fascinating aspect of complexity theory is that it analyzes problems and measures their inherent difficulty, in order to solve them at a more abstract level before they're implemented into algorithms and machines."

"I don't get it."

"Complexity theory identifies the difficulty of a problem in terms of its structure. Neither algorithms nor machines alter the problem's structure."

"How do you know?"

"Because deciphering, which I do as an archaeologist, begs for this kind of analysis."

"Cryptography too?"

"Cryptography, too. It isn't enough to have the key to a coded message. Deciphering takes time. In war, timing is of the essence. A message can be enciphered in such a way that it can be interpreted only by the time the information it contains has become useless."

"And how can this be predicted?"

"By examining the complexity of the problem. This is where complexity theory is useful. A basic approach is to examine unknown problems in terms of known ones—to try to find out if they are computationally brief, tractable, or intractable, requiring an infinite computational time."

"It makes perfect sense to relate new problems to old ones," she said.

"Sure. It also gives us a guide to making difficult questions into easier ones by the principle of 'divide and conquer,' breaking a large tough problem into smaller ones. It's like undoing a knot by unraveling each twist loop and pattern that you know—a running knot, a slip knot, a granny knot, a reef knot, a sailor's knot, a clove knot—one at a time, you're segmenting a new problem into subproblems that happen to be old ones."

She asked, "Is this problem solving by analogy?"

"No. They both reuse already structured knowledge to solve unknown problems, but the way they do it is altogether different."

She said, "I remember at school, when I had a hard problem to solve, I would immediately start searching for what I had already solved, and the solution would flash in front of my eyes, mysteriously. Is that 'divide and conquer,' or analogy?"

"Probably some combination of the two."

"Nobody ever told us anything about analogy at the Polytechnic. They only talked about deduction/induction. But the more I've been thinking about thinking, the more I find we use analogies everywhere."

"True. Analogy is omnipresent as something inherent, built into our minds, a primitive process, running wild in the interior of the jungle of our mind, as well as an artificial tool, a cultivated method of rational inference."

"And how does it produce hypotheses as a wild process?"

"By rushing back before leaping ahead, back through our brain's wiring labyrinth, across a system possibly like a system of lines Minsky called Knowledge Lines, which, like Ariadne's thread, the *nema,* after taking us to scenes we have been to before, where we have a good chance of finding a tool useful to our current problem, can take us to the exit, the solution."

"How do we know where to look for this information? What points to *the* relevant solved problem among all the others? How do we know which object to use? It's like asking someone to go to a house whose address is unknown in order to pick up the instructions for getting there."

"I would say it's more like trying to tighten a screw and going to the kitchen drawer to search among the knives and spoons for something that can be held by hand and used to rotate the head of a screw because you can't find a screwdriver."

"Why do something like that?"

"An imperative in the mind tells us that things that appear to share many characteristics have many more things in common, which goes to show that what is a solution to one problem might also be the solution to another. Whether in science or engineering, similarity in function between two different objects makes us look for similarity in forms, and structural isomorphisms search for functional resemblances. We invent by transferring forms from an old object to a new one. We discover by transferring the structure of an explanatory law from a familiar domain to an unfamiliar one. It's all based on the analogy principle. Similar problems may have a common solution."

"Hmmm. Very superstitious."

Hermes laughed. "Like produces like, said good old James Frazer. It's indeed rather primitive, wild."

"Who's Frazer?" asked Nina. "Sounds like one of your friends. Tell me about him so I can put him among the suspects."

Hermes went on laughing. "He was a specialist . . . in mythology . . . and magic . . . long dead."

"And what about analogy as an artificial method? What did domesticity do to analogy?"

"Tamed it—at least it's still trying to. It's like this. Analogy production is coupled with a mechanism that controls, tests, and filters its wild products. Analogy is actually more reliable as a method for creating hypotheses, better than those energetic monkeys of the British Museum Library fabricating candidate solutions day and night, or those tedious safecrackers of the Bank of England's vault tinkering away at its locks, and all this inspired talk about lightning and discharges of inspiration and intuition full of clouds and smoke."

"Go on."

"We said that given a new problem, analogical methods search systematically for an old problem that has already been solved, similar to the one at hand. That means we have to identify, compare, and match computationally any significant characteristics between the two problems. But we also have to have a stock of presolved problems, properly stored for easy retrieving."

"Funny," Nina said, "that you've brought analogy, so basic and primitive, so late into our talks, after you'd already discussed in such detail so many other methods much more removed from the way we think naturally. It's also strange that at the same time you had to use so many farfetched analogies, like wires and lines and Ariadne's thread, to explain it. Such an elementary mechanism, so personal and yet so universal, ought to have been self-explanatory or very well analyzed at the very beginning as a point of departure of any methodical thinking. Much more than search trees."

"Indeed, analogy hasn't been studied as much as other, more artificial ways of thinking. And although Aristotle had already written about it, we preferred to focus on his other works, like the *Organon*, where no mention is made of it. This may be because we're very familiar with it and, like the people who live under a church bell, we pay no attention to its ringing. Traditionally, we have been intrigued by other, distant rather than near, objects, like the stars and their orbits."

"Maybe that was safer," she said.

"There's something to that."

Suddenly she grabbed Hermes by the shoulders and shook him as if to wake him up. "Maybe the time has come to take risks."

"I'll show you only a very simple example. You'll have to work your way through the rest of the theory with the tutorial. Then you ask me questions. It goes like this." He typed and pulled up a diagram on the screen:

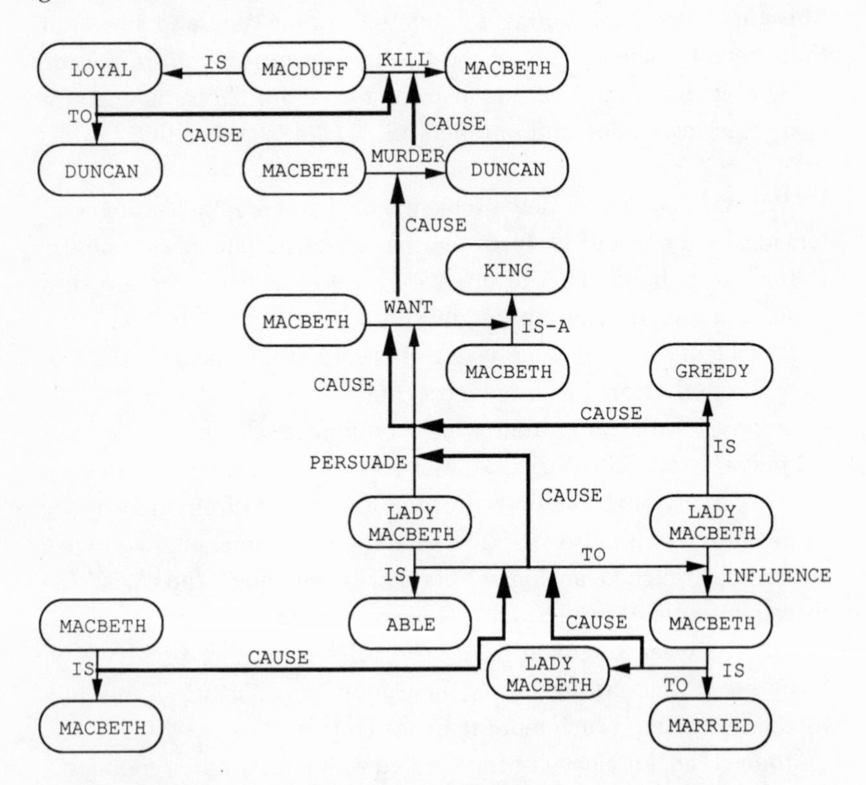

"You know the story about Macbeth, Lady Macbeth, Duncan, and Macduff."

Nina smiled impudently.

Hermes continued. "Here is how Winston represented the plot in terms of nodes and links. This plot abstraction is our structured knowledge, our precedent in memory. Suppose we face the problem now of a weak nobleman married to a greedy lady, and we are asked if he may wish to be king."

She said, "I can see where you're leading. Something like comparing and connecting semantic networks and frames. Macbeth's to the nobleman's."

"First we inquire if the actors in the problem match with the actors in the precedent. Second, we look into the problem to find out what the missing information is that would have permitted us to answer the questions. Third, we look into the precedent to find the corresponding link between matching actors. Fourth, we transfer this link. The transferred link permits us to answer the question. Indeed, the nobleman may wish to be king."

"But this is sheer speculation, besides being rather sexist in the way it puts the blame on women again."

"The latter is content, nothing to do with method. As for method . . ."

She interrupted, "It only gives us guesses. How can we be more certain?"

"It depends on the degree of matching."

She exclaimed, "I already see the Agraphiotis frame and the Golden Thinking Machine. I see links-known-to-be-true and links-to-be-shown-to-be-true."

He looked at the computer clock. "Promise you'll do that tomorrow. What am I saying? It's already morning. We should both get some sleep." Abruptly his face turned stern.

She noticed his face. "You look tired."

He nodded. "The kitchen window."

It had started rattling in the wind.

He jumped out of bed. It must have been past noon, but the overcast day was dim. The kitchen window was still rattling. He rushed to the living room.

She looked taller, with long, slender limbs. Her legs, arms, and palms were stretched out, her head leaned sideways, her face was longer, and her eyelashes were longer and darker on paler skin. She wore the same clothes as last night and they looked dull and crumpled. Her handkerchief, purple cotton with white polka dots, lay next to the computer, which was still running. Cold wind blew through the wide-open French windows, carrying inside the white muslin curtains that almost touched the girl's head. Something metallic was blown down somewhere in the kitchen.

"What?" She sat up, startled. "Oh. It's you," she said, realizing she had just woken up in front of the screen and that Hermes was looking at her.

"It's the wind. What are you doing here?"

"I'm sorry," she started to apologize.

"I thought you'd left."

"I did, I went upstairs and couldn't go to sleep. I paced up and down for a whole hour. Then I decided I'd had enough. I came downstairs to work. I was excited about what you said about analogy. I came in and you were reading. Thucydides. I saw you through the crack of the door, but you didn't see me and you didn't hear me. I turned on the computer."

"I'd just woken up. I couldn't go back to sleep either. That wind."

"I heard your book falling down on the floor. It was four hours later—I checked the computer clock. Then I heard you talking in your sleep about Macbeth, matching, murder, and Macduff. I didn't hear anything about Lady Macbeth though."

"It was because of all the talk we had about analogy."

"You were brewing a scheme."

"I don't think so."

"You were turning 'round and 'round."

"Maybe. What were you doing?"

"I kept on going. The system started responding. Slowly. I could hear the shops were opening downstairs and still no results, although I let the inference engine become more and more speculative, lowering thresholds of probability. Then having still no results . . ."

". . . you went to sleep leaving the computer on, still struggling for successful matchings. I saw it and I felt exhausted myself. You'd better go to bed. You've worked enough."

"What'll you do now?"

"Get myself some orange juice."

He made his way to the kitchen.

As soon as he left, Nina started working furiously at the computer again. A few minutes passed. Suddenly she shouted. "Hermes! Hermes! Come here! Quick! It worked! Look! We got a hypothesis. Sherlock 2000 with the collaboration of Macbeth Plus rounded them up. They're trapped. The link's identified. And—it's all very frightful."

But there was no answer. Nina rushed to the kitchen. Hermes was not there. She went through all the rooms. Hermes had gone.

A Medium's Memory Palace

It was ten o'clock when Hermes reached the cubical villa by the sea. During the early hours of the morning the weather had turned. A wind was whirling in the compound, and the cock had climbed onto the head of one of the terra-cotta sphinxes.

Elpis ushered Hermes directly into Melania's office. Inside the villa it was not more tranquil. The overgrown branches of an acacia tree rasped on the glass panels of the back door, and somewhere on the other side a loosely tied door coughed back an answer. The rest of the limbs and joints of the building followed, stuttering in chorus.

Melania and Hermes met for about a quarter of an hour. Once in the hallway she said, "I promised you something. I keep my promises. Follow me."

The landing at the top of the staircase led to a windowless hall surrounded by closed doors.

A long cicada's cry penetrated the space as if forced in by the wind.

Hermes asked, "Have you always lived in this house?"

"No," she said, "we haven't. My father bought it just before the war. My mother had just died. It was a late Saturday afternoon. I was taking a walk with my father. Our home then was half an hour from here. This was a peaceful spot, only a few villas surrounded by high walls and in between, open fields with sheep grazing. He liked to walk along this ridge and discuss hermetic knowledge. He liked the distant view of the horizon across the sea, and the perpetual change of the shades of the water. He spoke often about the physiognomy of the waves and the art of reading the history of our ancestors' lives and our future destinities from the way they unfolded.

"That afternoon," she continued, "there was great commotion in front of the garden gate. People were taking out furniture and loading it onto a truck. The house was for sale. We met the owner. We asked if we could visit it. He took us in. He said the villa had been built for a millionaire banker from Constantinople. The architect had been from Pontos. We went from room to room. I was taken by their vastness. My father noted how much the layout resembled the Plan."

"The Plan?"

"The Grid of Heavens, the Divisions of Thought inscribed in a Quadrated Circle, where every idea, every object, finds its proper place. My father said it was man's obligation to build in the image of the astral world that was in his own image, to keep the right numbers, measures, and weights. Perfect form and proportion turned matter to intellect, as Hermes Trismegistus of Egypt wrote. They can endow statues with an angelic spirit and make them move and think. And now here was this house, standing in front of us, for sale. My father arranged to buy it that evening. He died forty days later and in three months the war started. I took it upon myself to continue everything he left behind, consulting with my father's clients and moving to the new house. This way I brought together all the essential arts and sciences. I related every division of space to a type of divination so you can walk from room to room and, by directing your gaze upon the objects, understand, like reading the book of knowledge—*ut pictura poesis*. You climb the Tree of Wisdom, and the world within and outside becomes intelligible."

"A memory theater," said Hermes.

"A book on method," said Melania.

They entered a room with only one picture on the wall, an abstract figure painted in colors, ten nodes connected by links, that greatly resembled a tree graph. A bright line that started at the upper right node zigzagged from node to node all the way to the bottom left one.

"It is painted by Luria Safed of Poland himself," said Melania. "The Sephirot Tree, made out of ciphers and combinations. What is and what must be flow like lightning." She followed the course of the illuminated path with her index finger.

"The chosen path. It radiates like sapphire. This is why it is called Sephirot. Its nodes mark and enumerate the opportunities to choose from, its links indicate the ascent or descent we take in the ladder of being."

The next room to the right was dark, its windows covered with deep purple curtains. A bare bulb hung in the middle. Melania turned the switch and brought to life its feeble existence. Large, intricate hangings of gold-thread embroidery glittered on the walls.

"The Zodiac Pantheon," she said. "The Cosmic Correspondences, the Choreography of the Universe."

"They come from Agrippa's *De Occulta Philosophia* diagrams, a system of representation showing the relations among planets and constellations, seasons, and muses," said Hermes.

"They take long to construct," said Melania. "They have many applications. Most often they were used to calculate foundation charts, to specify when to start construction for a new building."

A door to the right brought them to a smaller space, furnished with three chairs and a low, round table covered with a white cloth and set with small coffee cups. Next to the cups a fragile paper rested flat, with a grid drawn on it in black ink. Inside each square of the grid was different blot.

She said, pointing to the grid divisions, "This is the Way, a voyage, and this is the Big Door, a passage, here is the Grave . . . the Letter . . . the Blonde . . . the Worry . . . the Meeting. The coffee dregs in a cup relate to one of the squares. You have to recognize individual features, marking contours, occlusions, lacunae. They can be the key to the matching, which means the person who drank from the cup will be confronted by the event the coffee reading announces in the near future."

Turning right, they stepped into the next room. A black-draped lamp illuminated an enormous line drawing of an open flat palm that covered almost a whole wall. Inscribed in it was a circle, and on it were drawn the position and orbits of the planets.

"It demonstrates the unity between the two major domains of esoteric knowledge—astrology and chiromantics," whispered Melania.

Continuing to the right, they entered a perfectly square room. A comfortable couch was set on a diagonal with an ebony stool next to it. On the stool rested an hourglass, an ancient instrument for measuring time by running sand, close to a bronze cube. A matrix of numbers was inscribed inside a grid on each side of the cube:

10	26	6		26	1	15		10	26	6
23	3	16		3	14	25		24	1	17
9	13	20		13	27	2		8	15	19

"Each row and column have the same sum," said Hermes.

"You're already meditating," said Melania. "The power of attraction of well-formedness. I know of nothing more pleasant than working out the harmonies of these planetary numbers and magical squares. They can describe anything we know about the movement of the moon and the sun. Its contemplation spreads the divine harmony over the body and restores the mind to order."

Similar charts were on the wall. Melania pointed out the numbers in the magic Jupiter square in a reproduction of Dürer's *Melancholia.*

16	3	2	13
5	10	11	8
9	6	7	12
4	15	14	1

"It counteracts the melancholic temperament under Saturn," she said. "Some of my clients rest here for an hour before they see me."

"Mathematicians have worked out such tables for centuries," said Hermes.

"Cryptology, the most faithful handmaiden of Occult Sciences, has used these tables too as a key to lock and to unlock secret messages." She took a step and said, "We will visit the cartomancy room now."

On a table covered in blue rested dozens of packs of cards.

"This is one of the greatest libraries of the books of Thot, the Egyptian Tarot, in the world," she explained. She took a pack, untied it, and threw the cards open. A rainbow of colors unfolded.

"They come from Venice," she said, "a gift of Julia Orsini herself, the great Sibylla of the Faubourg Saint Germain, to my grandfather when he visited her as a young man in 1870." She pointed to a picture of a man with a long beard and a conic hat, holding his hands over his eyes. She said "The Alchemist, or Folly. Next to the Seven of Swords it announces imminent catastrophe that can be escaped, but next to Victory, unavoidable failure. This is why the art of interpretation is so hard. It has to take into account the combinations and the position of each card within the framework of the others. It's the same with oneiromancy, the art of dream interpretation."

They moved to the next room. "They think each object in a dream means something specific. How simple it would be then," she said. She came to the middle of the room and took an old notebook, like the ones merchants used for accounting at the turn of the century, from the desk. She leafed through it. Hermes caught the picture, clumsily drawn, of a man slipping secretly through a door in a thief-like manner. Other pages were filled with scribbles, diagrams, or circles connected with single and double lines. Occasionally they looked like heavy fruited vines and other times more like complicated engines with wheels, pulleys, belts, bands, and ropes.

She continued, "These are the life-long notes of my grandfather for a book on the interpretation of dreams, an *oneirokritis*. It contains dream maps different from the maps people use. Each is drawn to describe a place conceivable in a dreamscape."

Hermes asked, "And did your grandfather make all the possible maps?"

"That would have been foolish. Instead he conceived a metamap, an *Ars combinatoria* for deducing all dreams, a true skeleton key to interpret them."

Now they found themselves in the largest room of all. It looked like a dining room, with a large table in the middle surrounded by almost two dozen chairs. Everything was white. A pedestal with what appeared to be a bust, covered by a sheet, was the only other object there.

"This is the seance room," she said.

They left the large room, passing through the door on its right wall again, and they were in the same hall their tour had started from. The cicada song was heard between two claps of thunder.

"What about the war?" she asked.

Hermes looked at her, confused.

She said, "Surprised?"

"What war?"

"There is only one, and you are in the middle of it."

Hermes kept on looking.

"You travel, you have contacts. I want to know more about what is going on. Don't ask me why I don't read the cards and answer my own questions—that is not what occult sciences are about. Oh, no. If all they could do was predict then they would already have been replaced by futurology. But they haven't."

"You've built a thinking machine here. But you seem reluctant to reduce it to an inference engine. Is it because you see divination as pure order, while everything seems chaotic today? I wonder, if I may ask, what you discuss with your clients in the end. Do you try to install a sense of order in their minds?" asked Hermes.

"Exactly the opposite. Disorder."

"Disorder?"

"Yes. Like any decent diviner, I consider it my duty to bring disorder to people's lives. People suffer from too much order. Their thinking is ruled by the compulsion for repetition. Divination makes them start all over again. You want order?" she continued as they started descending the stairs. "You've got artificial intelligence! And I want to know more about it. Not for professional reasons. My interest is purely academic, as they say."

"I think we'll find the time to discuss AI."

She looked at him as if weighing something in her mind. "And if you tell me about AI, I might be able to tell you about the stolen Golden Thinking Machine. And everything you want to know about it."

"You mean you know who has it?" asked Hermes. "How?"

"They came here asking after it."

"Then why wait? I have some ideas myself. But we weren't supposed to be exchanging information, according to the rules. Why not tell me now?"

At that moment the doorbell rang. Their talk was interrupted.

Elpis rushed Hermes out of the house and into the garden through the back door. When they arrived at the gate, nobody was waiting. The storm was menacing out in the sea. Sea gull cries rose above the waves, but the sea gulls could not be seen.

"The Meltemi," she said, "the northern wind of summer. The Dog Star is hungry again."

Out in the opening the wind reeled in circles, sweeping over roofs, walls, the ground, and blew a gust of sand into his face. A door slammed high up in an apartment building. The sound cracked through the air like a shotgun. A rag flew off one of the balconies, twirled around the arena, and was hurled straight into the sea. Shrieks of sea gulls came and went.

He was lucky to find an empty taxi as soon as he stepped onto the main street.

The driver was unusually polite. "Athens?" he asked, opening the door.

Hermes stepped in. "Thank you for stopping."

"My pleasure. I was afraid I'd have to drive back without a passenger."

"Isn't that rare?"

"On the contrary," the driver answered. "Say—are you from here? You seem to have some kind of accent."

"I never realized it."

"Have you been away for a long time?"

"Couple of years."

"Back for good?"

"Seems so."

"I can give you my telephone number. Call me when you need a ride. Ports or airports." The driver handed a card to him.

"Thanks," said Hermes.

"There are reduced rates," continued the driver. "Do you have anywhere to go tonight?"

"Thanks," said Hermes.

"Weather's changing," the driver insisted.

He switched on the radio. It was difficult to understand what the refrain was wailing about the wind, sun, and rain, but as the taxi headed north, the mountains seemed to be shining against a swiftly darkening sky.

Nina went on, ecstatic. "It's all here. We know who the murderer is!"

"Incredible," said Hermes.

They were both looking at the screen wide-eyed.

"Analogical thinking! It really worked marvels." She grabbed him by the shirtsleeves and shook him as if trying to wake him.

"Sure did." He ignored the shaking and continued eyeing the screen. "It even acknowledges degree of matching. Which is very weak."

"You mean the inference isn't trustworthy?"

Still mesmerized by the screen, he said, "It's all explicitly stated. The whole inference, right here. Conclusions, precedent source, and matching evaluations." He laughed and kept on talking, as if to himself. "And they say that commonsense problems can't be handled by symbolic representation. In addition it warns 'very weak matching: frame similarity very low. Slot value combinations ought to be reviewed.'"

"Keep reading," she said.

He did, loudly: "'Conjecture highly speculative.'"

"Of course," she said. "But this is only a hypothesis we've jumped to. The hypothesis we've been waiting for. Isn't it? Now what do *you* think? Do you realize what's been inferred? And what your next step will be?"

Hermes did not answer. He just looked at her. High winds blew the clouds so that their shadows ran across the facades of the buildings on the other side of the street. He said, "I have to see Melania again. Immediately. And I have to be very, very careful not to be followed. It might take me a few hours."

"Don't you want to see how the computer came up with this before you go? It's very intriguing. Don't you want to check first?"

He walked to the hall. As he was going out the door, he shouted. "You better get some *real* sleep now."

She repeated, "Hermes. Don't you want to check?"

But again Hermes was gone.

Against the Rules

The wind blew angrily from the passage onto his face as he stepped out of the taxi. It brought with it a taste of salt mixed with the sweet smell of smoke, the soft murmur of an invisible crowd, and the whining of a siren dying down behind the heavy parapet of the apartments. He reached the end of the narrow path. Reflections of red revolving lights licked the wall's edges. He entered the opening.

The villa was on fire. Smoke was billowing out of its windows. A crowd was milling around between fire engines and police cars. He moved among them. Somebody said they had seen a cock who had flown above the trees like a sea gull, somebody else referred to an ambulance that had carried away two or three or more injured. There were whispers about "senile old women," "pots forgotten on the stove," "robbers," "cursed," "witches," "terrorists."

The backs of the apartment houses formed a grandstand. Windows, balconies, and service staircases had come to life, jammed with people looking and pointing at the spectacle.

Hermes turned around and hastened to the trolley stop.

An hour later he was entering the hotel. He followed the same procedure as the first time. At the telexroom level he turned right twice and entered into the wide hall. Behind the opening he heard Kiki Nikolaki's voice and a client's.

She was asking questions in English. The client was answering. Hermes slowed down, then slipped into the alcove behind the potted palms.

The brigadier was standing, as if preparing to leave. He had folded his newspaper under his arm and was happily combing his mustache with his fingernail. He raised his eyes to Hermes and his mood changed.

"It's against the rules," he growled.

"I followed your instructions about how to get here unobserved."

"Not enough. You should have gone to Melania."

"That's why I'm here. They set the villa on fire. And I have a suspect for the murder."

"What do you mean?" Krypsiadis sprang up. He pulled Hermes by his sleeve to the door marked *Private.* Unlocking it, he pirouetted in, bringing Hermes along with him into a small cell concealed under a private staircase. "Tell me what happened. Tell me what you know," he said, pushing Hermes into an armchair. He himself remained standing.

Hermes spoke slowly, enumerating facts in as much detail as he could. Then he added his conjectures.

Krypsiadis listened, drawing short, fast breaths. At one point he murmured, "Necessary sacrifice." Later he interrupted, "It could have been worse. We could have lost the Queen in this chess game." When Hermes said, "But one should have acted, then," Krypsiadis replied, "No use. The disaster would have been postponed, but it would not have been prevented. The well-known 'horizon effect,'" he mumbled, and, turning to Hermes, "You did well. You pursued. Heuristic continuation or feedover." But a moment later Krypsiadis commented bitterly, saying, "Useless thrashing lower down," to which Hermes responded by accelerating his narration.

Hermes ended, recapitulating, "And as I told you, the suspect might be talking to your assistant here right next door. I think I recognize the voice. You have to verify the hypothesis. As for how it can be done, I leave it to you."

When Hermes finished, Krypsiadis said, "Let me handle it. We have to get you out of here fast."

They took the service staircase together, Krypsiadis first. They reached the bottom of the stairs. Krypsiadis unlocked another door.

"You can leave through here. You're on the ground floor. Just keep on walking." Krypsiadis stayed behind.

Hermes found himself in an alcove among brooms, mops, dustbins, and buckets. He turned the corner and entered a long passage with sinks and urinals on one side and toilets on the other. Then he crossed the hall, passed a small room, and entered the large hotel lobby. He came face to face with a man. He wore a white paper hat and held a cardboard sign. Both hat and sign bore in capital letters the word *HERMES*. Hermes came closer and read the word *tours* in smaller letters, under the first. The man offered Hermes a promotion smile and handed him an advertising leaflet.

"The boat leaves tomorrow at nine. Nine islands in three days," it read.

The Trench Coat

Hermes worked at his computer undisturbed that whole morning. Nina did not appear. At noon he had a light lunch. He returned to the dining room where the computer was waiting.

As he was sitting down, there was a knock at the door. He got up and went to the hall. "Up already?" he queried as he unlocked the door.

She strutted past him, straight into the living room. She was panting. An enormous heart-shaped doll rested in her creamy arms.

"Sorry I didn't call first," she said, smiling worriedly. "A friend of mine who lives downstairs from you just had a baby. I brought this for them." The doll smiled at Hermes. "It was a good excuse. I'll slip out of here in a couple of minutes. She's waiting for me."

Krypsiadis' rules, thought Hermes to himself, and said, "Kiki. What can I do for you?"

She stood in the middle of the dining room. She was wearing the same high-heeled shoes Hermes had first seen her in. She retained her world of fluctuating phenomena, surrounded by an even more ponderous cumulus of aroma, so strong and so dense that to cut it with a sharp knife would have been difficult.

"I'll just have a cigarette."

She looked around, smiled, and relaxed. She looked around again.

"There's no ashtray," Hermes said. "We don't smoke here. Wait. I'll get you something from the kitchen."

When he came back, Kiki was sitting comfortably on his chair in front of the computer, her fine heterogeneities of mass in a temporary state of peace. She had left the doll next to the computer and had already lit her cigarette. The tiny bluish particles streamed out of the aroma volume and levitated around it. She took the ashtray, put the cigarette in it, and left it next to the computer. She got up and came closer to Hermes. She opened her arms, held his head and brought his ear to her lips. She whispered, "Somebody will call and ask for the baker. Then you will have to hurry to Professor Votris' apartment. Without a second's delay."

She held the head in the prison of her fingers for a few more seconds in silence. Then she let it go. And in a tired voice she said loudly, "It is so nice to see you, even for such a short time, Hermes." More playfully, she added, "Make me some coffee, will you? I still have a few minutes."

Hermes left for the kitchen once more. He heard the heels going around the living room and sensed the aroma mixed with tobacco spreading throughout the apartment. When he came back, Kiki was sitting in the same seat.

"Nice apartment you have here," she said. "But you ought to take the dust sheets away. You're not being taken very good care of."

"I do most things myself," said Hermes.

"Washing and ironing?"

"No. I send them out."

"I must come one day and make some order here. You work too hard and you haven't got time to do it yourself."

"Oh, don't worry about me." Then he added, "I mean, this is a small apartment."

"I'll be back one day," Kiki said reassuringly. She had her last sip of coffee. "Now I really have to go." She stood up with determination, took the doll, and walked to the door. "But you'll see me again soon." She grabbed his hand desperately, puckered her lips, and blew him a kiss.

"Thank you for . . ." Hermes started to say, but she interrupted him instantly by reshaping her lips into a sign of silence and left.

Hermes came back to the computer, but before sitting down he looked out of the window at the darkening sky and the rolling clouds. He turned around and went to the hall. He opened the closet, went through his father's coats, picked up a battered trench coat, and examined it. He walked out of the apartment carrying the coat with him.

He headed toward the corner he usually stood at when he needed a taxi. At the kiosk he bought the last copy of the *Athens Gazette*. He leafed through it standing at the corner. His eye was caught by a title in the obituary section. It read: "Aby Wind, Billionaire, Archaeology Patron, Dies of Heart Failure. Leaves No Survivors." He turned to the classified announcements. There was no garage sale advertised.

Hermes continued on his way a block farther and stopped at a shop no more than five feet wide. The window was grimy. In it a printed sign on flimsy gray paper read "One Hour Dry Cleaning" in English and Greek. Exotic script had been added to the bottom with a ballpoint pen.

At the front part of the shop heaps of clothes were strewn on tables, on cardboard boxes, on the floor. Clean clothes on hangers were suspended overhead from hooks attached to strings on an elaborate system of lines and pulleys. Among them dangled half a dozen bird cages holding canaries. The birds were silent for the moment. At the back of the shop was an opening, partly covered with a faded, dirty red curtain. Behind the curtain there was darkness, the sound of agonizing machines, and a strong smell of gasoline.

At the center of this closed, tripartite universe of the shop, its proprietor lodged between an ironing board and a cash register. He was short, with fat, drooping shoulders. Long, black, wavy strips of hair greasily undulated around an expansive bald spot. He wore khaki shorts, a stained undershirt, and brown plastic sandals. The hair coming out of his armpits was wet.

Hermes stood in front of him holding the coat. The man looked at Hermes and said nothing.

"It just needs ironing," said Hermes.

The man did not respond. He grabbed a huge iron and brought it forcefully down onto what looked like a delicate woman's blouse. Hermes insisted, "Just ironing. Can I pick it up in an hour?"

The man looked at him angrily, grabbed the blouse and threw it behind him. Then he bent over a basket and picked up another even more fragile-looking piece of clothing.

Hermes said, "In an hour."

The man thumped his fist down hard on the ironing board.

"I do dry cleaning *and* ironing. And just forget those 'justs,' pal. Two hundred."

"Can I come back in an hour?" asked Hermes.

"Leave it here," the man growled.

"But the sign says it can be picked up in an hour."

"Leave that damn rag of yours here." He banged the ironing board with his open palm this time. "Stop playing around."

Hermes placed the coat where he was asked. "I need it for a trip. You're sure it can be done in an hour?"

"No answer," the man repeated, "I'm just not saying it won't be ready in an hour."

Hermes hesitated. "So it's a possibility," he said. He paid and turned around to leave.

Two young Africans loaded with enormous bags, like the ones used on ships for dirty linen, were trying to enter. Hermes gave them a hand as the proprietor stuffed Hermes's payment into the cash register, slamming the drawer shut with great force. Behind the two Africans came a skinny, pale man, inhaling the last draw from his cigarette and throwing it behind him in the street. Suddenly all the canaries started to sing inside the shop.

Blades, Handles, and Fur Cups

Hermes stepped out of the elevator. He found Nina in front of his apartment. She said, "I've been down several times to answer your telephone. It's been ringing a lot."

He unlocked the door and they both walked in. He took the dry cleaner's receipt from his coat pocket and left it on the dining room table.

"I shouldn't forget this. It's for my trench coat. I'm assuming it'll be ready in an hour."

"Who's been here?" Nina asked. She crinkled her nose.

"Nobody," Hermes said, irritated.

"Nobody?" she sniffed. "Strange. Are you growing lilies of the valley around here? Or is it camellias?"

Suspended up in the middle of the room, the bosomy volume of aroma that Kiki had neglected to take with her quivered slowly, sweetening the space, refusing to be diffused or vanish altogether.

"Did you have a good sleep?" he asked indifferently.

"Did you get the message to Melania?" she demanded.

"I was late for Melania. I was on time for Krypsiadis." He told her about Melania, about Krypsiadis.

She was neither frightened nor upset. Her face was stony hard but her eyes were restless, as restless as eyes can be. She said, "You see? It's getting late. They're getting tough. You think Krypsiadis will succeed?"

"We have a hypothesis. He probably has the means and the skills to test it."

"Will you go to Constantinople?"

"Yes."

"To set the bait as far as you can?"

He nodded.

"I know why you appeared so inactive all that time. At heart you're not a hunter. You're a fisherman!"

"I can't stand either analogy," he said impatiently.

She pursued him.

"Are you really relying only on our analogical inference, even though it is based on such weak matching? Crazy how Sherlock with Macbeth pulled such a far-out conclusion from such a chaotic mass of facts."

He smiled. "Indeed. It's quite a method. But you did quite a job yourself, recasting all the data and activating the analogy engine so effectively."

"I did a sloppy job, actually. I was pressed. I was just lucky. I didn't tell you—in the beginning I must have done something wrong. I had a strange experience. I thought I was just seeing things because I hadn't slept. The machine was running in circles, refusing to go beyond the source frame of data I wanted to match with the suspect's data. Eerie!"

"What did you do?"

"I switched off the computer and started again, lowering my matching expectations. This way, I thought, my search might start at some other point further away. It worked."

"You *were* lucky. Your search went into a crazy loop. You set up your analogy search in a such a way by mistake that your source data kept on matching themselves without realizing it. You should have safeguarded your system from falling into that. Next time . . ."

She interrupted him, "That was too much data for my matching procedure to go through. If I'd had more time, I would have thrown away lots of garbage. I shouldn't have let Sherlock and Macbeth waste time bumming around junk."

"But the truth is that a more meticulous job also would have applied lots of censors blocking infelicitous rules of inference and have prohibited the spectacular acrobatics across such distant frames that you got. Ultimately this would not have led you to a solution. You see, once more, it's a matter of circumscription, and a more constrained one might have ruled out a wild guess like the one you got."

"Is the moral of the story never to throw away your garbage, or that hobos make good investigators?"

"The moral is storage needs space and search time, and both are limited resources."

"Think what would have happened if we had matched the story of the peasant and his trio trying to cross the river. I wonder what that would have contributed to our problem." She laughed.

"A joke. In fact that is what jokes are all about, linking frames very far apart while censors are silent or out for lunch."

"You mean jokes are related to analogy, too."

"Of course."

"Could we add a joke inference engine to our system?"

"Sure. But then your system should be called Lewis Carroll or Freud rather than Euclid or Sherlock or Macbeth."

"Freud?"

"Freud wrote one of the best books about jokes."

"I thought Freud theorized only about the repression of sex."

"And jokes relate to censors and taboos."

"Is it possible to develop such a system, then?"

"Yes. But it takes more than analogical inference plus absence of censors to create funny things, like Freud's knives without handles and blades. You need procedures that actively seek the opposite to analogical inference."

"Disanalogous inference?" she asked. "Searching for mismatches, inviting dissimilarities between frames?"

"And a higher standing mental authority to examine mismatches and to distinguish between jokes and surrealistic art objects, objects like Meret Oppenheim's *Fur Cup*."

"What's that?"

"A teacup lined with fur."

Nina laughed.

"You see. You can look at it as a joke. But it's art. The mechanisms that produce them have a lot in common."

"I'd like to see a program capable of producing such garbage."

"Jokes and art are garbage?"

"They don't solve any problems."

"They do. They help to."

"You must be joking. How?"

"By making familiar things unfamiliar."

"That's absurd. You make things strange to confuse your enemies in enciphering, not to solve problems."

"That's true. Enciphering makes things strange but deciphering and problem solving need defamiliarization, too."

"Are you trying to convince me now that to solve a problem you have to abdicate knowledge by defamiliarizing analogies? That's negative thinking."

"Making the world strange is in a way the opposite of making it familiar, but it doesn't abdicate knowledge. It mobilizes it. You forgot circumscription. Getting out of routines, overcoming received presuppositions is circumscribing, part of problem solving. You know that famous nine-dot problem. You know why people fail to find the solution . . .?"

"I figured it out right away."

"Many people don't because as soon as they look at the dots, they're bound to the tacit assumption that they define a familiar square that circumscribes the area inside which the solution lies. If we were made to look at the nine dots as a strange world, outside the familiarity of the square, then the solution would have been easier."

"It seems like cheating to get out of the square."

"That's what Minsky called it. Conventions of problem solving assume an almost ethical appeal."

"And defamiliarization lasciviousness. Conclusion: Dirty jokes are exercises in problem solving. I wonder if we couldn't try to apply double analogy instead of a single one. One for solving, the other for circumscribing, one for familiarizing, the other for estranging."

"Thinking *is* like that. Like a knife, it has a cutting edge to cut through a knot with, to divide and conquer with. But it always needs a handle to give it power and direction, to connect it with a person and the rest of the world."

The telephone rang. Hermes rushed to pick up the receiver.

"No, this isn't a bakery," he said and hung up. "I have to go," he said gravely.

"Was this a joke or a delirium?"

"Right away."

"Has the moment to set the bait arrived?" she asked.

"We'll see."

"I hope there's no more backtracking. I'll stay here and work."

It was getting dark as Hermes arrived at the purple apartment house. There were few people around. It was as if the wind, stronger now, and the sudden drop in temperature had scared them all away.

An Emergency Meeting

The elevator stopped two floors before the top. He got out. Four doors surrounded the landing. One of them bore a large advertisement for a brand of miniature retractable scissors. People argued vociferously behind it. He turned to the stairway and started climbing fast and noiselessly to the last floor. There was no light. He felt his way to the door. He tapped at the panel lightly. The door opened instantly. Kiki Nikolaki stood in the opening. Votris was just behind her.

"Come in, come in," Votris whispered. He grabbed Hermes by the arm and led him through the side door of the hall to the kitchen. Kiki stared at Hermes without saying a word. Votris said, "Melania is suffering from some burns. But they're not serious. Elpis is in a state of shock. They're both in the hospital. Sophia's with them now. You realize, she is their sister. She wasn't there at the time of," he hesitated, "the accident." Then he added, "The villa has been destroyed." He pushed Hermes through a side door into a long dark corridor. He had difficulty breathing. The corridor was lined from floor to ceiling with piles of unbound magazines and pamphlets, tied neatly with jute string. They entered a large room. Kiki was left behind.

The room was crammed with complicated equipment resembling a museum of technology or a science-fiction laboratory. Floor and walls were carpeted. The door was, too. Even the ceiling was blocked up with some kind of insulation material. There were no windows, but the air was cool.

"It's very safe here," said Votris. "Nobody can hear us. It's information-leakproof. No instrument can penetrate it." He went back to the door to make sure it was completely shut. "We won't be asphyxiated. I have the best system of ventilation installed, a type used in modern submarines."

A huge round table, supported by six legs ending in bronze monopode lion's feet and covered with green leather, stood in the middle loaded with notes and books that were divided into three separate groups around three desk lamps. A fourth spot on the table was occupied by a violin. Next to the table beside the violin stood a sofa and in front of it, two deep, green leather armchairs. In the middle of the sofa sat, with a worried smile and a nervous tongue, Brigadier General Krypsiadis.

"We haven't failed," murmured Krypsiadis. "Only some material losses and some inconvenience, result of the horizon effect. We proceed to search through heuristic continuation." He stared at one of the lion's feet.

"It will never be the same again," Votris interjected. "But Phoebus," he cleared his throat, "I mean Brigadier General Krypsiadis, did a splendid job." And raising a bunch of papers in triumph, he exclaimed, "Ah. You're an incomparable methodologist, Phoebus."

Krypsiadis raised his eyebrows and lowered his eyelids modestly.

Two hours later Hermes emerged from the room, tucking an envelope into his shirt. Votris and Krypsiadis waltzed around him with great excitement, giving instructions.

"Hermes, my boy . . ." Votris hesitated. He looked at Hermes meaningfully. He swallowed. Then he continued, "Hermes, this idea of yours—I don't know if it is yours or your teachers' or your friends', about so-called nonmonotonic reasoning and analogy—it's full of fallacies."

Hermes turned to Votris, surprised. Votris resumed his advance.

"I'm afraid you're rediscovering the wheel. If all the trouble is about dealing with inadequate information, which in turn leads to uncertain beliefs rather than certain knowledge, then the answer is probability. Doesn't probability measure belief in a statement of fact related to the evidence in hand? You can express much more clearly all that you want to express about data with probability and decision theory, my boy. You don't need any new paradigms, as they call them, any neologisms. And what is this nonsense about 'all guns fire unless proved otherwise'?"

"That's because of circumstances when one doesn't have the time or the space to list all possible exceptions. And we want to provide for belief revisions in an ever-changing world," Hermes said dryly.

"Wonderfully said. Still, just a crooked way of saying 'The probability of a gun firing is such and such, between zero and one.' And I'm sure manufacturers, police, the army, and even serious crooks have the figure for you for the asking and that will account for belief revisions."

"But don't you see, by computing a probability number, you condense information about the evidence you have about a fact—which might be useful—but you also lose information about the origin of the information and the organization of your informers. This very information you have lost might be crucial for making a decision at a later stage of the process. As crucial as knowing the certainty of the fact."

Krypsiadis was at a loss, but Votris was inspired by the challenge. He countered cheerfully. "The mistake is clear: first you think you are excluding probability, which in fact comes back through the kitchen door."

At that moment the kitchen door opened, and Kiki entered the corridor holding a bag in her hand.

"Cheap effect." Then Votris resumed the attack. "You're still calculating coefficients of attributes of a belief, Hermes. You cannot avoid the problem of aggregation of individual choices. You can't avoid numbers or probabilities."

"But that was never the issue," Hermes protested. "The problem is to choose among alternative actions on the basis of information coming from different sources, of a different kind and from agents of clearly different credibility. Probability theory claims that the preference can be expressed by numbers. But how can we squeeze all kinds of information on which an action depends into one number expressing the reliability of your data together with the dubiousness of their sources? To say nothing of your confidence about the outcome of this action, which depends on doubtful sources."

Votris contested, "Haven't you heard about the market? They make those kinds of decisions every day out there. They express qualitative data in prices. What about parliaments? You'll find the same thing there. They do the same; they manifest qualitative attitudes by voting, and the votes are counted. One, two, three." Votris popped one, then two, then three fingers up in the air and went on. "Why can these new knowledge-based systems, based on statements extracted by psychoanalyzing experts, tell you anything more about the certainty of a given piece of information or of an outcome? Why are they more trustworthy than inferring the probability of facts directly from data or from observation, sampling, scenarios, and agreement and disagreement of points of view, always related straight to data."

"The market model. It appears to be determinable by few rules extracted out of masses of data. But it is not a model. Such extrapolations can break down any moment. It is not a predictable system. The same goes with a very large number of chaotic domains within which we exist," said Hermes.

"You mentioned chaos. There's a misunderstanding here," argued Votris. "Next time we'll go over it. In fact I hope you'll have changed your mind by then."

Hermes offered his hand.

Votris grabbed it. He looked jubilant once more and kept talking. "You see, Hermes, I've been following you. I've been giving a lot of thought to your project. What your friends have been doing is coming close to being exhausted. The situation will rapidly change. Your friends have been too much and too long under the influence of Descartes. Great scientist, but he advocated a very limited method, seductive as it was. He looked at the world in terms of cut-out domains that in turn can be cut further into parts that then have to be represented symbolically, analytically, logically, syntactically, through a corresponding formal theory. The approach never succeeded. It never will. A redirection is needed. The world is not facts and parts. The world is things and a whole. I clearly foresee a return to Spinoza. *There* is a great philosopher. I remember, it was the nineteen-twenties. No. Your father wasn't there. Yes. An overcrowded lecture. I will never forget how Einstein spoke of Spinoza and of his ideas.

How close he felt to him. For Spinoza, thinking was *in* the world and *of* the world, and *not about* it. Thinking has no other structure than what is given to it *by* the world. It is stated in his *Ethics.* 'The order and connection of ideas is the same as the order and connection of things.' Profound and clear. You must be thinking, of course, that I am finally becoming a mystic, or worse, a holistic phenomenologist," Votris continued. "Far from it. What I want to say is that the brain doesn't need any alphabet of concepts or physical symbol systems or inference rules to do its job. Forms *emerge* in the mind out of the world, just as when, during that sleepless stormy night I spent in the Alps I told you about, I saw shapes and objects emerge out of molecules of water and out of their local rules, a whole universe of shapes and objects, snowflakes into spinning, twirling, swaying patterns, patterns of pinwheel garnets, crystals, icicles. That's how symbolic thoughts emerge, but always as an outcome, as a result and not as a beginning. Like those patterns, symbolic thinking is a behavior. It's a replicating behavior emerging inside the brain, our information processing apparatus."

"Hermes has to go," said Kiki with an air of urgency and determination.

"Of course, of course," apologized Votris. "This isn't the time to resolve our differences. You must get going. One last thing. Be very careful with this Golden Thinking Machine. You have in your hands possibly the most important archaeological find of the century." He pointed to the envelope in Hermes' shirt. "When it comes to practice, you are the master. I couldn't make head or tail of it. Neither could Phoebus here."

Everyone turned to Krypsiadis. Krypsiadis shrugged his shoulders and smiled sadly.

Kiki handed Hermes a shopping bag. It bore the advertisement of a brand of imported retractable scissors.

"This is your cover," she said simply.

"I understand," said Hermes.

Krypsiadis whispered. "Rules are essential. Remember. Method!"

But Kiki was already leading Hermes back to the kitchen through the dark corridor before Krypsiadis had finished his phrase. The two men stood behind in the illuminated laboratory. They suddenly became solemn. The departure had something of a farewell to it.

Hermes walked down the two flights of stairs he had walked up a short while before. He pressed the button for the elevator. Behind the door with the scissors advertisement on it, people were still arguing. Voices rose and died in waves. The door half opened. The elevator arrived and he got in.

It started descending. Hermes stared at the two screens bypassing each other, the grid of the metallic cage of the shaft that seemed to go up, the grid of the metallic cage of the cabin that seemed to stand still. Votris was trying to make him believe that he did not want him to believe him. He wondered whether Votris could have eavesdropped on his discussion with Nina, thought about how very unlikely it was that Votris had referred as if by chance to all the points of the talk that he and Nina had had on "nonmonotonic reasoning" and analogy. He was still wondering, as the elevator slid down the slim well, if there was any reason after all to doubt that Votris was eavesdropping, and if there was anything else that had to be cleared up before getting into how the bugging had been orchestrated. The orchestrating must have taken several people, and who could have planted the bugs, considering that Kiki's visit took place after he and Nina had had their discussion about analogy and nonmonotonic reasoning, why had Votris let him know that he had been following them secretly, why had Votris tried to make him believe he wanted him not to believe him. His wonderings stopped. Grid rested over grid. The lift came to a halt with a jerk and a clang.

Outside, the shops had already closed and the streets were empty. No parked cars with loitering drivers and no casual bystanders. The wind was rolling torn newspapers, boxes, shreds of plastic, along the sidewalk, knocking the lamps that hung over the intersections back and forth, sending long shadows across the silent facades then pulling them back. A hollow can tumbled toward Hermes' feet. He felt the envelope under his shirt. Thunder died away toward the north and he hastened his step.

Breaking the Code

It had started to rain by the time Hermes reached the apartment. Nina was gone. A window had been left unlatched. The shutter had hit a small table and knocked down a glass, which lay shattered on the floor. Hermes shut all the windows. He pulled down the shades and drew the curtains. He got the envelope out of his shirt and left it next to the laptop. He pulled up a stool. The doorbell rang. He slipped the envelope back into his shirt. He neared the door silently. He stood behind it, listening. The doorbell rang again.

"Open up. If you don't, you'll have to go to Constantinople in rags."

He unlocked the door and Nina stepped in, trench coat over her arm.

"I saw the receipt on the table. I thought I'd pick it up for you." She threw the coat on a chair. "It was hardly worth the money. Pfff. He fixed the hem though. He said it needed mending and he did it for free."

Hermes took the coat and hung it up. "I hadn't noticed it needed mending."

"You've shut all the windows. It smells like a library in here."

"The wind," he said, adding, "they may be snooping from across the street and I have work to do."

He took the envelope out of his shirt again, tore it open, and laid the pages on the dining room table again.

"What's that?"

"I have work to do," he repeated.

"Back to cryptarithmetic?" she asked, taunting.

"Deciphering," he corrected her, "and I haven't even started yet."

"Another demonstration?"

"An application."

He had turned his back to her. She said. "Hermes? Aren't we in this together?"

He didn't answer. He placed the papers next to the computer.

"Are you angry I asked you who was here?"

He still didn't answer.

"Who was it?" she insisted.

"What difference does it make. Is it to complete your detective world knowledge model?"

"Hermes," she said, and there was bitterness and victory in her voice. "Somebody *was* here. Somebody came and dropped listening devices in the apartment. And she was a woman who smoked and used lipstick."

"You searching my wastebasket now?" He was ready to explode but nevertheless said in a tempered tone, "What's this about devices?"

She took three tiny brown objects out of her pocket and presented them to him in her open palm. "These are microphones. I deactivated them. She planted them."

"Where?"

"Under the table, here," she pointed at the table the computer was on, "under your bed, your *bed,* and even one in the bathroom. Disgusting."

"Jesus," said Hermes. "How on earth did you find out about them?"

"I've been checking for them ever since you arrived in Athens. I knew it would happen sooner or later."

"And how did you know where to search and what they looked like?"

"You're my client and I'm a professional."

"Cut it out," Hermes said brutally. "How did you know?"

"One of the assistants showed me in the lab. He knew all about them. He'd worked for a private agency."

"And he wanted to impress you," he said sarcastically. "And you believed him."

"Of course. Don't you think it has proved very practical? Why don't *you* trust *me*?"

"But I do."

"But you don't. You hid from me that Gerald was killed."

Hermes was taken by surprise. "How did you find out?"

"It was elementary. Reviewing the newspapers for relevant contextual facts for my data base, I found a complete description of the villa, the car, the body. It fit what you told me about your first trip to the Villa Euridice."

"How did you know I knew?"

"By the way you avoided speaking about it. I saw the corpse reflected in your eyes."

"Aren't you getting a little melodramatic?"

"Those are the facts. Why did you try to hide them?"

"You were already getting paranoid about everything else."

"That's not how one thinks about a collaborator. In this tracing you have been having me follow your footsteps. But you've also been covering your own tracks. Why are you angry? You ought to be grateful."

"Nina," his tone was changing, "of course I trust you, of course I'm grateful, of course we collaborate. I'm just angry at my slowness and I'm tense because this has arrived and it's lots of work." He pointed at the papers.

"How did you get them. What are they?"

"Krypsiadis intercepted them. I mean Kiki. It's a message."

"Kiki, his assistant?"

Hermes nodded. "She's the woman who was here."

"I should have known. That perfume! Krypsiadis really wants to keep an eye and an ear on everything."

"So does everybody else around here." He turned to the pages on the table.

"I see," said Nina, looking at the papers approvingly. "Good. The plot thickens."

"Yes, it does."

"Is the message from . . . ?"

"Yes. It's from him."

"Who's it to?"

"We don't know. It was sent to a nameless telex number."

"Is this what we've been waiting for?"

"Maybe. It might be just a business message. But it's the only long enciphered message sent, according to Kiki's books. You see, Krypsiadis keeps track of all the enciphered telexes that pass through there."

"What now?"

"It all depends on the message."

"What if you cannot decipher it?"

"I *will* decipher it."

"What if the message says nothing?"

He shrugged his shoulders.

"Will you backtrack?"

He stared at her and said nothing.

"Will you give up?"

"No. At least for the moment."

"Can you really rely so much on a hypothesis produced by such bizarre means, such low, low compatibility?"

Hermes went on, minutely adjusting the angle of the screen and the position of the computer on the table like a pianist before a concert.

"There must be something more."

He examined the screen carefully.

"There must be," she insisted. "You have to tell me what other support you have. You're hiding a clue."

He started to talk as if reading from the blank plasma surface:

"We were sophomores. In early April that year, T., you know who I mean"—Nina nodded—"was still alive, still venerated universally, still giving the occasional lecture. He was supposed to give a talk at the A. in Boston. The talk had been announced six months in advance."

He went on: "We were a small, tight-knit group, fascinated by what we called Mind Worlds. Naturally, the prospect of T.'s visit had excited us very much. We'd even joked about inviting T. for a late beer to Mather House, our house. Then a rather uncommon thing occurred. Esther, one of our inner circle, decided to write to T. She actually invited him. In addition to describing our admiration for his work and providing a detailed agenda for our eventual discussion with him, she enclosed a paper I had written that fall. The paper was one of my first algorithms and it had received some attention. She told us about her invitation, but not about the contents of her letter.

"Days went by and we waited. Paul, who was another member of our group, one of my roommates, and Esther's boyfriend, was delegated to pick up Esther's mail everyday. Much to his surprise, he found an answer from T. Paul took the letter to his room and, as he confessed to me afterward, he decided to keep it, to give it to Esther later that night in a kind of public ceremony. We'd all planned to get together for dinner.

"When he went back to his room, a few hours after, he couldn't find the letter. He didn't dare tell Esther, and as far as I know, she never found out. A few weeks later, we were all preparing for the summer. It was chaos. It was for this occasion that I'd developed an algorithm on how to pack—later I even wrote a program, KNAPSACK, for the same purpose. I gave it as an end-of-the-year present to my other roommate. In exchange, this other roommate gave me a book. I remember it was Gide's *The Counterfeiters*, a book he had been very much taken by. It was inside this book that I found the letter, *the* letter. Apparently he had given me his own copy of Gide by mistake. In the letter T. had accepted Esther's invitation. He had responded to all the points in her letter. He had even written that he was particularly interested in meeting me.

"I've never talked to anyone about finding this letter till now. I didn't even pay much attention to it at the time. T. died a month after this visit. It was a difficult spring for me. In fact I'd almost forgotten about the whole thing until yesterday, when I was having lunch with Robert. I was mentioning how much I admired Minsky, and he reacted by saying something about my always being fixated on father figures.

"The phrase itself meant nothing special to me, but there was something special about it nevertheless, the tone he used. It gave me a feeling of *déjà vu*. It wasn't so much the words as the tone and intensity. They reminded me of that other time. The night we attended T.'s lecture, I had been fascinated and had said so to our group. One roommate, who had been silent all evening, turned and said something about always 'being fixated on father figures.' What had been remarkable about the utterance, again, had not been the words themselves so much as their tone and intensity. They are what have always remained with me. That roommate was Robert."

"I see. Double analogy," she said.

Hermes shook his head slowly. "Two independently produced ones."

"I'll never forget the moment I turned my eyes to the screen and there was that matching, 'Donald, Gerald, and Robert,' the gang ring identified, thanks to that distant cryptarithmetic example you showed me in the beginning of our discussions and that I almost erased. Funny, they did come in a threesome in the end. And Robert, as the sum of the two others, part of the same whole.

"Yes. Robert," Hermes repeated.

"And Gerald is gone now."

"Uh huh."

"Do you have any idea who killed him?"

"I'm almost certain it was Pat. Pat thought Gerald had the evidence against him that could have destroyed him."

"How did he know?" she asked, looking at Hermes in the eyes.

Hermes shrugged.

"You gave him away, Hermes."

Hermes simply stared at her.

"I heard you giving him away on the phone that day to Robert. You gave him away to the person who was tapping your line. You knew your phone was tapped. I heard you. You were insisting that the man you met knew and was going to reveal who murdered Philippos. So Gerald is dead and Pat's dead, too."

Hermes shrugged again. Nina kept looking him in the eyes. She said, "I know it was the only way you could find them, making one fight the other, dividing each part of the problem, solving it separately. Divide and conquer by analogy."

"Well, not exactly," he replied.

"Again the matching is low," she said.

Hermes smiled and went back to his papers.

"So how long will it take to decipher the text?" she asked.

"I don't know, that's the problem. It might take some time. Hours. Maybe days. We have to start right away. And," he looked at her, "we are together in this."

He went over the pages on the table one by one, several times. Every now and then he wrote in the machine. Lists of groups of letters and matrices started appearing on the screen. Nina tiptoed out of the room, bolted the door, continued on to the kitchen, and returned with a bowl full of fruit that she left next to the computer. Then she took a chair next to him.

Heavy raindrops began to flog the shutters.

All Wrapped Up

Hermes eased himself out from under Nina's head. Gently he placed a pillow under it and stood up. He went out onto the balcony. The rain had stopped. The day was breaking, but a different kind of darkness was descending as more clouds drew in just over the television antennas of apartment roofs. A strong smell of ozone was in the air.

He came in from the balcony, passed the study, and went into the bedroom. He chose a few clothes from the closet, threw them on his bed, picked up his knapsack, folded the clothes, and put them in. He brought his packed knapsack to the dining room and left it on the floor. The laptop stood in the middle of the table, its display panel upright like an open, saluting hand. Scattered next to it were the telex pages. He turned on the machine, sat down in front of it, and typed in some commands. "It's all here," he murmured to the screen, holding the machine with both hands as if to congratulate it.

He looked at the knapsack, at his watch, and switched off the laptop. He no longer smiled. He collected the telex pages and hastened to the kitchen, pages in hand.

He set fire to the papers in the sink, one after the other.

"It smells of smoke in here. What are you doing?" Nina stood at the door holding his trench coat in her arms.

"The telex," he said simply.

"I see." She smiled. "It's getting more like a true spy story every minute. We must be close to the climax. They always burn something before the end."

"The code books! We don't have any!" He gathered the ashes carefully and flushed them down the toilet.

"Is everything OK with the deciphering?"

"I checked it once again. It all fits together perfectly."

"Hermes," she said, "I'm sorry I went to sleep. I thought there was nothing more to do."

"There wasn't. I was just confirming what we'd already found. We still have an hour to go."

"We're not done yet," she said.

"I know," he said. He made certain the kitchen window was shut.

She glanced at him. "I don't mean the detection."

"Neither do I." He tried the handles once more.

She went on, "We have a long way to go. And I can't believe how far we've already come. Of course *I* also anticipated the use of analogy when I tried to apply it from the first day, using the dangerous crossing problem as a source. Do you remember?"

He went around closing the drawers now while talking. "Of course. Well. That's Martin's Law. You can't learn anything unless you almost know it already."

She said, as if talking to herself, "Maybe we should have stayed there where we started and elaborated on analogy only."

He made certain the kitchen door to the balcony was locked. "But then you would never have learned how to represent all these data to feed your analogical engine with."

"Still, I have a strange feeling. I don't know how much of what is to come is based on what we've covered."

He stopped moving around and looked at her. "You mean now that the time for testing and action has arrived, you're worried that Sherlock 2000's value was just theoretical?"

"No. It isn't that. I want to understand the plan of your program," Nina demanded. "I have a feeling it was written in a funny way. It didn't build chapter on chapter cumulatively. It kept building and destroying. It forced me to do simple-minded, not just simple, things and then it overturned everything and made me start again. Strange. Sometimes I thought I was going through some kind of history of the field."

"That's not history. We just followed a chronology that had an implicit order of how things happened. History explains why things occurred the way they did."

"Was it what's-his-name Black's fault?"

"Black's fault? He never thought his Method Thesaurus was anything but a demonstration of tools. But don't you find negative experiences, mistakes, are often more instructive than positive ones."

She shrugged. "My feeling is that if a system like that is going to have common sense to cope with real-life problems, it has to be programmed in another way. Certainly not the way I did it, weaving together data day and night, trying to input the whole insanity of Athens in the machine memory, one fact statement at a time."

"What do you propose?"

"Probably develop a system that can learn about facts the way people do, just by *experiencing* facts."

"That would probably take an altogether different kind of representation system from the one we have used. I believe there is room for many complementary approaches. After all, the mind uses many strategies simultaneously."

"You know, I had a dream."

Hermes looked at her as if he had never heard of people dreaming before.

"It was an incredible dream. Incredible. We had left together, for America. We were living in Manhattan. It was all skyscrapers, avenues, highways, bridges, subways, and crowds, lights and crowds everywhere in an enormous cube. Suddenly I realized we were inside the connection machine you talked about as I was going to sleep last night. I saw it all working, the processes, the memory, the parallel data paths, the general network, the flags, the trees, the butterflies, and we were inside it, we were running up and down in all three directions, through the wires, the cells, the strings, the arrays, the matrices, never in one location, we were in many points at the same time. You said, 'This is how the brain is made. Let's do some archaeology now a thousand times a second. Let's think backward.' It was all very strange. There was no distance between places or events, no gravity. There was freedom."

Hermes said simply, "There's still a lot to do. Deciphering that text was only a preliminary."

"And after it's all over, what will we do? I want to see Manhattan. I want to work with the connection machine. I want to go away from the obscurity here, these evil people who have been doing terrible things to you. There is no meanness in Manhattan." He stared at her. She went on, "No tapping, no bugging, no tailing, no stupidity." She was shivering. "Look what they've done to you here." She showed the coat she was holding. "I just found it."

"I don't see anything," he said.

"Look at this," she shoved the hem of the coat close to his eyes.

"I still don't see anything."

"Here. Inside." She pulled part of the hem wide open.

"What's that?"

"Another transmitter." She handed him the small round object.

"You mean. . . "

"Yes. To keep track of you."

"How on earth did you think of searching for that too?"

"I have my own hunches. There was something spooky about your dry cleaner after what he said."

"What did he say?"

"He asked whether you were going to use the coat yourself. That's bizarre. The dumb pimp was dying of curiosity. It was obvious. He couldn't keep his mouth shut."

A lightning bolt came down near the building. It was raining hard again. They walked to the living room.

"You think he did it?"

"Probably not. They just asked to borrow the coat and then paid him for it. He suspected they had done something to it."

He took the transmitter and looked at it carefully.

She asked, "Are they the same ones who hired Kiki to plant the mikes here? Krypsiadis Inc.?"

He said, "They might be. But I can think of at least three other interest groups who might have done it." He gave her back the bug. "Put it back where it was." Then he added, "That was clever. Very clever, Nina." His eyes flashed. He continued excitedly, "We'll play an old trick. I won't even bother to cover up my traces. I'll make them follow my path and the closer they follow, the farther away I'll be. It'll be a great laugh." Hermes seemed almost ecstatic.

"What will you do?" she insisted.

He did not answer. He rushed to the closet, humming. He pulled out another coat exactly the same as the one she still held in her hands, only slightly more wrinkled and with a stain on the right side.

"My father owned everything in pairs. I'll wear this one." He put on the coat. "You wear my extra pair of pants and shoes."

He brought his extra pair of pants and a pair of sneakers from his bedroom. There was a second crackle of lighting, more distant now.

"I love it." Nina was beaming.

"You need a hat." He disappeared into the kitchen. He came back with two plastic bags. She already had on the pants and the sneakers, and she was putting on the trench coat. He handed her one of the bags. "It was the best I could get," he said.

She put one bag on her head and he the other one on his. "Wow! This is great." They took off the bags at the same time and looked in the mirror again.

"No wonder they say we look alike," she said. Then she recited, "With our plastic face coverings that turn us into two of the most truculent figures in Athens."

He said in a busy tone, "When you leave here, head toward downtown on foot and keep going. Don't try to shake them off. Try to keep them busy for three hours. That's all I need."

She sighed. "And what if I didn't exist? What would you have done?"

He smiled. "I would have invented my double. I would have found a way of making them follow my traces in the opposite direction."

She laughed. "Wearing your soles backward. But how can you do that with electronic tracing?"

"There are modern ways of being a trickster, by making your opponent think the means are the goal."

"Great Hermes. Will you bring back the Golden Thinking Machine to the house, like Philippos?"

"Off you go," was his response.

She put the plastic bag on again and pulled it down to her chin.

Hermes unlocked the door. "See you later in the afternoon," he whispered.

She leaned over, pressed her plastic-covered head on his cheek, and rushed out of the apartment. He closed the door and sat down.

He lingered momentarily, eyes wide open, fists closed tight, his knuckles turned white. Then he left the hall.

In the bathroom he searched in the first-aid kit. He found two rolls of bandages, some gauze, and surgical tape and put them into his deep coat pockets. Back in the kitchen he found a hammer and a screwdriver and put them into his coat pockets too. He picked up a card from the study, jotted something down on it, and put it in his breast pocket. He put the plastic bag on his head and left the house.

The rain was coming down hard again. The street lamps were still on. It appeared darker, as if the day wouldn't try to take over that morning, giving its place to the night without a fight. The van was still there across from the apartment entrance. There did not seem to be anybody around.

In less than a few minutes he arrived at the big hospital. It occupied two whole blocks, not very far from his apartment. There was some movement at the emergency entrance. A taxi arrived with a woman lying on the back seat. A driver was talking to the porter. A group of young women, night nurses, were leaving through the narrow side gate, talking about the rain. Two young doctors were debating. No one took any notice of Hermes, who slipped through the gate and the hall and down the stairs to the lower levels.

Much activity was also taking place at that level, marked *B-Laboratories.* Patients were being brought in on stretchers and in wheelchairs. Others just walked in, unaided. Doctors, nurses, and technicians were milling around. Hermes continued down the long corridor carrying the plastic bag. At the very end a sign on a door read *Fire Emergency Equipment.* He tried the door, entered, and shut it behind his back.

He pulled the bandages out of his pocket and wrapped them around his head, fast, methodically, tightly, using the surgical tape to secure them. He covered everything, leaving only a small opening for the eyes, another for the nose, and one for the mouth. He took off his coat and put it in his plastic bag. Then he opened the door and walked briskly out in the direction of the big poison-green exit sign, still carrying the plastic bag with his coat in it.

He emerged at the other side of the block he had entered. It was the main gate. There were marble steps, wet and slippery under his feet, and a row of taxis at the end of the monumental stairway. The drivers were standing arguing under the hospitable metallic marquee of the old café across the street. One rushed to help him into the first taxi in line. He opened the door of the car and tried to take hold of the plastic bag, but Hermes held on to it.

"That's quite a job," said the driver. "I'm sorry," he added. "Car accident? Where do we go from here?"

Hermes took a card with something written on it out of his pocket and handed it to the driver.

"Psychiko!" exclaimed the driver, and he started the engine.

Meltdown

The taxi drove almost to the apex of the hill, much higher than any of the other houses in Psychiko Hermes had visited, at the very edge of the suburb toward the west. The driver volunteered once more to help Hermes, but Hermes signaled he could take care of himself. The taxi went away, and Hermes disappeared behind the thick bushes at the side of the street. When he came out, there were no bandages on his face and he was wearing his trench coat again. He drifted one street lower and walked north for five minutes. Finally he stopped in front of a garden with big banana trees at the entrance. He passed the gate and took some steps downhill.

A spectacular panorama of the city was framed by tall pine trees. Clouds were still hanging over Attica, but in places gaps had opened up toward Mount Penteli, and a silver morning light was shooting through them. Ricochets of rainwater were running down from the top of the hill, down toward a group of tall trees through which gleamed a two-story, white, prismatic house.

Indifferently, like an inspector from the utilities company, he went straight to the door of the house. He rang the bell several times; there was no answer. The glass panels in the door reflected the sun rising low between the mountain slopes, under the clouds. He shut his eyes to avoid the blaze of light. At that moment, one after another, as if in the chorus of an ancient tragedy, the cicadas started intoning in their slow, insistent way.

He walked along the walls of the house, glancing at the windows one after the other. They all appeared securely shut. At the bottom, at the back of the building, there was a small, semicircular terrace. A cage-like pergola covered the whole space. Thick vines had grown over the gridded sides and the roof. The grapes that hung down from the roof were heavy with juice. It was a dark and dank spot, but it would have been bright and light around the marble-topped table on a summer night. Empty metal chairs surrounded the table now, and its top had gathered a layer of dead leaves. A sparrow landed on it, searched furtively through the leaves, took a quick side look at Hermes, and flew away.

Hermes tried the door that faced the terrace. It was also locked. He rested his plastic bag on the marble table and fished out a screwdriver, a hammer, and a bandage. He wrapped the bandage around the head of the hammer and secured it with surgical tape, the same bandage and tape he had used for covering his face an hour ago. He thrust the screwdriver next to the padlock and started pounding with the hammer. The door gave easily.

It was a square, comfortable, clean kitchen. Somebody had prepared ham and eggs but had eaten only half of it. Hermes started by inspecting every cupboard, every drawer, every box and jar. Then came the oven, the refrigerator, and the washing machine, including their mechanisms. From the kitchen he moved to the rest of the ground floor. It did not take him long to search the sparsely furnished living and dining room, the den, the small reception room—with no furniture—and finally, the main entrance hall.

The plan was easy to follow. The spaces succeeded each other like the episodes of a story that, although read for the first time, appear to obey a familiar plot arrangement.

He climbed the stairs. The landing was bordered by four doors. Only one was shut. He opened it and found narrow concrete steps leading down to the terrace. There was nothing there. He came back and continued his search of the rooms. The first was a bathroom.

Somebody had taken a shower not long ago. There was still water on the floor. The scent of shampoo, after-shave lotion, and strong lavender perfume levitated over it. The toiletry props lay on a chrome-topped table next to the basin. The pouch on the side was empty. Aside from the cosmetics there was little to examine. A photography magazine next to the toilet, a green sun visor on the top of it. A pair of white plastic slippers sitting next to each other. His fingers touched where the toes would have been. A blue-and-white striped towel hanging on the back of the door. He ran his hand along its damp sides. A yellow robe hanging from a hook on the wall. He reached inside its pockets. Nothing. There was nothing under the wet bath rug either. He checked the toilet lid, then around and inside the toilet bowl. Again nothing.

Ransacking is like concealing, thought out in a mirror. Both processes share the same constraints. The algorithm of the first is the reverse of the second. The same goes for the process of language use and acquisition of language, or for sound motivation and music interpretation.

Hermes went on, systematically retracing the possible steps, probable countersteps, placing himself in his quarry's frame inversely. Increasingly his face reflected what might be the other's facial expressions.

So this is what frisking is all about. Suddenly the spark of the thrill was gone. He moved around touching only whatever was necessary for the search, as if his hands, his feet, his eyes were polluting the place and were being polluted by intimacy with the body of a stranger.

Next to the bathroom was a bedroom, tiny, like a child's. It seemed that only one person had stayed in it, and that he had left in a hurry. The closet was open. A cream-colored linen suit and a few shirts were hung neatly inside. He went through them. The socks and underwear in the two pulled-out drawers, next to the closet, were in disarray, and silk pajamas were on the floor. The owner of the clothes had indeed been in a hurry. Of course he meant to return soon. The black leather attaché case that lay in the middle of the unmade bed was open. There was nothing in it but a small plain yellow metal bar, a bar that shone brilliantly in the damp morning light, a bar melted down crudely. Hermes raised it just a foot above the leather case. It was heavy. He put it back.

It was pure gold.

The other two rooms did not appear to have been used for a long time and he went through them fast. On his way to the stairs he noticed another green sun visor on the floor. He hurried back to the kitchen.

Back in the kitchen, he tried to force the lock to the door back into place. He succeeded. Using a paper napkin, he swept all the wood debris from the floor meticulously and put it in his plastic bag together with his tools and bandages. Fortunately, the door closed easily behind him. It started drizzling again. He reached the street and walked at a steady pace toward the top of the hill. When he reached the highest point, he encountered the ring road, turned left, and continued for a quarter of a mile. Then at the first major intersection he descended toward the highway, still holding onto his plastic bag. Rain came down at intervals, as if hesitating what to do next.

An hour later he was stepping out of his apartment house, carrying only his knapsack.

At the Airport

Crowds had descended upon the airport that Saturday afternoon. It took Hermes a great effort to reach the ticket counter. No Robert. But all was in order with the reservation and the ticket.

"Smoking or nonsmoking?" the attendant asked.

"No smoking, please," he said.

Hermes sensed a tapping on his back. He turned around. An enormous man with a well-shaved head and a badly shaved face, holding a wooden trunk in each hand, was moving his bushy eyebrows up and down. He eyed Hermes piercingly.

"Any baggage?" the attendant asked.

"Yes," said the enormous man.

"This is all I'm taking." Hermes raised his knapsack.

The woman smiled. "You travel light."

"Yes," insisted the enormous man, lifting both wooden trunks above his head.

"It's only a short trip," said Hermes.

"You never know," she sighed.

"Yes," insisted the enormous man, while Hermes moved on to passport control.

He had taken only a few steps when Robert's driver emerged, out of breath.

"Mr. Robert had to pick up two registered parcels at the last minute. He asked me if you could take this with you for him on the plane." He handed Hermes a black attaché case. "Mr. Robert will have to carry the parcels onto the plane. He's afraid they won't let him take his case along too."

"Sure," said Hermes.

"Perfect," said the driver. "Mr. Robert's already checked in. He said you should go on ahead to the gate. He might not get there until the very last minute."

Hermes, both hands occupied, headed toward Passport Control.

He was passing the passport inspection when he heard a cheerful voice exclaim, "Yoohoo! Hermes!" The Institute librarian's face stuck out in the crowd. "I heard you were taking some time off. I'm on vacation, too. And we're going to the same place. Imagine! Let's rent a boat together and visit the nineteenth-century villas on the Bosporus. It'll be such *fun*!"

"See you later," said Hermes waving only the fingers of his hand and smiling thinly. "I have to go to the washroom now."

When he returned to the main hall, there was no trace of the librarian. He approached the security check point. A tall, dark, mustachioed guard was helping the passengers put their luggage onto the conveyer belt to be X-rayed. "Your knapsack first, sir," he said. The knapsack started entering the scanning machine.

"Now the attaché case." He took the case. Then he whispered to him, "Step to the side please. I'd prefer to hold on to this, sir. I'm sure you'll agree with me."

Hermes turned to him. "What?"

"We know you're trying to smuggle a stolen archaeological treasure," said the guard politely.

"What are you talking about?"

"I think you know, sir. Would you please step to the side."

A queue of passengers was lining up behind Hermes.

"I don't know what you're talking about."

"Please step to the side, sir."

Hermes went on the side of the machine. A second guard came up to take the place of the first.

"This bag contains a stolen treasure," declared the guard. "Understand now?"

"No," answered Hermes stubbornly.

"I'm obliged to ask the police to come unless . . ."

"Unless what?"

"You see, now you understand," smiled the guard. "Unless you decide to cooperate and follow me to the office."

"Cooperate?"

"It's getting late, sir. I have been asked to tell you that if you refuse it won't be like the previous times."

"I want my luggage back."

"There's murder, too." There was menace in the guard's eyes.

"My luggage."

The guard put the attaché case on the belt next to the opening of the X-ray box but wouldn't let it go. Hermes pushed it forcefully through the opening. The guard could not catch it. It was all done very quietly, as if there had been no dispute and no force applied. The second guard grabbed the case from the other side. He turned to the first. "There's a funny metal object inside. Have a look?"

"My case," said Hermes.

The first guard said, "I think we've got something here."

Right at that moment a big man in short sleeves who had been standing and smoking a cigarette, looking absentmindedly over the hall, came closer.

"What's going on here? Give me this case," he ordered the guard.

"There's something strange inside. It appears to be an antique of some sort," apologized the guard. Then turning to Hermes, "Are you sure you want to take this bag?"

"You're out of your mind. Where's the police!" shouted Hermes.

"We have to call a customs officer," said the plainclothes man. "I'm anti-terrorist squad."

"I only have gold," said Hermes. "I'm entitled to."

"Not if it's in the form of antiquities," insisted the guard. He was joined by two more of his colleagues. More people were gathering around them as they continued arguing.

The plainclothesman said to the crowd nervously, "Keep moving." He pushed Hermes and the guard to the side and grabbed the attaché case. Another cigarette-puffing, stocky, short-sleeved man arrived.

"Get a customs officer," said the first short-sleeved man.

A customs woman arrived, fat, solemn, authoritarian.

"I would like to take some gold out of the country with me," said Hermes calmly. "This man insists I'm smuggling antiquities." He pointed to the guard.

"Give me the briefcase," demanded the woman, and she tucked it under her generous arm. She carefully placed the briefcase on an empty table farther down. The others followed.

"Get back! Let me breathe," she commanded, extending her arms and opening up a space around herself. Everybody stepped back as if they had been pushed, including the plainclothesmen. "You," she ordered, looking at Hermes, "Come closer. What are you declaring?"

"Gold."

"What did you find?" she asked the guard.

"Antiquities."

"Open it."

Hermes tried. The case was unlocked. Inside was only a folded red towel. The woman took it out and unfolded it. She revealed a shiny gold bar.

"This is no antique," she said flatly.

A representative of the airlines, a stewardess, and three assistants emerged.

The woman continued "You can't take gold like that out of the country, antique or modern. You need to apply to the Bank of Greece."

"It's Saturday today," Hermes protested.

"That makes no difference to me. I need a permit." The three customs officers nodded in support of the statement.

"I'll call the director of the Bank of Greece," threatened Hermes.

"You can call the Archbishop if it pleases you," said the woman, without a flicker of smile. The customs officers approved again.

"Where's a phone?"

"Right over there," said a plainclothesman and pointed toward a small booth nearby. Hermes went over to it. The woman stayed behind holding the gold bar in the red towel and arguing with her colleagues.

Hermes dialed. "I'm glad I got you . . . Yeah, it's me. I'm at the airport . . . I need your help . . . It's urgent . . . I'll explain everything . . . In the Customs Office in the departure hall. That's right . . . I'll stay here. Thanks." He hung up. The woman and her companions were approaching.

Hermes came out of the booth sweating.

"There's no air in there," he said.

They ignored the remark. One of them said, "Let's make some things clear. What's your destination?"

"Constantinople," answered Hermes.

"You just missed your flight," said the representative of the airlines, looking at his big watch.

Hermes did not appear shaken.

"Don't you mind?"

"Not really," said Hermes.

"Wait a second," said one of the customs men. "How come you're not concerned?"

"What's your job?" asked the first.

"Cognitive scientist."

The men looked at each other.

"May I see your passport," said the woman. She opened a wide palm under Hermes's chin. At that moment a man in a dark suit, dark glasses, and a deep blue tie approached from the direction of the passport control point. The woman seemed to recognize him. She lowered her hand. Two other men came from the opposite side. They also wore dark glasses, but no tie or jacket. The anti-terrorist man saluted them.

They made a circle around Hermes. The woman said, "Let's get back to work."

She walked past Hermes and kept on going. The other customs officers exchanged glances and dispersed quietly.

"The examining magistrate will be here in a quarter of an hour," said the dark suit to Hermes. Then he moved a few steps from Hermes and turned his back. The rest stood by pretending they were there accidentally. Since they were all smoking, Hermes was soon enveloped in a cloud of blue smoke.

Half an hour later, using one of the departure gates, Karras and his escort arrived. They were nine people, agile, fresh, with well-ironed suits and polished shoes. They looked like they had come for a christening party.

Karras was first. He appeared short compared to his assistants. He went straight to the man in the dark suit. The man raised his right hand halfway toward his forehead, took a step, and spoke softly to Karras. Another man with a walkie-talkie stood behind them. The representative of the airline came to Hermes.

"Sorry about the trouble," he said, abstractly. "You can come to our office in Athens at your earliest convenience. To reschedule your flight." He left.

Finally all were gone but Karras and Hermes.

Karras said, "We should have a talk in my office."

"By all means," said Hermes, taking a deep breath.

As they were leaving, they passed the X-ray control point where Hermes had been stopped an hour earlier. It was shut down now. There was no trace of the security guards.

Final Interview

Once again Hermes and Karras were riding in a car together. But this car was more spacious and a more expensive make than the first. The driver was an older man, well shaved, wearing a gray jacket, white shirt, and green tie. He drove slowly and meticulously. Throughout the ride nobody talked.

They entered a worn-down, seedy part of the city and arrived at a freshly renovated polychromic Neoclassical building standing within an enclosed garden. A few tall old pines were to the right and a small citrus grove was on the left. The car went through the gate and passed the ornate cast-iron barriers. A small group of men, presumably guards, continued their conversation.

They went through empty corridors and stepped into a small room on the first floor, followed by the driver, who carried the knapsack. The driver left the knapsack on the floor next to a large gray suitcase standing in the corner.

He closed the door behind him. Karras and Hermes were alone. Karras said, "Take a seat." Then he opened a small side door. The door opened onto a large space filled with voices, typewriter clatter, and heavy tobacco. Strange that all this frantic activity was enclosed within such a serene building on a weekend. Karras came back and sat behind the desk facing Hermes. Hermes had the feeling he was back where he had started from, the day he first met Karras.

But the place was very different from the office where Hermes had been interviewed before. There were pictures on the wall, mostly of Karras with people who looked important. There were additional displays, a university diploma *summa cum laude,* a diploma for Proficiency in English, and two other certificates from summer schools in the U.S., one in Criminology, the second in Urban Information Systems. A series of close-up photographs of wildflowers took up a considerable part of the other wall. Under the photographs of the flowers rested an ivory-colored computer. Next to the photographs and the computer a tall window, wide open, looked down on the orange grove. The window's light blue panels framed the radiant tops of the trees.

"We are not back where we started from," said Karras.

"Clearly. We're in a different room," answered Hermes.

"This is where I do all my real work. The previous office you saw is for routine," said Karras. "We'll have something to eat soon. I want to go over the whole case now. I hope you don't mind. This way we can leave the whole affair behind us as soon as possible."

"Ready," said Hermes.

Karras hesitated. "This must have been quite an ordeal."

"It was."

"It's over now."

"My last interrogation?"

"I never interrogated you, I only interviewed you. I needed your help and I need it now. I know it is very difficult for us to trust each other. But let us try. I have to understand the whole. It will give me a sense of coherence, ending, and finality."

"I never realized you people speak about crime in such literary terms."

"It's the other way round, I thought. Literature is all about lawbreaking and detection today," said Karras.

"You must read a lot."

"I do many things beyond the line of duty. My profession happens to be very routine."

"In movies, detectives always lead lives full of adventure," said Hermes.

They laughed.

"I'm sure you have a lot of questions for me. I have some of my own for you," went on Hermes.

"Should we bargain? Let's start with the Golden Thinking Machine, which could have been, but was not, in the attaché case, and with the gold bar, which was." Karras brought his palms together.

"The gold bar—the attaché case—where are they? I don't have them. They were left at the airport," Hermes exclaimed anxiously.

"Why worry? Were they yours?" Karras asked.

"Of course not," Hermes replied.

"They belonged to . . ."

"Robert," Hermes filled in.

"We know."

"How?"

"It just happens that one of my people overheard the discussion when you were given the case. No reason to be nervous about it. Unless . . ."

"I just hate to lose things. In addition, it might have been helpful for the investigation."

"No reason to worry about that, either." Karras got up and went to the large suitcase in the corner, grabbed it by the handle and lifted it high. There, where the suitcase had been, was the black attaché case.

Still holding the suitcase he said, "The big suitcase has no bottom. It's fitted with hooks that clasp the smaller case. It's an old trick, invented by Neapolitan thieves at the turn of the century, they say. It has since been borrowed by law enforcement authorities."

"But why did you use it today?" Hermes inquired.

"To save you from more complications and further red tape. As far as we are concerned, the attaché case has disappeared with all its contents."

"And now what will happen to it?"

Karras gave a dismissive smile. "Technically it's not my problem. The case stays in my office temporarily, that is, in the hands of counterespionage. I assure you we can explain the gold bar later more easily than you could."

"I never realized the counterespionage service was involved too."

"Everybody had to be involved. Now tell me, how did you know what was inside the case? Since you had just received it, you never had the opportunity to open it as far as I was informed. But from what they told me, you knew exactly what the case contained."

"I'd seen the contents before it reached my hands."

"Where?"

Hermes divulged how he had searched the villa in Psychiko.

"Why did you go to the villa in the first place?"

"I was after the Golden Thinking Machine that I was to be handed in the airport, in Robert's briefcase, to be blackmailed with. My idea was to destroy their plan by running away with the treasure and bringing it to you. When I found that it had been melted down, I decided to leave the bar there and see what would follow." Hermes paused and examined Karras, who was listening attentively, and added, "You'll find my fingerprints all over the place. I knew it was illegal."

"As is most police work," said Karras.

"You're encouraging me to confess all my illegalities."

"Yes I am encouraging you to speak, but I assure you that your 'illegalities,' as you term them, don't interest me per se. My interest in *you* is only incidental; I am interested in *them*. You see, there is only one of you, and I'm afraid very soon you will be leaving the country, and God knows if you'll ever come back. There are many of them, though. And they are here to stay. I had a hunch from the very beginning that there was more to this case than an academician shot in a robbery. Now how did you come to know about this villa in Psychiko?"

"I read about it."

"Read? Where?"

"In a telex."

"And what did it say?'

"Unfortunately for them, everything. It left nothing for me to discover. It said where to go, when there would be nobody around to bother me while I combed the house, and what to find. Finally it described what they were planning to do at the airport."

"All that in such detail?"

"But not in plain text."

"What do you mean?"

"I had to decipher it."

"I forgot temporarily, you're not only an archaeologist." He grinned. "I told you, I'm a kind of cryptography amateur myself. How did you do it?"

"It occurred to me they might be using the Enigma technique."

"Enigma? The system a Dutchman developed for the Germans in World War II?"

"Actually, it was developed by others before."

"But it requires a cipher machine. Do those people carry them around? Do *you* have one?"

"You don't need such machines any more. You use computers. There's a program that simulates them directly."

"I didn't know that. I told you my cryptography knowledge is tangential. And you? Where did you find this program?"

"It's published. As simple as that."

"But why on earth did you have it with you?"

"For sentimental reasons."

"That's rather strange, if you don't mind me saying so. Now, what I honestly cannot understand is why such sophisticated criminals used such an accessible cryptographic system."

"It is very understandable. The Enigma code system is well known today, which means any text encrypted through it is decipherable. But deciphering takes a certain amount of time."

Karras said with genuine impatience, "We've gone through that before."

Hermes smiled. "We have. But here is the trick. This deciphering time can be calculated very precisely, assuming, that is, that the decipherer is using the standard program and the fastest machines available."

"I see. That means that messages are considered practically indecipherable given certain time constraints."

"Correct."

"Which implies that it was safe to use this system to encipher messages, provided the messages referred to facts that had already become obsolete by the time the code was broken. Very practical. But then I don't understand how you . . ."

". . . deciphered the text ahead of time?"

"Yes."

"I'd improved on the method."

"When?"

"Some time ago."

"But why?"

"I told you, for sentimental reasons."

"That is strange indeed, but it is not my business to know more about you. Finally, I do have an additional question related to the whole affair. Where did you find the text?"

"That I can't tell you."

"Be careful. I might know already."

"All the better for you. But you'd better keep it to yourself, as I am."

"You might have a point."

"Do you have any idea who sent it though?"

Hermes told him who the sender was and how he fit into the whole plot.

"Indeed, we had some information from Interpol and other sources about the dealings of this Robert. Do you know who Robert was working for?" asked Karras.

"I only know he was linked with Gerald and Donald."

"But I do. The Mafia. We've been following Gerald also for some time. As for Donald, he remains a mystery," Karras said. There was silence. "You never suspected Robert, did you?"

"I always did," Hermes said.

Karras was surprised. "Always? What did you suspect him of?"

"Almost everything, but not of Mafia connections specifically."

"Since when?"

"From the moment we met ten years ago. We were classmates, roommates."

Karras shook his head. "That would probably have made it very difficult to suspect him in this specific case then."

"You're right. It took me some time to get beyond vague conjectures I had about him—a deep sense of mistrust—and pin him to this particular case."

Karras asked, "Was he ever aware of it?"

"Probably. He kept neutralizing my suspicions but encouraging them all the time."

"That is weird indeed. That is indeed a weird relationship."

"In a way, that suspense kept us together."

"Like hanging on to a puzzle?"

"Like collaborating on a puzzle."

Karras shook his head again. "And do you know who killed the Sloans?"

"I don't."

"Their ring did," said Karras. "We have proved it."

"It doesn't surprise me."

"And do you have any theories about why they murdered the Sloans?"

"To get the Golden Thinking Machine. Pat Sloan was the one who stole it from Agraphiotis in the first place. They grabbed it out of Sloan's hands as he was falling after being shot," said Hermes.

"How do you know that?"

"I was there. Sloan was bringing the machine to show it to me to convince me to work for him."

"Weird. But it all ties together. His fingerprints were at Agraphiotis' house. We only identified them after Sloan's murder though," said Karras. "The gun was mailed to us, anonymously, just yesterday. But I have my theories."

"Do you think Sloan killed Agraphiotis? It's my turn to ask now," said Hermes.

Karras replied, "Yes, Sloan did. The gun mailed to us had Sloan's fingerprints on it. But there was at least one other person in the house. We suspect that this other person was a competitor of Sloan's. Sloan and his competitor arrived by different paths at the house after you left. This much we have established. One through the door, which he unlocked with the help of a passkey, the other by climbing in the open window, clearly a young person. In contrast to Sloan, this young person didn't leave any fingerprints. Agraphiotis was taking a nap. He was surprised in bed. He heard a noise. He thought it was you and shouted your name. Sloan was surprised by the window intruder. He panicked and shot. It was a mistake. Your uncle got caught in the crossfire. Sloan was an experienced agent. He wouldn't have shot if he hadn't been really shocked. Or . . ." He added after a short pause, "If he hadn't been panicked by the fact that he had to retire by the end of 1983. He wanted to retreat with a big victory."

"Do you think it really happened like that?"

"In general it fits most of the facts. Certainly there are still loose ends. The cook who disappeared, your trip to the U.S. But it also fits the motives, and this is most satisfactory for detection work."

"You can ask me about anything you want. But which motives? What victory are you talking about?" asked Hermes.

"Motives. This is something you can help with. That's what I want to establish now. What were they—Sloan, Robert, the ring—after? The Golden Thinking Machine? You? Why?"

"I believe they were after me as much as the object itself."

"Because of your research? That's what I suspected from the beginning."

"I know you did. You asked me that before indirectly. I can tell you now. Yes."

"Is it really that crucial? I mean for intelligence purposes. Why?"

"What, the thinking machine?"

"No, your research."

"*I* don't think so," said Hermes plainly.

Karras looked surprised. "I received information to the contrary. And how can you explain . . .?"

"It's simple. It's like this. Somebody spots a paper presented in a scientific review and starts making approaches to the author, trying at the same time to keep it as secret as possible. Others notice the secrecy more than the paper. They conclude they have to join in. The more they compete to get hold of the researcher, the more they try to keep it secret, the more the perceived value of the research rises."

Karras looked even more surprised. "And all that didn't bother you?"

"Of course it did."

"Did you do anything about it?"

"I never had time. I never had time for anything outside of my research. I came to Greece to escape from all that and concentrate on my work. But then, I don't remember being as idle as I am now, even during vacations in high school."

"And you let them go on reinterpreting your work like that?"

"I was quite busy answering those who had legitimate scientific objections."

"But wasn't *your* responsibility . . ."

". . . I'm responsible for the quality of *my* research, not what *others* do with it."

"Wasn't it also because you looked down on them, those . . . snoops?"

"Snoops? It was a only a question of priorities. I didn't look down on anyone. I am sure they were interesting people."

"It takes of course a lot of knowledge for all that . . . that extrapolation they did parallel to spying."

"A lot of fantasy. Like the Golden Thinking 1 Machine."

"What's like it?"

"Imagination," said Hermes. He bent his head.

"I see. You think the artifact's value was exaggerated as well?" For once Karras looked Hermes straight in the eye.

"Possibly." Hermes said. He raised his eyes. Their eyes met.

Karras said angrily, "Thugs, melting down something like that."

"I wouldn't grieve too much without knowing more facts," Hermes said calmly.

"Facts about its value?"

Hermes nodded. "It was certainly worth the value of some family jewelry plus labor."

Karras looked at him askance. "You don't think it was—"

"I wouldn't exclude it."

"A real one?" asked Karras. "I mean . . ."

"Yes, a genuine fake. As for Donald, the person who probably melted the machine down to run away with the gold, he might have known it was not a genuine antiquity he was destroying. I have to remark, on the other hand, he seemed rather obsessed with melting down the world."

Karras said, "He is still at large. He might try it on something else." Then he watched Hermes, speechless.

"Of course I may be wrong," retracted Hermes. "It's possible that the Golden Thinking Machine was genuine. We'll probably never know, unless you discover something more in Agraphiotis' notes."

"We've gone through them and we didn't find anything. Agraphiotis. What a fool. In the end he outsmarted even himself."

"If it was a fake, he couldn't have made it himself. There's always the possibility that an accomplice will surface. We have to be patient. Anyhow, this is one of many unanswered questions, like who shot my uncle after all."

"Patience. I know this is the essential quality of an investigator but personally, I am running out of it. I've completed ten years in this kind of work." Karras turned his head toward the window and looked out, embarrassed.

"Ten years?"

"Yes, ten years. It seems like a long time, doesn't it?"

"Yes it does. But . . ." Hermes hesitated.

"You didn't realize I was that young, did you?" Karras said. "Authority adds years. Policemen always look older than they are." Karras continued, "During that time I have been amazed by how much people can invent," and added, "to deceive. Both sides."

"Which sides?"

"Cops and robbers."

"It seems you have some doubts about your work."

"I do. Although it offers opportunities for advancement, improvement, and education for people like me that other careers do not. I can take advanced courses, participate in conferences, do research, and keep on going."

"So you plan to perfect your knowledge?"

"I'll confess something to you, Hermes." He hesitated. "Policemen never confess. But I will be very personal." He raised his eyebrows. "I have been nurturing a dream to start a new career. I'd like to leave this country. I want to become a student again. I want to study artificial intelligence in the United States and then pursue a peaceful ademic vocation."

"Peaceful? You believe academic life will guarantee that?"

"I admit I've had some doubts recently." Karras spoke in a relaxed tone.

"I should think so. Is anything changing?"

"It cannot go on as it is any more."

"You mean people will reform?" asked Hermes.

"I'm not thinking about individuals, although that is what a policeman is concerned about. I'm thinking about institutions, our kind of world order."

"You want to say politics," Hermes said. "I know next to nothing about them. I didn't have time for that, either. But I know my history, my archaeology. I very much doubt anything significant has ever changed through politics, especially the way people think. Politicians always seem to be in a rush. World views, social structures, shift very slowly."

"But the process has to speed up," said Karras.

Hermes shrugged.

"Did you ever think how much all these secrets and snooping cost?" Karras continued.

Hermes said, "Four or five human lives."

Karras interrupted him. "I know what you're going to say. Murder doesn't affect anyone but the murdered person, and one out of two murderers, the ones we catch. I think a novelist said that. Robert might keep on living a normal life like you and me, like many others who participated in such a crime. You might find him back in Cambridge, back at business as usual. You might meet him again on the street buying newspapers. And there will be nothing you can do about it. I don't believe the world is governed by any imperative of justice or guilt. But I am not a nihilist. I believe in necessity and rationality. Now take a look at this specific case, our case. Count for a moment all the funds that went into it, into this industry of parainformation, misinformation, this industry of paranoia and hallucination, spying, lying, hiding, breaking in—not to mention the overhead. I know what these budgets are like. It's getting worse every year. Technology doesn't lower the costs—it escalates them, in fact. This cannot last more than five years. The costs exceed by far any benefits we get. Or anyone gets. We are in the middle of a fiscal explosion."

"Five years!"

Karras continued, "By then I know I will certainly feel more comfortable in academic life."

"And what will your first step be?" asked Hermes.

Karras turned his face toward Hermes. A shy, confiding look had come over it. "To be frank, I was hoping you could give me some advice."

At that moment there was a light tap on the door.

"Ah. Lunch has arrived," said Karras, beaming.

A man entered holding a folder. He handed it to Karras. Karras read it solemnly, his assistant staring at the telephone intently.

Hermes examined the photographs of the flowers on the wall. A constant contrast of sharp and soft, hard and brittle, close and far, but a little monotonous. The same effect again and again. In the meantime Karras dialed a number. His voice had an edge of urgency.

"Yes. It's me. Yes. I'm listening . . . don't interrupt . . . When? . . . exactly, exactly . . . Not now. Do you have a record? Go ahead . . . In a quarter of an hour, Here. Here." He put back the receiver and returned the folder to the man without a word. The man didn't say anything either and left the room. Suddenly neither Karras nor Hermes appeared to be interested in continuing the conversation. There was a pause.

Then Karras said, "There's been an accident." Hermes, still contemplating the flowers, seemed not to be paying much attention. "Your cousin Nina was hit by a car," he added.

Hermes turned his head abruptly, as if he had heard a scream from outside. But only the muffled sigh of the leaves could be heard.

Karras succumbed suddenly to his habit of meticulously inspecting the top of his desk. Without raising his head, he spoke casually. "She was knocked down by a hit-and-run car. It was outside an embassy of a 'controversial' country. It happened when we were still at the airport. The car inexplicably went over the sidewalk. It might have skidded at that point. It might, on the other hand . . ." He hesitated. "The blow wasn't strong but she lost her balance and fell, slipping on the wet pavement. She hit the back of her head. They reported to me that she died. On the spot. I'm sorry." Then he added matter-of-factly, "We'll find out who did it." He stopped. The leaves still rustled. Then he added in a dull voice, "I think we have covered almost everything . . ."

"Yes," Hermes said.

"Do you want us to contact her mother?"

"She's on her way back to Athens." He took a deep breath and brought his left hand up to his hair. "Her boat will arrive later tonight," he uttered with difficulty.

"Of course, if you need anything, call."

Hermes picked up his knapsack.

They both stood silent.

Karras spoke first. "Can we give you a ride?" There was no compassion in his eyes.

Hermes did not speak. He shook his head.

"I understand," said Karras, moving to the door. Hermes moved to the door too. As he came closer Karras took two steps back, keeping an arm's length distance from Hermes. Hermes also took a slightly indirect path away from Karras. They nodded at each other. They didn't seem to have exchanged a glance. They didn't seem to want to exchange anything further. Hermes was out in the corridor and they didn't shake hands.

Epilogue

Hermes passed quickly through the gate. The guards continued talking to each other, their eyes suspiciously following his colorful knapsack. He walked toward the large square. Hot weather was returning. But the light was weaker, as if the sun had aged during the last three days of storm. He went by a large parking garage shut for the weekend. A strong aroma floated in the air. There is always something blooming in Attica whatever the season, however squalid and polluted the surroundings, always some contorted sapling behind the tons of concrete blocks, between the half-empty drums of tar.

Hermes kept going, preoccupied with the source of the scent. A few steps farther down the fragrance ceased, as unexpectedly as it had appeared. He continued down toward the square. It was at that moment that he started thinking about the next day and there was nothing to think with.

He dug his hands into his pockets. He touched a piece of paper. An envelope. He took it out. It was from Cambridge. Still unopened. He tried to tear it as he walked but it was not possible. He stopped just as the traffic light was turning red before crossing to the large square. He started reading as the cars went by in front of him at great speed.

> Cambridge, July 10, 1983
>
> Dear Hermes,
>
> I heard from Sis that you came to Cambridge and that your presentation was a smashing success! I don't know if you tried to contact me. I've been away for a week. Paul's grandmother died and we had to fly to California. I haven't got your outline yet—you must be spending all your time in cafés and on beaches.

Here it's cold and raining—miserable. I hope next year I'll convince Paul to spend our vacation in Greece. It'll be better for both of us.

I trust your outline will be here by the end of the month. Sis told me your talk carried everybody away. Especially Old Moneybags. Sis also said that you arranged your speech like a mystery story, with a plot, deceptions, and disclosures. You always were so good at that. Do you remember when, our sophomore year, you, Paul, Sis, Robert, and I spent that weekend together in a cabin up in New Hampshire and you and Robert staged a plot contest? You won. It was a great evening. Plot, deceptions, and disclosures. Why don't you try something like that with your book? Fiction after all is an excellent way to demonstrate frames and circumscription. Or did I get it wrong? Do you know that Panofsky envied *The Maltese Falcon*? Plot and detection and some passion please. Take care. Best from Paul and Sis.

Love,

Esther

Bibliographical Postscript

Like any storybook, this one owes a profound debt to a multitude of other storybooks, although to acknowledge such sources is not customary. But unlike some others, this storybook also owes a debt to nonstorybook sources. Here is my list, very incomplete, of debts and suggestions for further reading.

AI in general

Winston, Patrick. *Artificial Intelligence.* Reading, MA: Addison-Wesley, 1984.
Charniack, E., and Drew McDermott. *Artificial Intelligence.* Reading, MA: Addison-Wesley, 1985.
Minsky, M. *The Society of Mind.* New York: Simon and Schuster, 1988.
Johnson-Laird, P. N. *Mental Models.* Cambridge, U.K.: Cambridge University Press, 1983.

Representation

Amarel, S. "On Representation of Problems of Reasoning about Actions." In Meltzer, B., and D. Mitchie, eds., *Machine Intelligence* 3, 1968, 131–171.
Newell, Allen. "Physical Symbol Systems." *Cognitive Science* 4, 1980.
Dennett, D. C. "Computer Models and the Mind—A View from the East Pole." In *Times Literary Supplement,* December 14, 1984, 1453–1454.

G.P.S. and Planning

Simon, H. A. *The Science of the Artificial.* Cambridge, MA: MIT Press, 1969.
Stefik, M. "Planning and Meta-Planning." *Artificial Intelligence* 16, no. 2, 1982.

Heuristics

Polya, G. *Mathematics and Plausible Reasoning.* Princeton: Princeton University Press, 1957.
Lenat, D. B. "The Nature of Heuristics." *Artificial Intelligence* 19, no. 2, 1982.

Nets and Frames

Marvin Minsky's 1975 essay, "A Framework for Representing Knowledge." Reprinted in many versions and included (together with essays by M. Ross Quinlan, Roger Schank, W. Woods, R. Moore, and Terry Winograd) in Brachman, R. J., and Hector J. Levesque, eds., *Readings in Knowledge Representation.* Los Altos, CA: Kaufmann, 1985.

Incomplete Knowledge about the World and Beliefs Revision

McCarthy, J. "Circumscription." *Artificial Intelligence* 13, nos. 1, 2, 1980, pp. 27–39.
Ginsberg, Matthew, ed. *Readings on Nonmonotonic Reasoning*. Essays by J. McCarthy, P. J. Hayes, R. Moore, R. Reiter, J. Doyle, D. McDermott. Los Altos, CA: Kaufmann, 1987.

Waltz Algorithm

Waltz, D. "Understanding Line Drawings of Scenes with Shadows." In P. H. Winston, ed., *The Psychology of Computer Vision*. New York: McGraw-Hill, 1975.

Vision

Marr, D. *Vision*. San Francisco: Freeman, 1982.
Fischler, M. A., and O. Firschein, eds., *Readings in Computer Vision*. Essays, including the R. A. Brooks essay on ACRONYM. Los Altos, CA: Kaufmann, 1987.

Language and Complexity

Berwick, Robert C. *The Acquisition of Syntactic Knowledge*. Cambridge, MA: MIT Press, 1985.

On the Debate over Nonserial- and Nonsymbol-Based Computer Information Processing

Selfridge, O. G. "Pandemonium: A Paradigm for Learning." *Mechanization of Thought Processes* 8, 1965, 513–526.
Hillis, W. D. *The Connection Machine* (Report, AIM-691 AI-Lab, MIT). Cambridge, MA: MIT Press, 1981.
Graubard, S. R., ed. *The Artificial Intelligence Debate*. Cambridge, MA: MIT Press, 1988.
Pinker, S., and Jean Mehler, eds. *Connections and Symbols*. Cambridge, MA: MIT Press, 1988.

Analogy

Polya, G. *How to Solve It*. Princeton: Princeton University Press, 1957.
Lakoff, G., and M. Johnson. *Metaphors We Live By*. Chicago: University of Chicago Press, 1980.
The MACBETH material is drawn from P. Winston, *Artificial Intelligence*, Reading, MA: Addison-Wesley, 1984. See also D. R. Hofstadter, *Gödel, Escher, Bach*. New York: Vintage, 1980.
Carbonell, J., ed. *Machine Learning*. Cambridge, MA: MIT Press, 1990.
Holland, J. H., K. J. Holyoak, R. E. Nisbett, P. R. Thagard. *Induction*. Cambridge, MA: MIT Press, 1986.

Jokes

Freud, Sigmund. *Jokes and Their Relation to the Unconscious*. New York: Norton, 1960.
Minsky, M. *The Society of Mind*. New York: Simon and Schuster, 1988.

LISP

Winston, P. H., and B. K. P. Horn. *LISP*. Reading, MA: Addison-Wesley, 1989.

0 00 02 0510564 6
MIDDLEBURY COLLEGE